Camino Tales

MARION DANTE

ISBN: 978 1 3999 4549 3
Also available as an e-book

Book design by The Art of Communication www.book-design.co.uk

DEDICATION

To my parents Frank & Patricia (nee Colivet) Dante,
my brothers Tim and Des and my sisters Pat and Bernie.

ACKNOWLEDGEMENTS

Bead Roberts, who gave me the title of my autobiography
"Dropping The Habit".

Gratitude to my nephew Mark Stay for his initial editing.

A huge debt of gratitude to editor Joanna Barnard
introduced by Maggie Farran through the secretary of the
Hampshire Writers' at Winchester University.
And to Christine Hammacott of the Art of Communication
for book cover design, formatting and help with publishing.

My thanks also to Mr & Mrs Singh for their insights into Sikhism.

CAMINO TALES

The life so short, the craft so long to learn,
The attempt so hard, the victory so keen,
The fearful joy, so arduous to earn,
So quick to fade - by all these things I mean
Love, for his wonders in this worldly scene
Confound me so that when I think of him
I scarcely know whether I sink or swim.

Geoffrey Chaucer
Translated by Theodore Morrison

1

CHALLENGING TIMES

*T*GIF! Thank God. Time to relax… if only.

Up until two months ago, when Richard and I arrived home from school exhausted at the end of the week all we wanted was to relax. School bags were dumped. A take-away was ordered and as soon as we'd coaxed four year old Dante to bed we would unwind watching a film or something on the television. Glasses topped up, all responsibilities were banished. But not now that Richard is in Italy.

Richard has already spent two months in Florence supporting his aged aunt Margherita as she copes with breast cancer. How much longer will he be there? There's nothing I can do about that. His two aunts were there for him when his mother died in childbirth. He needs to be with them. *But who is this nurse Angela? He's mentioned her several times. Each time enthusiastically.*

I am determined to cope while Richard is away, but it's not easy coping on my own with our young son while keeping down a full-time primary school teaching job.

There's all the housework too. Washing, ironing, cleaning, cooking were jobs that we shared. The weather during these first few months coming out of winter, hasn't helped either.

Take today for example. My plans to leave school early at the end of the day were thwarted when a parent was late collecting their son. I lost my patience when Dante toppled a box of coloured learning blocks all over the classroom carpet. Consequently when I was finally ready to drive home I struggled to keep calm driving through Friday night's rush hour. Stuck in a bottleneck I managed to slip into an alternative route only to end up in more congestion. The rain was teeming down, the windscreen wipers fighting off the rain. Headlights and indicators flashing. Dante was restless. I kept checking on him on my car mirror. Imagine my alarm as I caught sight of myself. God, I look like one of the chickens in our Kerry backyard being chased round the plot desperate to avoid being strangled. Puffed out feathers, shocked eyes and panicky squeaks coming from their protruding beaks. My fraught face and unruly, fiery auburn hair is an awful state. *What is happening to me? Why can't I be patient with my son?* He's tired too. No wonder he's tumbling around in the back seat. Sure, God love him, he can't be blamed.

'Why can't I sit in the front next to you, Mummy? Please Mum. I'm too tall for my booster seat. I'm thirsty. Daddy never goes this way. I need the toilet.'

I'm reaching the end of my tether. I want to scream.

We've made it. We're home. Dante's dumped his belongings and made a dash to get a drink from the fridge. I hope I'll be spared from what have become Dante's tantrums. He sure lets me know that he's missing his dad. He'll eat his supper alright. He can't wait for Richard to phone. He tells him everything and promises to be a good boy for Mummy. But as soon as they have finished chatting the battle begins to get him to bed. He doesn't want me reading him a story. After a lot of protests and struggles I somehow eventually succeed in cuddling him to sleep, smother him in kisses, tossing his blonde curly mob while I berate myself for my inadequacies.

I try to convince myself that I must cope while Richard is in Florence. He keeps telling me that I must look after myself. He means it, I know. That's the reason that dreading another lonely weekend, I have invited my friend Marion over for coffee in the morning and arranged a play-away-day for Dante.

Despite my tiredness, I'll have to get my lesson plans started tonight because they have to be submitted on Monday morning. I have cleared the kitchen table and opened my laptop ready to detail class three's maths progression. Oh God. Here we go again. Dante's piercing screams have started. I rush upstairs to stop him thrashing around. In his sleep he is calling for his daddy. I loosen his pyjamas and cradle him until his rapid heartbeat calms down.

Dante's nightmares began soon after his father left for Florence. When I consulted our doctor he seemed to presume that teachers know what to do and besides, all will be well once his dad returns home.

Just as I reached the bottom of the stairs my mobile rang. I rushed into the kitchen and closed the door so that I wouldn't waken Dante. Richard was late tonight so he missed chatting to Dante. I collapsed into an armchair while he comforted me. I told him everything. He was torn between his love for us and the care and support that he willingly showered on his aunts. We realised that we are fortunate in having enjoyed such a happy beginning to our life together in a lovely home with the precious gift of a healthy and good natured son. We concluded as always by counting our blessings and looking forward to the days when we can be together again. He was delighted when I mentioned that I had invited my friend Marion over tomorrow to help me relax while Dante is going to be collected to go to his friend's home to play.

But sipping a glass of wine while falling asleep in the armchair admittedly I struggled to analyse my muddled reaction to Richard's description of the nurse.

I love Richard from the bottom of my heart. Every minute we're apart I miss him. But why do I feel a twinge of jealousy when he mentions Angela? What's wrong with me?

Oh Good Lord, that's the News at Ten on the telly!

Focusing on anything else that night was beyond me. I turned off the television, closed down my laptop and crawled up stairs to bed. Quietly replacing Dante's duvet, I kissed him gently before creeping next door, stepping out of my dressing gown and slipping between my bed sheets.

The next morning Dante seemed to be transformed. He was as good as gold tucking into his Weetabix. There were only a few splashes on the table when he poured the milk and very little sugar sprinkled around his cereal bowl. I wondered if the thought of being away from me was calming him. As soon as he spotted his friend's car stopping outside, he jumped down from his stool, grabbed his bag as he sped to the front door. I followed him with his coat. I had to be satisfied with a wave as he seated himself next to his friend in the car.

Turning to go inside my contrived smile faded. I tidied the place in preparation for Marion's arrival. I washed the breakfast ware, boxed Dante's Lego and firmed up the sagging cushions on the settee. All the time I kept telling myself that I needed to take control of my life. Things had to change.

Spring is in the air. The clocks will leap forward soon.

Easter's on its way. It's almost eleven and the sun is peeping through a fluffy cumulus sky. I am only forty and according to Carl Jung, 'Life really begins at forty.'

I knew my friend Marion would arrive punctually at eleven. Sure aren't Marion and I products of years observing convent regulations. Rules, routine and order have given us a sense of discipline and purpose. We often laugh and refer to years we lived as nuns in the convent as 'time spent inside'. Fortunately for me it was only six years while for Marion it amounted to over thirty years. But even though I left the convent seven years ago, bonds continue to tie me to the observance of many of the religious principles and ideals that I imbibed. The fact that my wonderful husband Richard trained to be a priest keeps us conscious of religious obligations. We both continue to teach in the same Catholic school and our darling four year old son, Dante, is a pupil there. When anyone enquires about the reasons that prompted us to leave Religious Life, rather than revealing our personal conflicts we prefer to say that we look to our future through a prism. A multifaceted rainbow-hued vision of the world. *That's easier when the sun is shining.*

I was fiddling with strands of my wispy auburn hair when the crunching pebbles on the path made me look out and catch sight of Marion waving and carrying a bulging colourful patchwork bag. I suspected that it will contain yet another toy that she has found in a Charity shop. She never comes empty handed.

We hugged. Marion's got such an innocent face. Head up. Soulful eyes looking straight at you and the usual almost laughing smile that puts you at ease and assures you that all's going to be well. When I complement her on retaining her youthfulness she retorts with: 'Enough of the plámásing, Frankie. When I caught sight of my wrinkly face in the mirror this morning I was in no doubt that old age has crept up on me. But Thank God, I'm well.'

Put at ease I pulled the waist strings of my turquoise track suit around my wiry frame and thanking Marion for the puzzle, hung her long beige coat on our coat-stand. I noted that dressed in a green twinset and a three-quarter length black skirt Marion never seemed to have become fashion conscious. Since many nuns no longer wear their religious dress, with the silver cross brooch on her cardigan, you'd think that she was still a nun.

She followed me into the kitchen admiring how much we had modernised it by replacing the vintage dark brown, with lemon and blue, an expensive island table and spacious cupboards.

I reminded her that it was Giovanni, Richard's father who had given us his home when he decided to return to Florence in order to be with his two ageing sisters.

Marion chatted while I prepared the coffee and offered her fig rolls. These were her mam's favourite biscuits and mine too. It was comforting having her there with me.

As we reminisced I found myself folding my arms and rocking to and fro on my stool. A smile crept over my face as I reflected on Marion's courage at setting up a new life when she was nearly fifty. But has she been radical enough? She never married and is childless.

I cannot imagine life without Richard. Every day is precious. We made plans when we pledged our love to each other. We are fortunate enough to have a gorgeous son. Not that long ago, the average human didn't live past their mid-40s. Carpe Diem…I must seize every opportunity each day.

My mobile phone pinged. I glanced at it. A Google advert. I turned it off. Our eyes met. I was twiddling my necklace. I was restless thinking over how much I had struggled during the past six months while Richard was in Florence. Telepathically, Marion smiled before asking me when Richard was due to fly back home.

Furrowed browed, I steadied my stool and grasped the edge of the table. Marion's calmness was beginning to annoy me. Eventually I admitted to her that I barely coped. She pulled her chair nearer as she enquired about Richard's aunt's prognosis. While I topped up Marion's coffee I explained that fortunately Margherita's cancer was diagnosed as ductal carcinoma at an early stage and that it was in the ducts of her left breast and the lump has been removed and that at present she is undergoing radiotherapy. She is the eldest of the two aunts and she'll be seventy-five in September. When Richard's mother died in childbirth, it was these two aunts who were determined to do all they could to replace her.

Marion made the sign of the Cross: 'May Almighty God bless each of you. But, Frankie, what did you do to help you cope while Richard's has been away?'

Conscious that I was rolling my lips and clenching my fists, I confessed that sheer willpower kept me going. Routine took over. Getting my son dressed, fed and out into the car and fighting my way through the dreadful morning traffic, required a lot of stamina, but the more determined I was to achieve the more I seemed to be failing.

Marion reminded me that we had both developed strong characters in order to survive hard times in the convent.

Exasperated, I sighed and combing my hands though my hair, I exploded:

'I've tried everything, Marion. Tiring Dante out playing in the park after school means that I am doubly exhausted after teaching all day. By the time he is fed I could readily collapse into bed with him. But no, I have to prepare my school work for the next day.'

Marion's silence is infuriating me. I'll have to tell her about Dante's nightmares and tantrums.

Marion must have realised my dilemma. She wasn't

doing her usual doling out advice. She was just rubbing her hands together and looking into the distance. *Maybe she's taken to praying for me.*

After this uneasy pause in the conversation I stood, ready to carry the cups to the sink. This seemed to prompt Marion to acknowledge her ignorance about child rearing. She also said that she presumed that I had discussed these situations with Richard.

After sighing a lot, I accepted that Marion most likely would not really be capable of understanding my present, trying circumstances. How could she? She was still steeped in religion, as she had never married and her knowledge of children was restricted to the ones she taught and maybe her niece's children. She only has herself to care for.

Marion smiled and complimented me:'You've both been strong. But I don't see what more either you or Richard can do until his aunt fully recovers and you are both back here together in Wimbledon, Frankie.'

I nodded and reflected.

I like Marion. But she is pious. She is older than me. I am being challenged above my strength. What can I do? I am resolved not to give in.

'You've got that far-away look, Frankie.'

'Yes indeed. I was half way up a huge mountain. I think that I was running away from the rut I dread being in.'

Dear God, I hope that she's not going to come out with some sanctimonious platitude. Oh no. *Her eyes are watery. Tissues. What's triggered this?*

I pulled my stool nearer. We sat quietly clasping each other's hands.

Eventually Marion began in a wobbly voice: 'Please forgive me, Frankie. I sense that I probably come over as being heartless….Oh, I don't know. Sanctimonious? Not able to see where you're coming from.'

What could I say? I'd misjudged my friend. Time

elapsed before we eventually moved to armchairs with more coffee and lots of tissues.

When we were both in the convent I looked up to Marion. She always seemed to be happy, observant and was an excellent teacher. Children and parents adored her. The parish priest even bought her a guitar when she took charge of the music at Mass on Sundays and feast days. Consequently everyone was very surprised and concerned when she left the convent. But times were changing and they wished her well presuming that the Convent Superiors would help her to settle into her new life. I never thought that she might need some support. I waited tentatively watching her rubbing one hand over the other occasionally glancing around the room as though she was trying to focus her thoughts. Silence. Was she swallowing lumps of disquietude in her throat before she came out with:

'I'm sorry, Frankie. You have enough to cope with and here I am trying to come to grips with my own concerns. It's not fair on you. I'm really sorry.'

God Almighty. What's happening? She can't go home in this condition!

When Marion didn't reply I cautiously invited her to stay on for a while and maybe have some soup. Once she was assured that Dante would be with his friends until late afternoon, she agreed. When we had settled into our armchairs Marion seemed to be unable to prevent the flood gates from releasing a torrential surge of tears that must have been dammed for many years.

What's all this about? Again there was silence.

Maybe it's that she's remembering the sexual abuse that she suffered soon after she left the convent. The nuns didn't support her in spite of the fact that this incident happened when she was recovering from breast cancer. I heard that Marion complained to those in authority and in fact I know that she has a file of letters pleading with hierarchy in both the male and female branches of the Religious Order that this priest belonged to. They all fobbed her off. Correspondence between her and bishops, clergy and even the Cardinal lengthened as she pursued her plea for help. The nuns reminded her that she had voluntarily left the convent and therefore was no longer eligible for support from them. For over twenty years each and all the Catholic hierarchy failed to reprimand the priest for the sexual abuse that she had suffered from him. Finally only a few weeks ago the Cardinal invited her to discuss the matter with him. She said that although he was gracious, kind and understanding, on reflection she wondered if his prime concern was his anxiousness to prevent further sexual scandals surfacing.

All these things were going through my mind. I didn't want to say anything in case I had jumped to conclusions. Something else could have been troubling her. Who was I to intrude. I was relieved when Marion started to ask me how Dante was finding school and what reading scheme they were using now. But I could see that she was struggling with this change of topic. She must have sensed my concern because after she asked me if I would promise not to divulge the real reason for her tears and I had assured that anything she wished to say I would regard as confidential; gradually she relaxed.

I was surprised when Marion revealed that for many years she struggled with her adhesion to the Catholic Church. But then I also worry among other things about some aspects of the Religious Education syllabus being taught in our Catholic schools. For instance our obligation as teachers to expect seven year old children to go to confession in preparation for the reception of their first Holy Communion. The Sacrament of Reconciliation formerly known as the Sacrament of Penance and also still commonly referred to as a child's First Confession is based on asking the children to reflect on times when they did not live as Jesus asked them.

Marion agreed with me. She too was concerned about the harm that can be done to children in inculcating a sense of guilt and sadness in them and associating God with punishment and negativity. We talked about the fear of God notices that were posted throughout the convent warning us that GOD SEES YOU. A God of fire and brimstone being promoted instead of guiding us to look to a loving father helping us to develop our moral compass.

Suddenly while we were sitting there the heavens opened. Rain lashed against the windows and winter darkness descended on the room. However, once the side lights dispelled the darkness, the heating was increased, we pulled our armchairs nearer to the electric fire and placed rugs over our knees, a sense of cosiness and relaxation enveloped us.

The age difference between us and the fact that she had been someone that I esteemed for many years seemed to disappear. It was as though we were equals now. For a while Marion gazed into the distance, rubbed her hands together and then scanned the room as though making sure that there were no intruders. I'm not sure if she was aware of her slow process of unwinding. Maybe she was checking that it was safe to share details about her early life.

The phone in the kitchen rang. It was the friend entertaining Dante telling me the time she would drive him home. I came back into the room with tea and cake. Reaching out Marion thanked me, took a sip and looked straight at me. She placed the cup on the table next to her and began to talk about her early life as though she had been propelled into a stream of consciousness. There was no stopping her. The brakes were off.

She explained that she had only recently discovered that she could have been caught up in the Bon Secours

Mother and Baby Home scandal that operated between 1925 and 1961 in the town of Tuam, County Galway, Ireland. That there was a strong possibility she could have been left in that maternity home for unmarried mothers and their children.

When I questioned the fact that Marion's family would have put her into such a home she explained that she did not doubt that her parents would have battled not to have done so but once they had been refused a normal wedding ceremony in the Catholic Church, with that knowledge they could have demanded that the child conceived outside of wedlock would have to be surrendered.

Stunned, I needed clarification:

'But surely your parents were married, Marion? You would not have been accepted by the Sisters in the Religious Order that we joined if they had not been.'

'My parents had to hasten the date of their marriage in order to avoid the scandal that was attached to unmarried mothers at that time.'

Marion explained that she had been a member of the Religious Order for ten years when the nuns eventually permitted members to visit their parents and that it was on one of these visits that she learnt that she had been *conceived outside of wedlock*. That they were only permitted to marry at a side altar of the church with only two witnesses present. Of course there was to be no white wedding dress. This disclosure came about when she enquired about their silver wedding celebrations. She was prompted to do so when another nun friend had been invited to her parents' Silver wedding celebrations.

'Are you sure that had your parents not married Marion, your mother could have been sent to this Bon Secours Mother and Baby Home in Galway?'

'Yes, Frankie. I have no doubt that my parents loved me. Of course they would not have wanted anything to do with this dreadful place. But if you have followed the latest investigations you will know that many of the children taken away from their mothers were sold for adoption and furthermore that apparently the bodies of 800 were discovered in huge grave in the Bon Secours Mother and Baby Home in Galway.'

'That is disgraceful, Marion. Thank goodness your parents married. It's no wonder that you struggle with your relationship to the Catholic Church.'

'You are familiar with the saying: *Once a Catholic, always a Catholic*. Naturally having been immersed in the Catholic religion for so many years I often ponder on what continues to motivate us most, Frankie. Possibly others had similar experiences. Despite the fact that many people say that some don't adhere to religious norms, folk seem to search for principles that promise to make their lives thrive and bring them peace of mind and a healthy existence. Maybe they find that compliance with certain behaviours and customs provides them with a sense of security. Ethics, cultural and religious practices give them a framework. Besides, you only have to take a walk in the countryside to be reminded what a wonderful world God created.'

'Indeed Marion. That seems to be the case. What was that quote from Dante? Yes. He begins the Divine Comedy with the words *Nel mezzo del cammin di nostra vita: "Midway through the journey of my life."* He continues: *"I found myself in a dark wood—"* '

'Woe! Haven't we both emerged from the darkness? That quote is from Dante's Inferno. Remember he guided his pilgrims through purgatory and on into paradise. My journey to Machu Picchu started me on a new beginning in my life.'

2

COGITATING

*M*arion and I had not noticed the time racing by until the main light in the room switched on automatically.

'So sorry for out-staying my welcome, Frankie. Your little son must be on his way home.'

I spontaneously invited Marion to stay the night.

Why shouldn't she? She lives alone, she seems fragile now and besides I am already learning a lot from our discussion. After protesting a little Marion did not need a great deal of persuasion.

I felt the benefit of having Marion with me when Dante came bouncing through the door after being dropped off by his friend's mother. Marion hugged him and while I prepared supper Dante was happy to give Marion an account of all that he had been up to with his friend. He also enjoyed assembling the puzzle depicting a map of Britain that Marion gave him. When I called them to eat he continued to chat about the lovely time he had enjoyed at his friend's home. I was delighted that our son was at ease with Marion. She offered to read Michael Morpurgo's 'Colly's Barn' to Dante before he fell asleep. I hoped that there would be no tantrums that night. Thankfully, after he had run out of questions about swallows and owls he nodded off peacefully.

Back in the lounge, curious over some of Marion's opinions, I hoped that she would continue with her tales about her struggle with the church. When I watched her settle cosily into the armchair I was glad that she seemed to be restored to her old self. She smiled and as time passed she recounted how much she had gleaned from many of the more trying experiences that she had coped with. While I had always looked on a cancer diagnosis as being life threatening Marion told me that although naturally she was scared that she would die, that frightening experience seemed to give an inner strength and determination to take on other challenges. After all what was there to lose? Grateful for the treatment that she was receiving and conscious that compared to others undergoing cancer treatment she was fortunate that her diagnosis was not as serious as others, she wanted to repay the NHS for the care that she had received. She was particularly delighted that her radiographer Charlotte had taken such good care of her. When Charlotte informed her that she and two others were intending to set up a therapeutic centre within the hospital, she volunteered to help them raise funds for this cause. Marion was excited at the proposal of climbing Machu Picchu as one of the many events intended to raise funds. Each volunteer was to be sponsored and helped to raise funds. Marion recounted how she formed many friendships both training and even more so as they trekked from Cusco to Machu Picchu.

There was not a sound coming from Dante's bedroom. Wondering if he had really been cured from his nightmares I crept quietly upstairs to check. But yes, a smile of contentment radiated from his innocent face.

I was so pleased that I opened our drinks cabinet, pulled out a bottle of Baileys, poured some into glasses, ripped open a packet of amaretto biscuits and placed them beside Marion. Once I had put large pouffes next to our armchairs we sunk back in comfort for a night of sharing.

'The proposal, Marion? Tell me?'

We both laughed.

'All the result of a half a pint of Guinness! In my mam's day sure, doctors recommended that stout was a healthy option for pregnant woman. Mother's milk. A good source of iron.

'But tell me Marion what happened?'

Marion explained that it was true that they had been instructed to abstain from alcohol up at three thousand metres altitude but that she had regarded Guinness as a tonic. She was delighted to celebrate their arrival with reminders of the homeland in Paddy's Irish Bar. However, she soon became lightheaded and had to be escorted back to their hotel. Consequently on the following day when their group of twelve set out slowly on a preparatory acclimatising walk up to four thousand metres chewing the recommended coca leaves, she became sick and had to be escorted back down the mountain to their coach. The driver aware that she would be resting most of the day offered to give her a reiki treatment. They struggled to converse but with smatterings of English, Spanish, and Italian they discovered that they were the same age and both teachers. When Luz learnt that she was single, about to receive a state pension and lived on her own, he suggested that maybe they could help each other. Perhaps even marry!'

After another drink and a good deal of laughter Marion continued to relate that when the walking group arrived back at their hotel a doctor was called and she was given injections, pills and oxygen before being sent to bed. In fact that evening when everyone else was given their kit bag to pack ready to commence the trek the following morning, hers was not delivered.

'Oh, so you didn't join them, Marion?'

'Yes I did. The following morning the doctor appeared in my room when everyone else was at breakfast, took my temperature and told me to pack. It was when I was seated in the front of the coach that the planning for the wedding began. It was great fun. I was teased, encouraged and cajoled. Some volunteered to be my bridesmaids, others to help me choose a dress and one of the men promised to give me away. This proposal provided us with great hilarity for the rest of the trek. I never saw Luz again.'

'I envy you in climbing Machu Picchu, Marion. What a wonderful experience it all must have been.'

Glasses topped up we reclined further into our upholstered armchairs. Marion continued to relate the challenges, conquests, achievements and the sheer beauty of the trek.

She marvelled at the wonderful Peruvian countryside and in Bolivia when they ventured over the border to see Lake Titicaca. She spoke of the Andes Mountains and mentioned that this area is claimed to be the birthplace of the Incas, and one of South America's largest lakes and the world's highest navigable body of water.

'Sounds absolutely wonderful, Frankie. But such a different countryside.'

Marion agreed recounting memories of the terrain, the crumbling and slippery rocks, swampy parts, woodland, lakes, streams, huge rivers and the necessity of adapting to the weather. Then she stressed that in retrospect she had come to realise that it was what she had learnt from the people who she walked beside that proved to be even more significant.

When I asked Marion to explain what she meant by

this she replied:

'Isn't it what we learn from other people that provides us with the hugely treasured part of life's journey? Although fortunately our convent lifestyles have helped us to ponder, meditate and reflect on life's journey, it's our contact with believers of other religious persuasions and none, that have sometimes been limited?'

'I think that maybe that is true, Marion.'

Silence ensued. I noticed that Marion appeared to be cogitating. After a while she asked me if when I was an Aspirant training to become a Sister, Enid Blyton's 'The Land of Far Beyond' was read aloud while we were eating our evening meal. I said that indeed that book had been read to us.

'I hope that you'll find this relevant, Frankie. It's just popped into my head. But long before you entered the convent, I remember that one evening when our group of trainee nuns were seated in silence along three rectangular tables in the refectory, this children's tale was read aloud. Can you imagine our reaction? All twenty-six Aspirants ranging in age from twelve to twenty-seven were surprised when the reader at the lectern started reading: *Once upon a time, in the great City of Turmoil...*'

This propelled Marion and I into a huge discussion on a topic that had intrigued us both. The scaffolding that supports us on our journey through life. It soon became evident that we needed more time to continue pondering on the colossal subject of the place of religion in our lives.

Encouraged, Marion continued to stress that walking side-by-side and in the footsteps of those who hold differing views proved to be very enriching. She referred to Dante, John Bunyan, Milton and even Enid Blyton's 'The Land of Far Beyond', the fundamental as having that message. She concluded with: 'Each of us is on our own journey pondering universal truths that have even greater significance.'

'Okay, Marion. So you're saying that we may have been blinkered by being soaked in Catholic perspectives on life?'

Marion reminded me that the so called Smiley Pope, Pope John XXIII, transformed the Catholic Church when he convened the Second Vatican Council. Up until then Catholics were taught that they had the one true Catholic Faith. We recited this in the words of the Nicene Creed:

'I believe in one, holy, catholic and apostolic Church.

I confess one baptism for the forgiveness of sins,

and I look forward to the resurrection of the dead, and the life of the world to come.'

'Pope John XXIII opened the windows of the Church. He blew away the cobwebs and reminded Catholics that each of us are on the one journey through life, didn't he, Marion.'

It was almost midnight. Marion and I crept past Dante's bedroom and settled into peaceful sleep. After breakfast the next morning the world seemed a much better place as Marion set off on her way home. As she started walking towards the front door she turned and patted my arm thanking me profusely for all that we had shared. Then she added:

'No doubt things will improve for you when you discuss everything with Richard.'

'Our flights are booked for Monday next.'

'Excellent, Frankie.'

Dante seemed to be much better behaved when I took him swimming after we had been to Mass that Sunday. I wondered if this was because he had sensed that I seemed to be more at peace with myself. Having tired him out and putting him to bed later that evening I checked that he was sleeping peacefully.

He is the image of Richard. Curled up with Peter Rabbit.

Hopefully Richard will phone tomorrow. Off to dreamland.

My mobile rang, I guessed it would be Richard.

'*Cara, Charisma Frankie.*'

'Richard! I knew that you would be busy all day Sunday.'

'My heart's aching. You have been out of my arms for too long. I can't wait to hold you and our darling Dante.'

'Me too. Today's nearly over. We'll be with you next Monday.'

'I'll be the guy who is jumping up and down near the front of the exit gate at the airport.'

'I love you, Richard, especially when you're acting the eejit.'

'I'll try and control my excitement. Kiss Dante goodnight for me.'

'Of course. I do that every night. He's so excited.'

'Papa is delighted with the photos you email. You bring joy to Margherita. Rosina says that your love and support helps Margherita get better. Nurse Angela says the same.'

'Love you!'

'Ti amo di più.'

So much to ponder. Surely sleep will come easily tonight. Richard loves me. We are very fortunate. Happy memories. I'm swimming in Richard's love. We are enjoying the warm Sicilian seas a few weeks before Dante is about to be born to us. Sheer delight is trickling through my sleepy body inducing wonderfully sensuous dreams.

'Ti amo di più.'

But sleep did not come easily for me. After tossing and turning I eventually decided that if I was going to really make big changes in my life I needed to make definite plans. I searched for a notebook. Marion's disclosures had resulted in both kindling my enthusiasm and creating a dilemma. I realised that I could not abandon the Catholic beliefs that were embedded in my very being. But had I confused piety and devotions with spirituality? What motivated people from other faiths and none? Eventually I headed the first page of my notebook with:

'The unexamined life is not worth living.' Socrates

1 I need to take stock and evaluate what is going on in my life and acknowledge that I have not been coping.

2 What is causing this? I am forty, healthy, happily married with a gorgeous son. I might be half way through my life.

3 Maybe I am no longer expected to be dominated by strict religious norms.

4 Taking time out from our busy, buzzing lives is not going to be easy. Richard may well have had opportunities to reflect while he was caring for his aunt. We need to discuss this.

5 I am convinced that if we are to live fulfilled lives our journey must be enriching. Our goals are important and the journey to our destination too.

6 Whatever challenge Richard and I embrace must stimulate us both. When he returns from Florence we need to kick-start our lives.

7 Marion stressed the importance of walking besides and listening to others.

8 My mother suffered depression that seemed to stem from jealousy. She had low self-esteem and always longed to go somewhere different. But wherever she went she continued to be troubled. Will my urge to escape from the humdrum and take on a challenge really help me consider my priorities in life?

I fell asleep with my notebook beside me on my pillow.

3

UNITED

A week later Dante and I landed in Florence.

Dante clung to me as I pushed the trolley through the barrier at the Airport. He couldn't wait to see his dad. *I've tried to look my best but sure Richard won't care what I am wearing! There he is waving! Puppy eyes and dimples. Handsome as ever. That's my man.*

'Papà, papà!'

'Mia cara, Fran! Dante, amore mio! Ma guarda! You've grown…'

Wonderful! Tears of sheer delight spilling. Dante jumping into Richard's arms. Three of us cuddling and kissing. So much to say. Richard's hugging Dante into his booster seat.

What's making him gurgle so contently?

Richard swivelled round to witness the cause of his delightful outburst.

'Pooh Bear. Daddy, he's strapped in. Come here, Pooh. How did you get in here?'

Dante is happy, chatting, sucking grapes and feeding

some to his furry friend. Richard's squeezing my knee and chancing another hug and a kiss while waiting at the traffic lights. We're revelling in our love.

'More grapes, please. We're hungry.'

'We're nearly at Aunty's house. You're very quiet. Has Pooh gone to sleep?'

'No. Pooh's hungry too, Mummy.' Dante leans forward. Richard laughs, then reassures Dante.

'Tell him that your two lovely aunts are sure to have plenty of food ready for us.'

'Here we are, darling. I'm just about to drive through their gates.'

'Clever daddy.'

Richard was delighted that in spite of Margherita's cancer treatment, both his aunts were on their doorstep to welcome us. I assumed that the tall, athletically slim, young lady standing next to them must be the nurse that Richard told me was taking care of Margherita.

Somehow I didn't visualise Angela as being so attractive. Fine cheek-boned, bronzed complexion. She's a cross between a mermaid and a seraph. She looks gorgeous in that flowing white, pinafore dress. Her large aster-blue eyes are scanning me as she comes forward to hug us and swing Dante around.

'Again! Again!' Dante cried out.

I was struggling to cope with a whirlwind of emotions when Richard introduced the nurse to me: 'This is Angela. She's such a tremendous help to Margherita. I don't know what we would do without her.'

So she's a wonderful help. What am I to make of that? Then again being immersed in an Italian welcome is very special. Warm embraces. Kisses and hugs. All these genuine expressions of love.

Margherita linked arms with Richard. 'Mi dispiace.

Sorry. Giovanni is not here to welcome you. He is with Lucia, his friend's wife. He stayed with her after the funeral of her husband Carlos. He was only seventy-one. It was cancer.'

Richard reminded Margherita of how he and I experienced the loving kindness of these friends, when Giovanni and his lovely wife, Lucia, came to visit us in England. Margherita was pleased, and Richard immediately volunteered to collect Giovanni from his home and drive him back to join us the following morning. Richard's other aunt Rosina beckoned us to follow them into their kitchen.

'Venite, for lasagne. You must be hungry.'

She'd pulled on a wrap-around blue denim apron over a beige blouse and an ankle length, brown, plaid skirt. The button-through floral paisley-patterned dress that Margherita was wearing seemed to accentuate her weight loss, presumingly resulting from her cancer treatment.

'Grazie. Rosina. I love this kitchen. It's so rustic. The lighting. So cosy. And the smell of the lasagne bubbling in the oven? Thank you. So lovely to be here again.'

Rosina beamed a huge smile and from the grin on Richard's face he seemed to be in a jovial mood. Excited, he started fooling about. *By the look of things he's up to something.* Grabbing Dante's hand he began to dance.

'My shoes make a noise, Dante. Listen. These are terracotta tiles you're standing on. This is a real Italian kitchen.'

'Oh, stop dancing, Papa. You look funny.'

Egged on by Dante's remark and eager to prevent him from being overawed while surrounded by so many adults, Richard acted the eejit. With a smirk on his face, opening his arms wide and curtseying he started speaking in a clipped Italian accent:

'Welcome, Signorina Francesca, to our typical Tuscan albergo, our hotel. The lasagne will be served with a tomato salad and a fluffy piece or two of perfectly cooked garlic bread. The lasagna is irresistibly yummy and it will be accompanied by a glass of your favourite wine.'

'Daddy! Now you're pretending to be a waiter. You're acting funny.'

'Così carino! I lift you up. Dante.'

'Yes, please.'

Angela hoisted Dante onto a stool next to her. Margherita thanked her for looking after him.

Angela certainly seems to be part of the family.

The homely, happy surroundings made us feel relaxed. We chatted as we devoured the fresh, flavoursome, sun-kissed Italian cuisine. Enjoying such fabulous homemade food Richard remarked that it surely couldn't be surpassed. After such a delicious meal, Margherita suggested that Richard and I go for a walk. Angela volunteered to look after Dante.

'Ponte Santa Trinita, here we come.'

'Oh, Richard that's wonderful.'

In an alcove on the bridge overlooking the river Arno, Richard and I embraced and kissed passionately. Wrapped in Richard's arms, I delighted in feeling his heart beating with love.

Ponte Santa Trinita, amongst the most beautiful in the world, is steeped in romance. This is the bridge where it is believed the great Dante met Beatrice all those years ago. I gave Richard a picture of that famous meeting on the very first Christmas we shared our love. I long to be here in Richard's arms forever.

'Stay in Florence. I miss you. Stay with me. Margherita does not have to have chemotherapy. She has only two more sessions of radiotherapy. While she is recuperating, we can enjoy being a family again.'

'I would love to stay. Could we? What about school? My contract? Dante's schooling?'

'I love you. I want you here. Oh, what can we do?'

We discussed the limitations of the amount of time that we could spend together and how we wished that we had planned things differently. Richard was granted six months' school leave, and I was committed to staying in my post. We had to accept the consequences of our decisions and resolve to enjoy every second of the remaining time together in Florence.

When we eventually returned to Richard's aunt's home, I heard Dante chatting in the kitchen.

'Look! Orech… Orecchte…'

'Orecchiette!'

'Little ears. Like my ears.'

Dante was perched on a stool making pasta shapes with Angela.

'Margherita sleeps. I show Dante how to make.'

'Yes Mamma. For dinner. Angela helped me. Look, the flour is sticking to my hands.'

Dante thanked Angela. 'Grazie, Angela.'

She encouraged him. 'Bravo, Dante.'

Dante seemed to be at ease with Angela. They appeared to have thoroughly enjoyed themselves. Not sure how to respond, I came out with :

'Thank you, Angela. Come with me now, Dante. I'll change you out of those clothes. You've got flour all over them.'

'Angela knows lots of things about pasta, Mamma. She is very clever.'

After supper, Angela offered to put Dante to bed while the rest of the family chatted, sipped wine and relaxed. Richard thanked her and promised to pour a glass of Chianti for her to enjoy as soon she returned to join them. Her generosity prompted both aunts to praise her. 'Angela. Angelica! An angel. So good.'

'We are very fortunate in finding such a good nurse, Francesca.'

Richard added, 'I have been teaching her English. She wants to nurse in England. Perhaps she will learn more from Dante and she can teach him Italian?'

I wondered what it was like when Richard was teaching Angela? Were they seated close together, leaning over a phrase book, hands touching, eyes meeting? Him laughing at some of her silly mistakes? Italians are so tactile.

When Angela joins us in the lounge, I find myself deliberately speaking quickly. Am I hoping that she will find it difficult to follow our conversation?

That night I realised that our bedroom was situated between Dante's and Angela's. Therefore Richard had been sleeping next door to Angela. Margherita's bedroom was on the other side of Angela's. I wondered if Angela could hear what Richard and I were saying?

Determined to prove my love, I changed into my white flowing, floral lace night gown hoping that I might remind him of our wedding. When I stepped out of the bathroom, Richard leapt off our bed to carry me and dance around the room singing 'O solo mio'. I was stretched out in his arms as he sang:

'O sole mio

Sta 'nfronte a te!

But another sun

that's brighter still

It's my own sun

that's in your face!'

He gently laid me on the bed and enclosed my face in his strong, caressing hands.

'Oh darling, my love at last we... oh...'

'Oh, oh...'

'What's that?'

We heard a sharp knock on our bedroom door. I sat up in Richard's arms. The door opened. Dante ran in and jumped on our bed. Angela stood at the open door.

'I'm so sorry. Dante was crying. I tried to comfort him. Mi dispiace. Sorry.'

'Grazie. Thank you, Angela.'

Angela closed the door.

Dante cuddled in between us. We both consoled him. 'Poor Dante. No need to cry. You're safe with Mamma and me. Come. Sleep now.'

Why did Angela disturb us? Surely she could have comforted Dante? Richard is so gentle. Two pairs of amber eyes, father and son radiating love. I wonder what the soundproofing is like between our bedroom walls? No, I must not let jealousy rear its head. Dante's already asleep. Richard has settled him on his side of the bed and hugged me closer. How I have missed his love.

4

FATHERLY LOVE

The following morning Richard and I were seated at the kitchen table happily chatting away to Rosina while enjoying coffee and Panettone when we heard the door open behind us.

'Buongiorno, Francesca!'

Richard's father, Giovanni, had arrived. There were hugs all round. He apologised for not being there to welcome us and explained that his friend Sergio drove him over to meet us as early as possible. I threw my arms round him assuring him that I understood that of course he needed to be at his friend's funeral.

'You look as lovely as ever, Francesca. That's a beautiful blue dress. And Dante. I peeped in to see him. He has grown. Forse. Perhaps he will be tall. I'm longing to hear his voice.'

Rosina, anxious for everyone to vacate the kitchen so that she could begin preparing the ingredients for lunch, ushered us into another room. Richard and Giovanni jokingly curtsied and Richard lead the way. We all seemed to be in good humour so having been complimented for my dress I turned to Richard and pretended that he was a model. He took up the challenge and began to stride around the room as though he was walking down a catwalk while I commented: 'Casual sophistication. Taken from Giorgio Armani superb Men's latest style. Modelled elegantly by Richard. Italians sure know how to make a statement, even when partaking on their debut designer collaboration show.'

There was laughter all round. I added: 'In comparison, as the Scots would say, I am stuck with a peely-wally complexion, freckles and auburn hair.'

After breakfast, I admired the way Richard organised everyone. Margherita's hospital appointment was at eleven. He and Angela were going to drive her there. Rosina had enlisted Dante to help her make the pasta for lunch. Giovanni invited me to accompany him into town to buy a present for Lucia, the wife of the friend who had died.

I was delighted to take a leisurely walk with Giovanni. As always, he proved himself to be a genuine gentleman. I had forgotten how narrow the pavements are from Via Pinti up to the Duomo, but I needn't have worried. Giovanni insisted on hopping on and off from the pavement onto the road, often grasping my hand. So fatherly. Much like I imagined my own father to have been.

Turning into the Piazza della Repubblica, I was once again overcome with the splendour of the scene before me. I gasped. Flinging open my arms I exclaimed, 'Il Duomo. Beautiful. What an awesome sight. No wonder this piazza is perpetually filled with admirers.'

I continued to gaze up to the cupola and the tower, the prettily decorated exterior with a festive cladding of white, green, and pink marble coloured brickwork and so much else. Giovanni put his arm around me as reminded me. 'Davvero. But because we cross this square so often...'

'I know. I'm seeing it all again and I just love it. It's

full of happy memories too.'

We stood together while I continued to marvel at it all. 'So cosmopolitan. Oh look, the horses are at the ready to take people for a jaunt just like they do in Kerry.'

Then Giovanni tugged at my sleeve and stretching his arm round me guided me towards a restaurant situated in full view of the Duomo. He ordered my favourite caffe macchiato and an almond croissant.

'You remember everything, Giovanni. Grazie mille.'

Just like his father! I dote on the warmth of Richard's love. How did Giovanni manage to store all that love inside him for all these years since his beloved wife died?

A group of Japanese tourists blocked our sight of the Duomo. Giovanni leaned over the table and patted my hands. He said nothing for a while. We looked into each other's eyes.

'When my darling wife Laura died, I felt that I did not want to go on living. Our love. My love for her. Our love for each other was as Dante Alighieri says, 'L' amor che move il sole e l'altre stelle.' It moved not only the sun and stars but my entire world.'

Giovanni's eyes moistened. I squeezed his hands. We sat in silence.

'Riccardo misses you, Frankie. Nobody can replace you. Not even Dante, whom he adores. You should be together. I know that he loves me and his aunts. But a new life began when he married you, Francesca.'

'Grazie, Giovanni. You are always so understanding. Margherita needs him while she is having treatment. The bond that they have formed is mutual. We respect that. This school term is short. We will be better able to look to our future after that.'

'Davvero. You are right. We have a great future before us. Come. Let's make our way to the Supermercato, in Via Lorenza.'

The Supermarket is chock-a-block. Foreigners and natives babbling, mingling, pushing trollies, examining and weighing produce. It resembles my muddled, questioning mind. Love and duty? Our past. Our future. Am I jealous of Angela?

'Ah! Vino Nobile Di Montepulciano! This is one of Tuscany's most renowned red wines. Lucia will love this one.'

Intent on purging any jealousy of Angela that might be erupting in me, I checked with Giovanni that Angela hailed from Sicily before purchasing a bottle of Sicilian limoncello and Bacci ice-cream balls to share at the promised celebration that night.

Later I was happy when Angela thanked me for my thoughtfulness in choosing the limoncello. But I wished that I had not been so encouraging when Richard suggested that Angela accompanied us the following day when we planned to visit Fiesole.

'It will be a great place for Dante. Would you like to join us Angela tomorrow? Perhaps you could show Dante around the Roman amphitheatre while Francesca and I visit the Etruscan exhibition?'

That night, as Richard released me from a warm embrace before going to sleep, I wondered what it was going to be like with Angela at close quarters. But, determined to purge myself of jealousy, I resolved to use this opportunity for that purpose.

5

EVALUATION

*I*t was already a warm April day when Richard, Dante and I accompanied by Angela set off for Fiesole. I listened to the lovely way Angela began to speak in Italian to Dante when she pointed to the landmarks en route. When I looked in the car mirror, I saw our son cuddling up to her.

Dressed in a flowing blue top over a figure-hugging pair of white leggings, Angela is undoubtedly fit, attractive and attentive. Dante obviously feels safe with her.

Once we arrived and parked, we made our way to the entrance of the beautiful gardens, inserted our tickets to release the gate, and entered. Dante grasped Angela's hand, and they jumped down the steep steps towards the amphitheatre.

Richard enfolded me, kissing my forehead. 'What a difference time makes. I treasure the memory of how wonderfully understanding you were with me when I was tormented with my fears that Christmas, Fran.'

Richard nestled my head further into his chest. I whispered, 'We were all worried. You had every right to be afraid.'

'Huntington's disease. The consequences would have been… well…'

'Thank God, you needn't have been so scared. Come on, let's have a coffee before we go into the museum. Let's immerse ourselves in this wonderful place. It's so beautiful here. Tuscan hills and a cloudless sky. What's that psalm? *I raise my eyes toward the mountains. From whence shall come my help?*'

Richard joined me:

'My help comes from the Lord,
the maker of heaven and earth.
He will not allow your foot to slip,
or your guardian to sleep.'

We finished together:

'The Lord will guard your coming and going both now and forever.'

'We share so much, Richard. We were steeped in religion. You stood by me when my future seemed hopeless. What would I have done without your support?

'What is the saying, Richard? Was it St Peter who talks about gold being tested by fire?'

We watched Dante enjoying himself down in the amphitheatre. He looked happy with Angela, so we decided to enter the museum. We admired the superb collection of Etruscan pottery and other exhibits. Conscious that Dante's concentration span might not last long, we restricted ourselves to a quick glance round. When we emerged, Dante ran up the steep, stone steps, landing in Richard's arms. I was delighted at the way he swung him around into a huge hug.

Angela retrieved our sandwiches from where she had hidden them in a cool spot behind a fence on a little balcony overlooking the site. The sun shone from an azure blue, cloudless sky above the undulating hills.

Mesmerised by its beautiful panoramic scenes, while Dante tried to catch a lizard bathing in the sun we discussed different artists who used various mediums to depict such splendour. Among others, we mentioned Bruno Chirici famous for his sensitive use of oil on canvas for his portrayal of Tuscan Villages. Lost in the wonder of it all, I reminded Richard that there's a copy of the Red Poppies in the dining room in his aunt's house. Hearing the word 'poppy', Dante interrupted.

'Poppies. What are poppies? Are they like puppies? I wish I had a puppy.'

'Poppies are lovely red flowers, Dante. Let's see if we can find some.'

Angela volunteered to take Dante for a run around, freeing Richard and I to spend more time together. Grasping Angela's hand, Richard said, 'Are you not too tired, Angela? You have been running around amusing Dante. You set out our lovely picnic, too. Would you like to see the exhibits in the museum?'

'Thank you. The pottery is very beautiful. I enjoyed looking at it last month when I come with my mother. No. We have fun. True, Dante?'

When Dante and Angela skipped down the steps again, Richard put his arms around me. 'It's so good to enjoy this precious time together. I'm so sorry to have left you on your own. It must have been so lonely for you.'

'It's true that I struggled, Richard. I missed you so much. The house was empty without you, and Dante kept asking when you were going to come home. But, I was determined to be strong. Admittedly, getting Dante ready for school, and driving through the traffic during the rush hour was hard, but haven't we both learnt to face up to difficulties? Besides, we are still young. We can do more than cope.'

I snuggled closer after his tender kiss.

'Oh darling, I'm so sorry...'

'No. No. Dearest Richard, none of this is your fault. This is life. Margherita has been a mother to you.' I traced my fingers across his brow and tossed his hair. He held onto my hand.

'But that is not to deny that it's difficult, too. You have proved your love for me many times. Returning here today reminds me of how generous you are.'

Dante shouted to us, 'Mamma. Look. I can jump down from here. Watch me!'

'No! No! Don't, Dante!'

'Oh no!' I shouted. 'He's… Why doesn't Angela…?'

Richard was already half way down the stone steps. Dante had fallen. He was crying. Angela enfolded him in her arms. I was about to follow Richard with some wipes.

Angela hugged him tighter. 'Poverino. Non piangere… don't cry.'

'Why did you do that? I've warned you before about jumping down steps.'

'I didn't. I thought… Mamma, I…'

I wished that I hadn't raised my voice when I saw Dante putting his arms around Angela's neck and she kissing him.

'I'm sorry. I should have stopped him.'

'No. Don't blame yourself, Angela. That's what boys do.' Richard continued, 'You have to build up to doing long jumps, Dante. But not on hard stone steps. Come here. I'll make you better.'

I walked behind Richard as he carried Dante to the top of the steps. Angela used the wipes to clean his cut. Once back in the car to begin our journey home, Richard tried to dispel the silence by playing the cheerful 'Poppa Piccolino' song.

That night in bed, when I apologised to Richard for being so abrupt in dealing with Dante, he admitted that if I hadn't, he most likely would have done the same. I felt better when he also said that Angela should have prevented him from jumping down concrete steps.

I agreed and added that had she not looked after Dante, we wouldn't have been able to enjoy precious time alone.

He concurred, but then defended her. 'Yes. Poor Angela is still learning. She hasn't any children of her own yet. Perhaps we expect too much of her? Or maybe we could explain things to her?'

Why would we need to give her instructions? Is Dante going to be with her on other occasions, or does Richard intend Dante staying on here while I return to England? What does he have in mind? Why is he defending Angela? I decided to probe.

'Her English is improving. You are a good teacher. Where do you conduct your lessons with her?'

'Usually in the dining room. When the older members have their siesta, we spread our books out on the kitchen table.'

'Do you work through a text book?'

'We started in that formal way but decided that conversation about everyday things would be more relevant.'

'So you must know a good deal about each other by now?'

'Yes, we do. Very interesting.'

'Tell me about her?'

Richard filled me in on Angela's background. 'She was born in Sicily. Her mother moved from Austria when her father died young of a heart attack. Her mother began working as a nanny when she and her sister were growing up, and she later trained as a nurse and is still working in her sixties. Angela's older sister, Ursula, chose a nursing career.'

'So they are all in a caring profession, Richard.'

'Yes. That is why we selected Angela. In fact, she was highly recommended. She intends to complete further qualifications in the same profession.'

Richard is really animated talking about her.

'You appreciate Angela very much, Richard. Inevitably working so closing you have developed a close relationship with her.'

'Inevitably. She has proved to be of great support to Margherita and to Rosina too. Giovanni was with me when we interviewed her. She adapts very easily. She is punctual and fits in with our way of living. Yes. All round we are pleased with her.'

'She has lived with your family longer than I have had a chance to do. I can imagine her sitting cosily next to you each afternoon…'

'Oh, Fran… we… I make sure not to become… You're not jealous? Oh, what am I saying? You. I love you more than anyone else in… why wouldn't I? I love you. You must know that? You do, don't you?'

Good Lord, Mammy used to cut people out of the family photographs. God rest her soul. She suffered intensely from jealousy. I hope that I have not inherited that debilitating streak.

6

RICHARD IS PERCEPTIVE

The following day, once again, Richard and I decided to take advantage of the warm weather.

When I joined the family at breakfast, Giovanni asked, 'Hai dormito bene, Francesca?'

Richard was winking at me so I replied, 'I'm not used to this hot weather, yet. But thank you, I did eventually manage to sleep.'

'Brava, Francesca. I'm delighted that Riccardo has invited me to accompany you to the Boboli Gardens, today. Margherita needs Angela to stay at home to help Rosina in the kitchen.'

I felt my face breaking into a smile as I replied, 'Richard knows how much I love those gardens.'

While it was still early, we set off to drive to the Boboli Gardens.

As soon as we parked our car, bought our tickets and entered the gardens, Dante became excited when he saw the hills. The scratches on his knees must have healed, because he began to run.

Giovanni encouraged Dante. 'Let him go. He needs to run off his excess energy and I need to lose weight. You two take your time, and I'll challenge him.'

Richard managed to convince his father that even if he took a side path, he would not be able to keep up with the speed that Dante would run up the hill. Giovanni agreed to accompany me into the Pitti Palace first, so that we could enjoy its unique treasures. Watching Dante race up the hill, Giovanni seemed delighted that his grandson had already reached the top of the path making it difficult for Richard to catch up with him.

Then Giovanni put his arm round me guiding me to sit on a low wall outside the Pitti Palace.

He thanked me on behalf of all the family for letting Richard stay with them for so long while I remained alone to cope with everything in Wimbledon .

I wondered if this opportunity had been planned after my discussion with Richard the previous day.

'I am delighted that Richard has been able to support Margherita. She and Rosina have been so good to him. Cancer can be so frightening. And yes, I have missed him. I...'

'You and Dante alone in a big house. You have been mother and father to our little boy. I know something about that. Alone, loneliness. It's a struggle.'

Giovanni reached over and kissed my forehead.

Tears began to trickle. When I reached for my hankie, I realised that Giovanni needed one, too.

'Francesca, I have been thinking. Wondering if... well, you tell me what you think. When Richard was training with the Carmelite priests, there was another chap who we befriended. He left the Order too. He became involved in fundraising for a cancer charity.'

'Could we help him? A cancer charity? Of course.'

'It's not straightforward, Francesca. Joseph. That's

his name. He has committed himself to taking part in a fundraising trek organised by the Oasis Cancer Centre in St Gerard's Hospital in Wimbledon. Richard told me that he might be coming to Florence soon.'

Could this be the challenge I was searching for? If he is one of Richard's friends, maybe this might be a way of assuring Richard that his friends are mine too? I need to find out what is involved.

I immediately assured Giovanni that I would be delighted to sponsor Joseph. Adding that after seeing how much support Margherita has received from centres like these, during her cancer process that Richard and I would be only too pleased to help other cancer patients.

We continued to discuss this proposal while groups of visitors shuffled over the pebbled path at the side of the wall where we remained seated. I was delighted to learn that Joseph hailed from County Limerick, and was intent on selling Irish memorabilia, old Irish coins and linen on eBay as a prerequisite to raising the minimum of two thousand pounds in order to join the group taking part in the trek.

'Richard is waving to us.' Giovani told me that there is a playing area and a lake half way down where they could enjoy themselves while we went into the palace.

I wondered why Richard had not mentioned Joseph. Especially since there was the possibility that he may visit Florence. That night when I was already in bed, I asked Richard about him.

Before preparing to join me, perched on our bed, Richard explained that he thought it strange that Joseph had written to his father to ask if he would sponsor him.

'Joseph and I were not that close. Well, you know what it's like, Fran. Friendships weren't encouraged.'

'Oh. I suppose he knew that your father would be willing to support a cancer charity.'

Richard agreed adding that he suspected that Joe might

be hoping that they might help him too. As he would be remaining in Florence until the end of the month he didn't feel it was fair to decide until they both discussed this.

'When Giovanni mentioned it, I said that we could support him. I would like to do my bit for a cancer patients. You have been very much involved through Margherita, and after the scare you had we should prove our gratitude.'

Richard combed his hands through my hair.

'You're always so generous, Fran. Shall we wait and see what my father does? He might have already invited Joseph. I wouldn't be surprised if he has sent him the fare.'

Sure enough, two days later, what my mam would have described as a thin, lanky fellow. A fine cut of a man, turned up. Curly flaxen hair, blue shorts and t-shirt, matching his baby blue eyes. Joseph radiated a winning smile, immediately finding favour with everybody.

'I see you are wearing your Fáinne. Conas ta tu?'

'Go han-mhaith, go raibh maith agat.'

'What was all that?'

'Were you speaking Italian, Mummy?'

'Ah now, this needs a bit of explaining, doesn't it, Fran?'

I tapped a cushion on the chair where I was seated, inviting Dante to sit next to me. 'We're speaking in the Irish language. Gaelic. I knew that Joseph would understand because he is wearing a Fáinne.'

'Yep. This gold circle brooch shows that I am a fluent Irish speaker.'

'But what did you say to each other?'

'*How are you?* To which, she replied, *Very well, thank you.*'

Dante jumped off the chair to face us. Pointing his index finger towards us he said, 'Clever Mummy. You speak three languages. Italian and Irish and English.'

'If only I spoke them well,' I admitted. 'You can

already speak two languages.'

Joseph added,'Sure with a name like Dante, you should be very proud of yourself. You've a lot to live up to.'

'Have I?'

Joseph was friendly, much liked and soon absorbed into the family circle. Angela eagerly volunteered to show him up to his room. I was pleased when I noticed that Angela appeared willing to accept him correcting her faltering English.

I was delighted that, since the arrival of Joseph, the dynamics in the house became more joyful and lighthearted. Margherita seemed to be coping well while recovering from radiotherapy. Angela volunteered to take on some of the cooking, and Giovanni succeeded in driving her and Rosina to Fiesole. Then Richard made a welcome suggestion:

'It's so busy around the Duomo. How would you like to go to Lucca? We could travel by train. It's such a lovely walled city.' Dante responded: 'Train? On a train? Yes, please!'

All was arranged and the following morning we set off for Lucca.

Clutching Pooh bear, Dante clung to Joseph's hand as he lined up with Richard and me to make our way over the pedestrian crossing onto the forecourt of SS Maria Novella train station.

Everything was new to Dante, so Richard explained that we would have to search for the train departure times on the information panel and then find the correct queue, buy the tickets, and move to the appropriate platform. Dante enjoyed using the machine to validate our tickets before boarding the train.

We filed onto the upper deck. Dante sat near the window. He held Pooh up so that he could look out of the window and, much to the amusement of a couple in seats opposite, proceeded to tell Pooh that our destination was Lucca. Joseph sat next to him.

'Thomas the Tank Engine. Mammy reads those books to me. I wish I was on one. Are we?'

Joseph laughed. 'It would take us ages to get to Lucca on that kind of train!'

'It can go fast?'

Joseph tossed his blonde curls and began to explain the difference between steam trains and electric ones. He did not mention the fact that their journey would take one hour and forty-six minutes. Instead, they began to play 'I spy with my little eye something beginning with the letter 'B''. This was followed by the 'Banana' game that requires each player to find the letter 'A' somewhere on a sign, license plate, or similar. The player then moves on to finding the letter 'B', and so on. After they reached the letter 'E' they changed and played 'Simon Says.'

I was happy that Joseph seemed to bond so quickly with Dante. The long journey appeared to speed by. When we had lunched at Lucca, we walked round part of that beautiful walled city.

That evening, Joseph joined Richard and me as we relaxed in our aunt's garden.

'We owe you a huge, thank you, Joe, for all your help today. Especially for whiling away the time on the train.'

'Away with you, Richard. Sure, the little fellow is a dote.'

'You have no idea, Joe, how much we are usually repeatedly pestered with *Are we there yet?* Isn't that right, Richard?'

'I suppose up till now, I have only experienced the easy side of parenthood. But, hopefully things could change as a result of taking part on this trek that I have signed up for.'

'I'm curious, Joe. What exactly is involved?'

Joe explained that what attracted him to going on this trek was the need he felt of moving his life forward. He wanted to prove himself and face his future. The thought of making friends within a group of caring people who commit to causes like this, seemed appealing. He hoped that he was explaining himself, properly.

I assured him that we were very happy to sponsor him. We were impressed by all that he had told us about the great benefit that is available in Oasis Cancer Centre. But while we had both been on a pilgrimage to Lourdes and we knew about trekking, we wanted to know what's different about this pilgrimage. How many miles was the walk? What type of the terrain is covered? Does it involve a lot of praying and penance?

Joe laughed, before saying that Richard might want to opt in if it were more like the pilgrimage described in The Canterbury Tales.

'Canterbury Cathedral. Indeed, 'tis a grand place. We were taken there as novices, Richard, weren't we?'

'Yes, Joe. And you disgraced us.'

Joe's face has broken into a smile. He looks as if he enjoys life to the full and is friendly and personable. I wonder what constraints were put on him and Richard in the seminary.

'I did. The memory still haunts me. How was I to know about Adam Delving?'

'Can you imagine us, Fran? Our guide was pointing up to, was it three windows, Joe?'

'Three. Yes I think so.'

'Anyway, he asked us to admire the precious portrayal of Adam Delving. And Joe piped up with, Who's Adam Delving?'

Joe pointed his finger at us. 'Well might you both laugh, but I have a sneaking feeling that the rest of ye didn't know either.'

'Maybe the two of ye would have been more interested in the bawdy tales in the accounts described in The Canterbury Tales?'

'Of course. I've lured you in. Ye want the facts about the pilgrimage to Santiago de Compostela. But at this time of night, I limit it to just a few. Okay. After you have refilled your glasses, I'll begin.'

As Richard and I lay in bed that night, we discussed what we had learnt about the Camino de Compostela. I told Richard about Marion's suggestion of going on a pilgrimage. Initially Richard said that we would have a big enough challenge just getting our lives back together. He had been away from teaching for over two terms, and I had been coping on my own. I agreed that we had both been stretched, but that we had coped. But that surely at this stage of our lives we didn't want to resort to the same routine. Richard retaliated by reminding me that routine had served us both well for most of our lives.

I knew that I had to tread carefully. I told him that I was not suggesting that we should put the kibosh on following a well-regulated lifestyle. That it's a matter of balance. But that I do not want to become predictable, content, or just satisfied.

Not convinced, Richard said that traipsing off through Galicia is alright for a single man, like Joe, but that we have responsibilities to each other and our son. 'I'm happy as I am. I am content. Why shouldn't I be? I have a beautiful wife and an adorable son.'

'And I count my good fortune in having a wonderful husband and a handsome son who is the image of him. However, is being content enough?'

Eventually, Richard agreed that perhaps I was right. He rested his head on his chin and seemed to become more pensive before admitting that although his father Giovanni adhered to fairly strict schedules while he was lecturing, once he retired he suddenly decided to return to Florence and now he delights in just enjoying life. Since then he has taken his sisters to visit places that they never visited before. Giovanni benefitted from the routine life that he had followed. He is financially viable. But we are not in that position yet. However, we need to keep aiming high so that we can make our dreams a reality.

'Dreams. We need our dreams. Shall we sleep on these ideas, darling, Frankie?'

'My eyes are closing, too. Hopefully, I'll enjoy dreams instead of nightmares tonight.'

I like what Joe has told us about the Camino. Those who have opted to join the volunteers taking part in the pilgrimage seem to come from varied backgrounds and age groups. Joe says that he has been given to believe that although we start and finish together each day, we can choose who to walk beside or opt to walk alone.

The added factor is that at the same time as challenging myself, I can prove my love for Richard. Killing off jealousy is not that easy. That slimy green snake wriggles and writhes. I'll need to get St Patrick on the job. After all, he succeeded in banishing the snakes out of Ireland.

The next morning, Richard and I carried our bowls of fruit and muesli to the bottom of his aunt's garden. We wanted to breakfast in the shade of the spreading branches of an ancient olive tree.

'You seemed to sleep peacefully last night, Fran. I think that I can guess where you were.'

'Walking towards a field of golden stars. Compostela.'

'What I noticed last night, is that Joe appears to be in the same place that you and I were in when we first met. He talked about being with committed people. Do you remember how vulnerable we felt?'

'Raw! I felt like an egg without a shell. I sensed his anxiety, too. At the same time, he seems to be driven. I liked the way he was talking about being a parent. Obviously he needs to take things gradually.'

These considerations began to lead Richard to conclude that it would be good for us to support Joe as he makes new friendships and decisions. We recalled how when we left religious life, even though we were mature adults, we needed support when we emerged from the closed environments that we'd live in for years. Not only our relatives, but people that we befriended, didn't appear to appreciate how fragile we were. We felt that it was important for us to be there for him with the proviso that we would take care while not verging towards becoming over protective of him.

After some hours of discussion, Richard rubbed the top of his nose and then waved his index finger. 'Okay. The trek's scheduled to take place during the autumn term. So you'll be at home to care for Dante.'

'Grand. I was about to ask you about the date. Perhaps, when I return home, maybe we could invite Joe over to our home so that he can fill us in on further details.'

'Yes, Richard. Here he comes. Shall we tell him the good news now?'

It's lovely to watch the wide smile on Joe's face as Richard tells him about our decision. Hugs, thanks, smiles, heads nodding and slapping of hands. They're happy.

At the end of the Easter holidays, Richard and I were delighted that Joseph was flying back to Wimbledon with Dante and me. My agreement to sign up for the fundraising pilgrimage to Santiago de Compostela brought Joe closer to us. I looked forward to the end of the next school term when Richard was to travel home to reunite our little family.

7

SIGNING AND PLANNING

*T*he Saturday morning after we had arrived back in Wimbledon, Joseph knocked at our front door. It was only nine o'clock. I was enjoying a lie-in. Now that we had returned to our seven o'clock school day timetable, even Dante was tired.

I opened our bedroom window. Joe waved up. Delighted to see him, I grabbed my dressing gown and flew down the stairs to open the door.

'Forgive me Frankie! There's no accounting for my coming here so early!'

This will-o'-the-wisp fellow is beguiling. A slender, ghost-like creature emerging from the morning dew. My hand nearly reached out to this cupid fellow and tossed his golden curls.

I rubbed my eyes.

'Ah, 'tis too early, altogether.'

Clutching my dressing gown tighter I laughed and welcomed him inside.

'No. Come on in, Joe. I'm… I was exhausted. The first

week back to school. Just as well you woke me. Here he comes, Dante. He'll be delighted to see you. Maybe you could entertain him while I go upstairs to get dressed? I won't be long.'

Dante rushed to hug Joe. I showed them into our front room where Dante pointed to the castle with a moat that he had succeeded in building.

I was surprised at how quickly arrangements to sign up for the fundraising trek moved on while we enjoyed a substantial breakfast. Mark, at the Oasis Cancer Centre in St Gerard's Hospital in Wimbledon, had supplied Joe with the necessary forms.

I questioned him for further details. 'So, Joe, we each have to raise a minimum of two thousand pounds. What did you decide about holding fundraising events?'

Joe explained that, as he didn't have much room in his flat, he was thinking of maybe of selling rare stamps or coins on eBay.

I am going to have to be careful telling Joe that I don't consider this suggestion to be very practical. Unconsciously, my hand rose to my lips. I didn't want to discourage him, but he must have sensed my hesitation. I was relieved when he asked what I had in mind.

I confessed that I had never used eBay, reminded him that as both of us teach, our time is limited. I suggested getting involved in social events where we could enjoy ourselves while we support our chosen charity. Something like making a deal with a restaurant, ensuring the proprietor that we could fill his place on a night when he doesn't usually have many customers.

Joe clapped. 'Brilliant! Back in our days in the Friary, we used to put up stalls at our fetes. *Name the Teddy* was a good one.'

Dante licked his spoon, put down his cereal bowl and pulled at Joe's top. 'Pooh's my teddy. I love him.'

'Ah! Come on, give me a hug, Dante!'

'Where's my dad? Is he hiding?'

'He's nearly ready to fly home. He'll be here soon, Dante.' Joe tickled him.

I waved my finger and reminded Dante that he had better get dressed ready to go to Ram's house. Their car would be there to collect him soon and he had not finished eating his breakfast.

'Can Joseph come with me?'

'I'd love to, Dante, but your mammy and I are trying to help people, like your lovely aunt Margherita, who have been sick.'

Once Dante had left to enjoy the day with his school friend, Joseph and I completed our application forms and made a list of fundraising events. Firstly, we researched advertisements for locations and dates of local car-boot sales. I had agreed to ask my colleagues at school to donate.

We listed other possibilities such as holding a raffle, hiring a bouncy castle, organising a game of Beat the Goalie or Hook a Duck, tea/coffee/strawberry parties, setting up a tombola and a cup cake stall, name the teddy or doll, count the sweets in a jar, coconut shy, hula hoop stall or darts.

As Joseph didn't have a car, I invited him to sleep in our home overnight on these occasions.

'Gosh! Where has the time gone, Joe? There's Ram's mother drawing up outside.'

'Well, you know what they say, 'Time flies by when you're enjoying yourself!''

'I'd better get the door. It's been really lovely having you here, Joe.'

I can see myself mirrored in Joe. He, like me, and indeed Richard too, seems to be vulnerable and emotionally fragile. I imagine that must be similar to a mother of a teenager, caring and protective while trusting that each person grows stronger through creating their own life story.

8

THE CAMINO AND CROAGH PATRICK

The day that Richard returned home….well… it was all we'd dreamed and more.

We managed a quick get-away from school. Dante chanted 'Daddy's coming home' as I manoeuvred my way swiftly through the Friday night traffic. The welcome home poster that he had made was twirling around on our front door. Everything was ready inside. As we rushed through the door my mobile phone rang. Richard was already well on his way from the airport.

While I hastened in to put the lasagne in the oven and place the salad on the table Dante was glued to the window occasionally dancing around.

I've relived this happy scene so many times since.

As soon as our gates opened and Richard drove through, we were there. Dante jumping into Richard's arms. Him lovingly swinging him round. All three of us in a tight embrace. The hugs. The kisses. We were a family again. Once seated for our family meal we interrupted each other catching up on everything.

Then seamlessly we somehow became immersed in all things Italian. Richard was thrilled that Dante unconsciously responded to him in Italian as he unpacked his rucksack and laid the best chocolates — Baci from Perugina and packets of nut and nougat 'Terrone' on the dining room table. Still savouring being together, we relaxed as Richard poured a red blend of Chianti wine into our glasses, and Dante began to read aloud from an Italian copy of *The Adventures of Pinocchio* that Richard had just given him.

Our family was reunited. We enquired about Margherita, Rosina, and Giovanni and slept contentedly.

In the morning, as soon as Richard moved I skipped down the stairs to join him for breakfast. When I reached the final step I scooped up the post from our door mat. As I sat next to him he pulled my stool nearer to his and enfolded me in his arms. We kissed while he assured me that I had done more than my share of looking after everything while he was in Florence.

'Frankie, dearest, from now on it is I who will take good care of you and Dante.'

When he took my porridge from the microwave, he noticed Joe's writing on the envelope on the top of the pile of post.

I reminded him that I had signed up for the Camino when Joe came over to our home. But that because I had been tied up with end of term commitments, such as SATS, reports, open evenings, sports day, I had not enquired about the training walks in preparation for the trek.

We read the letter to discover that Joe was asking if he could visit us the following weekend. He had returned to his job as a peripatetic music teacher and Wandsworth County Council Education Authority was sending him to schools mostly around the Battersea area.

We were glad that the Carmelite Friars helped him in renting a room with the Salesian priests.

'Small steps into the secular world. You had to do the same, Frankie. Fortunately, I was able to return to live with my father when I left off training for the priesthood.'

'Hard times. All the more reason why we should look out for him as he takes these huge steps.' We agreed to invite Joe over to our home on the following Sunday. Richard offered to cook the meal.

'I used to dread Sundays when I left the convent, Richie. Sunday meant Mass so no lie-in for me.

I no longer believed that is was a mortal sin not to go but I do know…I was fed up being preached to . Besides I was questioning everything.'

'Did you go to Mass, though?'

'Guilt! That's what made me get out of bed and toddle off to join the faithful. Sure we had bags of guilt. I suppose it was different for you being at home with your father, Richard.'

I suggested that while Richard and Joe were together they might want to go down memory lanes.

Richard collected Joseph from Wimbledon Station at eleven the following Sunday.

Dante had positioned himself at the window in order to see the car returning with Joe. He shouted into the kitchen to let me know as soon as the automatic gates into our premises began to lift. He rushed to the front door, pushing me aside in order to jump into Joe's arms.

Joseph began swinging Dante around. Dante wanted to show him his dinosaurs. Obediently, Joe allowed himself to be dragged into our front room.

'D'you like my triceratops? Mummy and I have been painting fridge magnets. Green with white spiky horns. Stegosauruses next and then T Rex.'

I followed into the kitchen. Dante showed Joe his

dinosaurs. 'They're so enthusiastic, at that age, aren't they, Frankie?'

'I love Joe's child-like qualities.'

'You're right, love, he's all excited about his discovery that Croagh Patrick has connections with Santiago de Compostela. Did you know that, Frankie?'

'Croagh Patrick and Santiago? No. I don't remember hearing that.'

'Fellows in the seminary used to talk about that place. They called it the holy mountain. Is it in Donegal?'

'It's in Mayo, Richard. Third highest in that county. I suppose like Santiago it has always been a place of pilgrimage. We call it the Reek.'

Richard jokingly accused me of checking on his cooking. I explained that I had purposely left Dante with Joe so that he could benefit from his full attention. We both agreed that Joe showed signs of being a good father. Peals of laughter enticed us to carry our drinks in to join Joe and Dante.

'Daddy, is Uncle Joe going to live here?'

'This little fellow has grown. He'll be as tall as you, Richard.'

'As my mam used to say, Joe, 'He's got a fine frame!''

'Meaning a good bone structure, and he has too, Fran. God Bless him.'

'Now Dante, uncle Joe is going to tell us all about a high mountain in Ireland, the country where I was born. *If you ever go across the sea to Ireland.*

I couldn't stop myself from singing *Galway Bay* and Joe joined in.

Richard praised us: 'Gosh, you have a lovely voice, Joe. Both of you. Together, you sound so melodic. The harmony is lovely.'

'Why are you crying, Mummy?'

'These are happy tears, darling. I just love the country

where I was born. Come here till I give you a cuddle.'

'We'll have to go to Ireland. Mummy needs to show you the land that she loves. We've seen some of my country, Italy, haven't we?'

'You said that there is a big mountain there too.'

'Well now, they are not as high as the ones in Italy. Shall we have our drinks, and then uncle Joe can tell us about this Irish mountain?'

'I can build a mountain with my Lego.'

'Good idea, love. Drink your orange juice. Careful, don't spill any. Then you can take your Lego out.'

'Is it going to be like school, Mum? Will I have to be quiet?'

'Not at all at all! You fire away building your mountain with Lego and sure we'll talk around you. If you want to ask about anything, just ask. Okay, Dante?'

Richard and I were puzzled about the connection between Santiago in Galicia, northern Spain and West of Ireland's Croagh Patrick. Joe relayed he learnt that scallop shells and burial places, is the answer. That these shells have been found in many places in Ireland but it's in the west and particularly around Kerry, Galway and Mayo that are of particular interest.

Richard pointed out the scallop applies to any one of numerous species of saltwater clams, and that they can be found as far afield as Canada and, of course, in the Atlantic.

'What are scallops?' Dante asked.

'Scallops. I knew you would ask me that,' answered Joe. 'They are like fish or crabs. They taste sweet, buttery, and delicate. Come over here and I'll show you, Dante. I've brought some of the shells that they live in. See, they are found inside this lovely shell. Look how it's got a top and a bottom.'

'It's crinkly and hard. Mine's a different colour to yours. There's nothing inside!'

'Yes. Feel the ridges. They spread out like a fan. I asked a chef in a restaurant near where I live to let me have these shells after he had taken out the meaty food.'

'Daddy's one looks the best. It's more yellowy. Can we swop Dad?'

Joe went on to answer Richard's query, explaining the connection between scallops found in Croagh Patrick and Compostela. That St Patrick is believed to have come to the Reek in 441 AD. He spent his time in prayer and doing penance in preparation for bringing Christianity to Ireland. On this holy mountain St. Patrick is said to have fasted for forty days and nights as he wrestled with demons and banished snakes from Ireland. He understood the importance of the sun for the pagan people, but he wanted them to consider Christ as the true sun, the light of the world, the creator of the stars.

'Okay. So now the Irish are being converted to Christianity, but—'

'I know, Richard. Santiago de Compostela and the scallops? 'Tis often said that the Irish have itchy feet. Sure, won't you find the Irish wherever you travel? That's exactly what happened. They went on pilgrimage too.'

'Of course you are aware that St James was a fisherman before he abandoned his life to become one of the twelve apostles. Legend has it that when his body was cast to sea after he was martyred, and the boat washed up on the shores of Galicia, a horse and rider went into the sea to retrieve him. When they emerged from the water, they were covered in scallop shells. So, Santiago became one of the three major places of pilgrimage.'

'Fair enough,' Richard agreed. 'But is there any proof?'

'Of the story about the body of St James? Not really. There are many versions. Myth and legend makes it almost impossible to separate the development of the Camino from the 9th century and the great fight to rid both Spain and France from the Moors. The Catholic Church wanted to rid these countries of Islam.'

'*Compostela*? That is the field of stars,' Richard enquired. 'How did that come about?'

'Sheer good luck. In AD 813 a Galician hermit Pelayo, heard music and saw lights above a place known as campo stella, the field of stars.'

'Was that where St James was buried?' Richard asked.

'Who knows! It is told that Bishop Teodomiro confirmed that the remains in graves there were those of St James the Greater. Now James may even have been related to Jesus through Mary, his mother.'

'Was there any connection between St James and the scallop shells in Ireland?' Richard enquired.

'That's it! Scallop shells were discovered during excavations at St Mary's Cathedral, Tuam, County Galway, also of thirteenth or fourteenth century origin. A further shell-associated burial site has been located during excavation of the Augustinian friary at Galway. An exciting discovery was made by Fionnbarr Moore in 1992, underneath the wall of a late medieval tomb at Ardfert Cathedral. He found a pewter scallop shell, on which a little bronze-gilded figure of St James had been mounted. The shell was attached to a brooch, clearly defining it as a pilgrim's badge.'

'Sounds convincing,' Richard agreed. 'So, the shell emblem is important.'

'Mighty important. The emblem of the shell has always been connected with the apostle James and its occurrence in a burial usually indicates that the deceased had been a pilgrim to the grave of the apostle in Santiago de Compostela in Northern Spain.'

Richard nodded. 'I see.'

'Scallop shells became a significant badge for the pilgrims walking the Camino. They also used to serve a practical purpose. Worn by the pilgrims, others knew who they were and what they were doing so that they could offer hospitality to the pilgrims along *The Way*. The shells were also used as vessels for food and drink. When pilgrims went searching for food and drink, churches would offer them as much sustenance as could be scooped into a scallop shell. Scallop shells also served as proof of completion once they arrived at their destination.'

Dante stood up and pointed to his Lego building. 'Do you like my mountain, Joe? It's got lots of steps. The green steps are bigger on this side. I think Daddy will have to climb these steps. Mummy has pink steps. Her feet are smaller.'

'Brilliant, Dante! Well done. Do you know that this is an excellent model, because just as the Lego steps are hard, so are the sides of Croagh Patrick. It's like walking on the kind of slates that cover roofs and the rain runs down and they become slippy.'

'I've heard it said that it takes the best part of four hours to climb up and down Croagh Patrick,' Richard said.

'Indeed. And it's no wonder. It's mighty high. 2500 feet. 7 kilometre climb. It's challenging.'

Ah, but it's well worth it, even though it is often misty up there. As you reach the summit, a white chapel becomes visible. The view from there is simply wonderful. I know I am biased but, for me well, there's nowhere to match it. There's St Patrick's Bed, the remains of an ancient stone fort. Straight ahead you have an exquisite view of Connemara, Clew Bay, the Nephin Beg mountain range, Achill and Clare Island. What more could any mortal wish for?'

'The Apennines Mountains?'

'Ah now, Richard, you know full well that there's no comparison with the Apennine mountains. But I bet you haven't got a famous bell up there?'

'A bell?'

'Of course I'm joking, Richard. However, in all seriousness, the "Clog Dubh" is mentioned by De Latocnaye in his Frenchman's Walk through Ireland. Let me read this to you: 'On the summit there is a little chapel at which Mass is celebrated on the Fete day and in it is a black bell for which the inhabitants have a peculiar veneration. It is used as a thing to swear on in legal matters, and no one will dare to perjure himself on it. They have strange ideas on the subject of this bell and believe that the devil will carry them off immediately if they dare to affirm on it anything that is not true."

'I've heard mention of this black bell.'

'I'm not surprised, Frankie. I hope now I have managed to convey to you the reason why elders and children, believers and hikers, tourists and locals, they all come with walking sticks and hiking boots, guide books and rosary beads.'

'In March?' Richard asked.

'No. Well, you're partly right because you can climb Croagh Patrick throughout the year, but 'Reek Sunday' is the last Sunday in July. Traditionally the holiest day to climb, when up to 30,000 visitors flock to the slopes.'

Richard stood and beckoned us saying: 'Come on. Time for lunch, Joseph. You've certainly earned it. Sunday roast is on the menu, thanks to Richard. If we'd have known the relevance of scallops, we could have had them as a starter. However, we do have a fishy starter. Prawn cocktail with salad. By the time that we have consumed the first course, the roast beef and trimmings will be ready. So, follow me into the dining room.'

Joe thanked us both for inviting him to lunch. Rubbing his palms together he apologised if he had spoken for longer than we had expected. Richard reassured him, 'Not at all, Joe. Although I knew about the Reek, I was ignorant about its connection with Santiago.

'It won't surprise you to know, Joe, that Frankie is still educating me about Ireland.'

Richard was quick to applaud Joe for being a keen student. He reminded him of all the research he had done while they were both in the seminary. 'Was it about that historic place outside, was it Tipperary?'

'Not Tipperary. Newgrange. County Meath. North of the River Boyne. Built in the Neolithic period, around 3200 BC. Indeed, it's older than Stonehenge and the Egyptian pyramids. Another sacred place.'

I observed the caring way Joe helped Dante to wash his hands before giving him a piggyback into the dining room.

'Joe is great with Dante, isn't he, Richard? I hope he meets someone lovely and settles down before he is much older.'

Having Joe over today appears to have helped to strengthen his friendship with Richard. Richard seems to be as enthusiastic about this pilgrimage as I am now. I suppose we both wish to support cancer patients while challenging ourselves. Then there is Joe. He has done his research, he's committed, certainly unsophisticated, unaffected worldly wise, maybe, naive.

9

NUALA

I was content, now that Richard had returned to his school headship. It was such a relief to have him back home doing his share of helping us get ready to leave for school each morning.

'Take your time, Frankie. I'll get our dreamer up and dressed. I know what it's like to write thirty-plus end-of-year reports.'

Richard insisted that I sit and enjoy my porridge with Dante while he took everything to the car. He advised me to conserve my energy for the parents' evening that night. He pulled out my chair and settled me in, smiling all the time.

'Thank you, darling. I hope the Johnson parents don't knock on your door to question why I wrote 'Has a tendency to flout the rules', on his report.'

'Don't worry. Both parents ignore the fact that school begins at nine. They seem to think that if Ryan manages to join his class line on the way into assembly, that he is on time.'

I told him that I had already called the register and it has been taken back to the secretary's office before I lead my class into the hall by the time he arrived.

When my phone vibrated I checked that it was a WhatsApp message and surmised that as it was probably from the Camino walking group I could answer it later. Richard bent down to kiss me and suggested that walking might free my mind from the end of term pressure.

'I can take care of our son if you want to take a breather tomorrow. We could even join you part of the way, couldn't we, Dante?'

That night, while we were sipping wine and recovering from the children's Parents' Evening, Richard reminded me to check my WhatsApp message. I discovered that the prep walk for the Camino was to take place in the village of Shere at four o'clock the following day.

'Shere. That beautiful, quintessential English village. What could be better? We could have a lie-in and start out after a leisurely lunch. If we take Dante's wellies, he will really enjoy paddling in the stream. We can play Pooh Sticks and count the ducks. I'm beginning to unwind already.'

'You're so enthusiastic, Richard. I'm so tired that I wonder if I am beyond sleeping. But it's a lovely idea. Let's see how we are in the morning, will we?'

The following afternoon when we arrived in Shere, Joseph waved to us as we were walking from the car park. He was with five others leaning on the bridge over the stream. Richard had to stop Dante rushing across the narrow road to fling himself into Joe's arms.

'Gosh, I've only got my trainers, Joe. You're wearing proper walking boots and that lady over there has walking poles.'

'Ah now, Frankie it's not important today. We're only going for a short walk over fairly level ground. Come on. Let me introduce you to the others.' He patted me on the

shoulder. The group turned round to greet me. I immediately
picked up an Irish lilt from among them. I learnt that was
from an Irish colleen who hailed from the kingdom of Kerry.
There was Mark from Guildford who gave her a polite
handshake and was well spoken had a good physique. He
seemed to be the athletic type. Then there was Emma from
Farnham who is the mother of two girls. She looked lovely.
A smily blonde wearing bright pink walking gear complete
with a matching hairband. There was Bahis from Holland.
A tall, fair-headed guy. Next there was Karam from Kenya.
Another friendly chap wearing a turban and a twinkle in his
eye. Greeting with two hands and a huge grin. A slender,
attractive guy. Too many introductions all at once!

'Well, shall we start? I'm Mark. As I'm local, I have
been chosen — ha! ha! — as the leader today. That is, I
have been handed the map. Apparently I volunteered!'

Everyone laughed.

Having been introduced to so many new people
so quickly I remembered Marion telling me about the
importance of listening to and learning from others in order
to glean a better understanding of what motivates them. I
started off walking beside Nuala. I discovered that she was
also a teacher. But unlike me, she taught in a secondary,
Independent Girls' private school run by Holy Family nuns.

*Judging by appearances, Nuala is the kind of lady that
perhaps would be good for Joe. She's Irish, and a teacher
and also good-looking. With her ginger hair and hazel eyes
she, like me, could be regarded as a typical Irish woman.
My hair is auburn, and hopefully we have both not inherited
the fiery attitude, too. But then again, where would I be if I
was content with the humdrum of life?*

What was also beginning to endear Nuala to me was
that she decided to fundraise for Oasis Centre in St Gerard's
Hospital in Wimbledon when one of the pupils' mothers,
aged thirty-two, died from ovarian cancer. Ciara was only

twelve and an only child. Nuala explained that the survival rate is low and that overall, around half of women with ovarian cancer live for at least five years after diagnosis. Furthermore only about one in three survive for at least ten years. She told me that because this type of cancer is not easily detected, unfortunately two years had gone by before Ciara was diagnosed with ovarian cancer. Sadly, the earlier ovarian cancer is diagnosed and treated, the better the chance of a cure. But because in Ciara's case it had already spread, a cure was no longer possible.

Nuala and I were so involved in our discussion that we didn't notice Joe creeping up behind us. He seemed to be happy that we were relating well to each other. I explained that Nuala was telling me about the mother of a child in her class who died of cancer.

'Tragic. An only child, too. Her father is helping to raise funds. He'd join us, only he has to work. It was Joe who encouraged me to do the Camino. Wasn't it, Joe?'

I watched Nuala grasping Joe's hand.

So Joseph's found a lady friend already? I'll drop back, leave them together, and chat with Bahis and Karam, the fellow wearing the turban. But as the walk was only three and a half miles, we were soon back and seated round a table in the garden of the The William Bray pub in Shere.

Dante became the centre of attention as soon as Richard brought him over to join us. Joe started us off discussing our progress at fundraising. He confessed that although we were already nearing the date when we were scheduled to depart on our trek he had barely raised a thousand. He wanted to know how the rest of our fundraising efforts were going. Immediately Nuala offered to share the three thousand pounds that the parents at her school had helped her raise with Joe. She also volunteered to support him with some of the events that he was planning. Joe gladly accepted. Richard said that his father wanted to contribute too. He said that when his aunt in Italy was diagnosed with cancer he was impressed with the great support that she received.

Karam gratefully assured him that the Oasis centre really appreciates his generosity and that when he clocked-in to Oasis on Monday, he would bring them all up-to-date on all our promises of support.

Before the deliciously freshly cooked meal of fish and light, crisp chips was over, we had organised some of the walking practice dates and the fundraising events.

In bed that night, Richard and I commented on how glad we were that we'd noticed a relationship developing between Joseph and Nuala. We surmised that they were probably aged about thirty-five.

'That brings back memories of our urgent hurry to conceive before it was too late. Aren't we lucky to have such a lovely boy? Sometimes I marvel at the things he comes out with.'

'What are you laughing at?'

'Oh. Oh! When he asked Nuala why her hair was a funny colour.'

'Surely there must be someone at school with ginger hair?'

'The Molloy twins. But then they're boys. They've got short hair, neither is it as bright red and it's not as full of curls.'

'It's strange that he didn't remark on Karam's turban. Now that's different.'

'Sabal. His friend Sabal is a Sikh. He wears a junior type of turban. They've been friends from play-school.'

'Oh yes. Lovely family. He came to his birthday party when he was only three.'

As Richard cuddled me closer, I felt even happier when he said that he was looking forward to catching up with his father-son bonding and regretted having missed out on so many occasions when he was looking after his aunt. He promised to take Dante places and spend valuable time with him while I will be engaged in taking part in preparatory walks for the Camino.

I can sleep peacefully tonight. Richard has reassured me that he is eagerly anticipating enjoying the full responsibility of caring for our son while I am preparing for the Camino.

The walking has tired me, but I am also looking forward to learning more about the other pilgrims who will join us.

10

FUNDRAISING CAN BE FUN

Richard and I were not surprised when Joseph rang to ask if he could bring Nuala with him to our home. Joe and Nuala had been working together with a group of teachers on a music course.

When Nuala's car pulled up outside our house, I went out to welcome them.

'Lovely car, Nuala. Red, too. My, we are flash. Come on in to our abode.'

They followed me inside. Nuala explained that she had always wanted a red Mercedes-Benz and it was a perk that she could now enjoy because of her private school salary.

Joe did a slow clap, teasing her. 'Good for some.'

Nuala retorted, 'Why not? Where exactly do you hail from, Joe? It must be out in somewhere remote down the country for your parents to have had a vintage car.'

'Now that would be telling. How old do you think I am, Nuala!'

Richard welcomed them and showed them into our lounge. They sat next to each other on the sofa. Nuala spread out her tie dyed multi-coloured tiered skirt, and flicked her ponytail free from her dangling green earrings. Joe watched her every movement. His dark blue jeans and jacket were the smart type, but his flyaway hair gave him that Peter Pan appearance.

Joseph obviously has not disclosed much information about his background to Nuala.

'Joe tells me that you have already been in contact with an Italian restaurant to secure us a fundraising deal, Nuala?'

Nuala informed us that Antonio Vivo, the proprietor of Villa Bianca restaurant in Battersea, had been very accommodating. He agreed that if they could muster up enough guests to fill his restaurant on an evening when he wouldn't otherwise have many customers, he would be very happy to help them. Joe added, 'Fair enough. That would work two ways. He would be on the make, too.'

Nuala filled us in on the further details. If they invited a minimum of forty guests, he would offer them a three course meal with two choices at each course for twenty pounds per person. That would ensure that if we were to charge everyone thirty pounds, they would make four hundred.

Richard suggested that running a raffle with some attractive prizes would help to increase the amount raised maybe by another hundred. He offered to provide the wine and other prizes, and he thanked Nuala for contributing half the money that Joe required to take part in the pilgrimage. Nuala put forward the idea of forming a band and putting on a musical event.

Joe was enthusiastic:'The very thing. We could even play dance tunes and encourage folk to really enjoy themselves. That's a grand suggestion. Why don't you and I organise that, Joe?'

Joe agreed, and I suggested they could add to the

enjoyment were they to provide nibbles or run another raffle. I added that I expected that people would be more willing to give if they could have a good time while they are donating to helping others.

Everyone nodded, then I asked Joe if he would be leading the walking groups.

'No. Peter, who is a volunteer therapist at Oasis, will guide the walks. His son, Mark, makes sure that he is up-to-date with all the modern gizmos, orienteering, the lot.'

I was surprised that both father and son were involved. Joe replied that he had asked the same question and learnt that Peter is a well established reflexology therapist, who also leads and promotes walking in the Oasis centre. His son, Mark is the quite stocky, muscular fellow. Apparently, some years ago, Peter trained to be a therapist in Farnborough College of Technology. One of the people who volunteered to take part in his study case told him that they were looking for volunteers in Oasis. He saw it as an opening, especially when he heard that Oasis offers further training there. And his son, Mark, perhaps followed in his father's footsteps. So both Peter and Mark are numbered within the volunteers. Peter is officially a volunteer walk leader, and reflexologist, and that he leads walks for patients who frequent the Oasis centre. He explained that Mark led the first walk because Peter wasn't with us that day.

'And Karam? What's his background Joe?'

Now, Frankie, I was informed that Karam, our Kenyan Sikh, is one of the three founders of Oasis and is also the coordinator of the three members of staff employed to run this therapeutic Centre in St Gerard's Hospital. He is also a nurse and also an acupuncturist guaranteeing that we will be safe hands on our journey.'

'Acupuncture, Joe?'

'Acupuncturist. Wonderful. You should try it, Frankie. He's always over booked. Very popular.'

'I'll have to confess my ignorance, Joe. I don't really know anything about acupuncture.'

'My aunt Marguerite vouched for it. At first she didn't want to go anywhere near needles and, of course, acupuncture applies needles into certain places on the skin.'

'Did she darling? Does it hurt? You must feel the needles.'

'Margherita said that while you are conscious of the insertion of the needles, there is no real pain involved. Of course, it's a skilled occupation.'

Nuala enquired about how people become volunteers. Joe informed her that Oasis asks would-be volunteers to apply and they are taken through a number of procedures determined by the hospital and become part of the hospital set-up. The centre depends on volunteers. Each day, at least two volunteers welcome cancer patients, provide them with information, book them in for a therapy session, and offer them a drink while they are waiting for their cancer treatment elsewhere in the hospital. Some of the volunteers are trained therapists.

By the time they were ready to go home, Richard and I were very happy with the enthusiasm shown by Joseph and Nuala. On the following Monday, each of us the group who had volunteered to take part in the Camino pilgrimage, received an information pack. It contained three A4 pages listing preparatory walks and two dates set aside when the twelve people would assemble at Oasis Centre in St Gerard's Hospital in Wimbledon. It also stated that two persons who had previously followed the 'French Camino route' had kindly offered to share their experience at the scheduled meeting.

11

RECALLING AND REASONING

*A*fter enjoying a good rest, I crept down to our kitchen and flung my arms around Richard. He was sitting at the table reading a newspaper. I was glad to have him all to myself.

I love the way that he holds my face between his hands when we kiss.

I switched on the microwave to warm my porridge. Following a well established routine, I had soaked three heaped spoonfuls of Flahavan's porridge oats in a bowl of milk the night before.

'You're relaxing. No tossing and turning now that we're on holiday, Fran.'

'I was in a deep sleep. I was walking up steep hills. It was a lovely dream. It must have been the all that discussion about the Camino.'

'Those two, Joe and Nuala, they seem to get on so well together, don't they?'

'But, Ricci, did you notice that when Nuala asked him about his family, he didn't answer? In fact, I sensed an uneasiness, and felt compelled to chip in and change the topic.'

'Well, remember that I was also cagey about telling you that I had been studying for the priesthood. In fact, I didn't until our secretary, Paula, let something slip about your background.'

'You're right. *I was a nun*, or *I was nearly ordained a priest*, aren't good opening lines to forming a relationship. Anyone I know that left the convent, rarely admits to it.'

'I thought that only Paula and head teacher Sr Sheila knew about our backgrounds. Of course Paula is dead now. May she rest in peace. Sr Sheila wouldn't tell anyone.'

'What are we afraid of, I wonder?'

'Well, Richard, in Ireland, long ago, a man who left the priesthood was referred as a *spoilt priest*. I suppose that was because it was believed that a priest couldn't renounce that state. *Once a priest, always a priest*. Or is that *once a Catholic, always a Catholic*? I've heard it said that it was very difficult to leave, anyway. But then you were not ordained.'

'Very nearly, Richard.'

'*Going on for the priesthood*, is what they would say, Fran?'

'Do you think that there is still a certain stigma about letting people know?'

'Richard, people nowadays let others know if they are divorced, but I still think that if you were a nun or priest, people regard you as a failure. I don't know. Some think you naive and they are very careful about what they say to you. Especially when they tell jokes. They wouldn't discuss sex in your presence.'

'Maybe *our time inside* has made us puritanical, Fran?'

'Sins of the flesh! Lots of guilt. Going to Confession. Constantly examining our conscience. I still feel embarrassed when people are too explicit about certain things. Actually, I don't really think that it is necessary to speak about many private matters.'

'We'll have to be careful what attitudes we pass on to our son.'

'I suppose you're right. So, to get back to Joe. Do you think he will eventually tell Nuala that he too was training for the priesthood, Richard?'

'Eventually, he surely will tell her. But of course being Irish herself she's more likely, please God, to understand.'

Richard wanted to know more about Karam. He said that people are often curious about the reasons why Sikhs wear turbans. I recounted how when little Tanvir enrolled in our after-school club his mother came to explain why he would be wearing headgear tied in a bun. She wanted to make sure that the children in the group would be told about Sikh religious practices.

'That was a good idea. Children just accept differences?'

'They were fine. He was the first Sikh to join after we opened the club to anyone whose parents would be late returning from work.'

Tanvir. I seem to remember her telling me that his name meant *Brave and strong in body*. She mentioned names for the boy's headgear, too. Was it something like patka? Joora? I can't really remember.'

'That settles it. We'll have to invite Karam around for a meal.'

'Maybe after the meeting on Monday organised for us pilgrims? That's our title now. Isn't it grand? We are preparing to go on a pilgrimage to Santiago Compostela. Granted, we're only completing the final hundred miles on the French route.'

'Just checking, is it miles or kilometres?'

'D'you know, Richard, I'm not sure.'

'Quite a bit of difference, Fran.1 mile is equal to 1.6 kilometres.

I'm glad that we have agreed to invite Karam to our home. Once the Catholic Church vouched to be more ecumenical, we began to meet with people of other faiths, but it was often superficial. We have so much in common, it will be enriching to share and benefit more from each other.

12

SUSTAINABILITY CENTRE

*W*e carried our coffees into the lounge so that we could relax after breakfast. Richard had started on The Times' crossword, and I was just about to curl into a comfy armchair when I noticed the postman passing our window. As I picked up our post, I saw that it had the Oasis Centre logo on the envelope. I opened it to find that it was from Karam, our leader, recommending a weekend at a Sustainability Centre for our group. I hoped that Richard would be enthusiastic when I showed it to him.

'I've heard of a centre in the beautiful Meon Valley, Frankie. Is it the one not too far from Petersfield?'

'That's the one, Richard. It's becoming popular with folk who want to improve our environment. Apparently, the people who run it are very friendly, and welcome people from all backgrounds and ability.'

I handed Richard the enclosed leaflet that explained that Environmental sustainability doesn't mean living without luxuries, but rather being aware of your resource consumption and reducing unnecessary waste.

1. Reduce household energy use...
2. Eat locally...
3. Dispose with disposables...
4. Plant seeds...
5. Recycle...
6. Re-sell and donate items...
7. Drink from the tap...
8. Save water. Just what it says on the enclosed leaflet...'

Our chatting must have woken Dante. He bounced into the room and onto Richard's knee, kissed him and pleaded to go training with Mummy again. Richard cuddled him closer. 'Last time I looked in on you, you were sound asleep.'

It's moments like this that I treasure. Our son is so spontaneous and loving. He makes funny faces when he sees us smiling back at him.

We soon decided to take advantage of this learning experience.

Dante came over to lay beside me while I explained what was involved in this adventure.

I am delighted about this venture. I wanted to get to know more of my fellow pilgrims. When Karam reminded us that our stay would necessitate them leaving behind luxuries, I recalled my convent days.

We booked the triple room. Richard read out extracts from the leaflet. From rolling hills to bustling market towns, the South Downs National Park's landscapes cover 1,600 km of breathtaking views, hidden gems, and beautiful English scenery. A rich tapestry of wildlife, landscapes, tranquillity.

The following Saturday, I drove Richard and Dante to the Centre. As we approached I spotted a peaceful looking lady getting out of her car. Careful not to startle her as we approached the group, I whispered to Richard:

'The sight of that lady with those greying curls at first glance, reminded me of my mam. Only, God forgive me, if it was her, she would have been eyeing everyone else.'

'The way that she's purposefully lacing her boots now, gives me the impression that she has come prepared for a walk, Frankie.'

'Can we get out? There's Joe.'

Richard and I were preoccupied — preventing Dante from running between the parked cars to Joe — while we unloaded our provisions for our overnight stay. I lost sight of this lady. However, once the walkers assembled around Karam, I saw that she was standing to her full height, peeping over the heads of one of the men. I realised that Karam must have assumed that we had already been introduced. As soon as the instructions had finished, I moved over to befriend this newcomer. But she made the first move.

'Hello. I'm Catherine. When I saw you in the car park, I hoped that you were in our group. Is this your first walk?' She gave me a firm handshake and asked if I would like to partner her. Just as we agreed Karam issued instructions to head for the opening on the left of the field.

'Bye, Mummy. I love you. Daddy and I are going to explore.'

'Have a great time. Love you both!'

'They're yours?' Catherine asked. 'Lovely.'

'Thank you.'

'Well, as we'd say in Wales, 'Bore da.''

'Great. I'll respond with Dia dhuit. *God be with you.*'

'Irish? Both Celtic.'

We continued chatting. I admired Catherine's walking outfit. She explained that it was well worn and the matching trousers and top were at least five years old. The jacket had retained its blue even though it'd been through the washing machine less frequently. She explained that her late husband loved walking in the Welsh mountains and that they had learnt over the years that it worked out cheaper when they shopped around for good quality gear at sales prices. She recommended some online stores.

Karam must have been working his way down the line of walkers to check on how we were all progressing. He arrived beside Catherine and me.

'How are things, ladies? I see you are making good use of those poles.' I replied that I was trying my best and Catherine assured him that she had always used them as she found that they help her to pace herself. She added that she felt that she needed to exercise after the sedentary work that she was engaged in.'

Curious, I quizzed Catherine about the type of employment that she was involved in. I wasn't surprised when this intelligent looking lady disclosed that she is a clinical scientist in healthcare, researching and developing new equipment. Her occupation necessitated using life sciences, including biology, microbiology, genetics or biochemistry and in physics, engineering, anything relating to medicine.

'Now that is impressive, Catherine.'

'Maybe, Frankie. But when you are diagnosed with breast cancer, you are reminded that life is precious. As a survivor, I want to payback for the support that I have received. That's why I am on this pilgrimage.'

'Oh Catherine, you have been coping with cancer.'

'I am a lucky survivor ready to move on with my life and try and help others, too.'

Karam and I praised her generosity and then Karam moved forward to speak to the other walkers. I noticed that they seemed to walking quite quickly on ahead, and would soon be out of sight. When I looked back and saw that Joe was falling behind, I suggested that we wait for him to catch us up.

'Are you alright, Joe?'

'I'm so sorry Frankie, but I think I will have to... I don't know. The group is disappearing out of this field. I'll just take my time. It's my left leg. Had trouble with it before. I'm sorry. You'll lose sight of them. You carry on.'

'But what about you?'

'Don't worry. Look, here is a farmer on a tractor. I'll be fine. Catch them up.'

'You sure? Karam is waving. I'll let him know. You take care. See you later.'

When I saw Nuala turning round I suspected that she must have overheard our conversation, explaining to Karam the reason why Joseph had decided to abandon the walk to return to the centre. I was proved right when she suggested that she guessed that Joseph would be disappointed at having to drop out and that it might help if she invited him to prepare the fruit for the mulled wine that she had brought along. Everything was in her car and she had hidden the keys in a place that could be accessible. Karam took her up on that idea telling her to go ahead and phone him.

Late that afternoon, when we had all returned from the walk and were all seated around a table outside the centre, everyone was thanking Joe as they quenched their thirst, sipping mulled wine. He told us that the farmer who drove him back to the centre in his small truck was a young man clutching a nine-month-old baby in one arm, while managing the steering wheel with the other.

'Generous chap.'

'Very grateful to him, Bahis, but I admit that I was scared when I realised that he was driving over dried furrows and besides minding his baby, there were no doors on the truck.'

I noticed that Nuala offered to give Joe's legs a massage in her bedroom.

This friendship is developing quickly.

'Daddy showed me where people sleep when they stay overnight - in a yurt. A massive big tent with a hole at the top.'

He is so gorgeous I had to smile. 'A hole in the roof? Glad it's summertime.'

'It's so you can see the stars in the sky when it's dark, Mummy. That's what Daddy said.'

Richard explained that it was a traditional Mongolian yurt or Tipi more inviting than the bedroom that they had been allocated in the building that they were sharing. It had a wooden floor and a front door. It was tastefully decorated. He said that he might even suggest it for a staff outing.

'Did you see the burial site?'

'Yes, Catherine.'

'Dead people, Daddy.'

Richard clasped his hands and looked at me reassuringly. 'We hadn't planned to, but we nearly bumped into a funeral procession, darling.' Then he hugged Dante. 'No need to be afraid, my pet. One day we'll all go to heaven, and if they're all as colourful and happy as the people singing as they made their way down to a canopied site under arms of broadleaf and yew trees, I'm all for it.'

'We had a picnic with them, didn't we, Daddy?'

'We did, and you were very good. You ate all your salad and fruit.'

Anxious to convince the others of the value of the centre, Richard added that he had become convinced that this concept of sustainability was becoming part of the South Downs Natural Park. He was sure many families have found great comfort laying their loved ones to rest with natural and simple dignity.

I winked and mouthed to Richard, signalling that death might not be an appropriate topic for Dante. I need not have worried because Dante was soon rescuing the football way down the hill.

Then I noticed Bahis smiling. He explained that he had just overheard Emma saying that she visited the Muslim burial site in Brookwood. She said that all the men had beards and or moustaches, and that only men were permitted to attend. 'Well, as you might know, I am a Muslim and, as you can see, I am clean shaven. I guess we Dutch interpret the Qur'an differently.'

'That's the thing, isn't it, Bahis? We Irish like to bury our dead within three days of their death. Well, that's how it used to be. We had a wake. We followed certain customs, but we've had to adapt to the times. In the Catholic Church up until comparatively recently, cremations were strictly forbidden.'

'Cremation of the body is still strictly forbidden in Islam, Frankie. Sharia calls for burial of the body as soon as possible, preceded by a simple ritual involving bathing and shrouding the body, followed by salah.'

I hope that Joe's knee problem is not serious. It would be a shame if he had to drop out, especially now that Nuala seems to have linked up with him. We will have to look out for him. I'll speak to Richard about this.

13

MEETING AT OASIS

*A*s soon as school finished I got away as quickly as possible in order to avoid the usual build up of evening traffic in the Wimbledon area and drove straight to the hospital for the Oasis meeting. When I was searching for a parking space, I wondered if the red car that I had spotted behind mine might be Nuala's. It was. She waited for me. We both remarked that we had not realised that Oasis was actually inside the hospital in the same corridor as the chemotherapy centre. We presumed that a therapeutic centre, such as Oasis, would be a separate building. We agreed that it was much better to have it right next to where cancer patients come for their treatment.

Following the signs at the end of a corridor we found the Centre and immediately saw Joe. Both he and Karam were waiting at the entrance to welcome everyone. Still in accountable teacher mode, no sooner had I entered the room than I counted sixteen people seated in a circle chatting to each other.

As we sat, I caught sight of Joe winking at Nuala.

Karam clapped his hands to gain our attention, gave the usual Safety Rules pointing out the fire exits and where the toilets are situated. Then we were thanked for volunteering to walk the final hundred kilometres of the Camino and for the two thousand pounds that we had pledged to raise. We were reminded that this would be a tremendous boost in helping us to support cancer patients and their families. He told us that we would receive hand-outs with all the information before introducing us to Jane and Linda, members of the Oasis Staff. They looked smart in their royal blue open necked t-shirts with the yellow Oasis logo embroidered on them.

Karam then informed us that as well as the twelve of us there another lady called Roberta and her carer friend Joan, would bring our numbers up to fourteen. As she had chemotherapy today she was not well enough to join us tonight. He said that Roberta would complete as much of the Camino as she can. Sometimes she will most likely have to travel some of the way by other means. Buses, taxis, etc. Roberta was to be a constant reminder of the reason why we are walking the Camino. There was also Chris and Angie who had come to join us tonight in order to share their experiences of having walked the planned route the year before.

Linda promised to be brief in what she had to say and that she was aware that some of us might have rushed in here from work so she wanted us to enjoy some of the nibbles and drinks.

When Chris and Angie had finished speaking Nuala nudged me. 'Ah, Frankie aren't they lovely. They must be in their sixties. That's so encouraging. I mean, if they can manage all those miles, why shouldn't I be able to? They were very good to bring along all their walking gear too. Basic stuff. Tops, bottoms, strong, proper walking boots. Instead of style, it's utility that matters.'

Karam then encouraged everyone to mingle. After we had done so he said that Linda, Jane and he had taken the liberty of temporarily partnering us for sleeping accommodation. However as they were unaware of individual needs we might wish to change these.

Oh dear. I hope that I will be with someone who values privacy. My convent background has not prepared me for unnecessary exposure.

I was delighted that I was partnered with Catherine. When each person's name was called we sat next to our partner.

So many different characters. I wonder what the chemistry will be like between us? Good, though, that Joe is with our leader, Karam.

After the meeting, I drove Joseph back to our home and invited Nuala to join us for a drink. Richard quizzed us on the meeting. Full of enthusiasm I declared that the team that runs Oasis was very well organised. I handed Richard the booklet that each of us had received. Richard offered a glass of wine to us, while I related how the three people who run the Oasis Cancer Centre have been granted permission from St Gerard's Hospital to set up this therapeutic centre actually in the hospital. I also said that I was delighted that I had been partnered with Catherine and reminded Richard that he had met her briefly at the Sustainability Centre.

'We got to know each other on our walk. She's in her forties, she's Welsh, and was a member of the Baptist church. She's really lovely.'

'What about you two?'

Nuala laughed and waved her arms about. 'I'm with a very animated Sonia. She seems to be quite …well, loud. Hope she calms down. And Joe, you are with our leader, Karam?

'Yeah. I'm delighted to be with Karam, but you, Nuala?…'

'Well, we'll be able to walk with whoever we choose. Let's hope that as we are all pilgrims, we will get on. People are kind. Not perhaps like the folk in the Canterbury Tales.'

'Hopefully not, Nuala.'

We all laughed.

Richard was impressed when he began to read the booklet that we had been given. It detailed everything from the currency, flight, the holiday company that Oasis Centre had engaged to plot out the route via accommodation each evening. Our luggage was to be forwarded by them so we would only have to carry bare essentials in our rucksacks.

'Gosh, Frankie, this is the type of preparation that we are required to do when we take our classes away on educational breaks, this compares well with it.'

I then explained to Richard that Karam travelled by train to the Confraternity of St James on Blackfriars Road to purchase Pilgrim's Record Booklets that are referred to as 'The Pilgrim's Passport'. These have to be stamped as we reach each destination to verify that we have walked the route for a minimum of a hundred kilometres in order to merit a certificate. They are dated, signed, and numbered, so it's all official.

Flicking through this booklet, Richard was amazed that so much was itemised, even down to suggestions that we visit a local fish shop or restaurant to get a scallop shell to attach to our rucksacks. Lists of everything from Compeed to prevent blisters, Aloe vera to treat sock rash, tissues and even toilet paper. Cold remedies and sun protection. A container called a platypus in which to carry our water.

We had also been reminded that every one of us that our preparation would include being careful in purchasing the type of clothing that had been suggested. Basically dressing for the type of climate and remembering that good hiking base layers move sweat off the skin, dry fast, and are super comfortable next-to-skin. Other gear that were necessary to consider including were walking poles, rucksack, rainwear and a sunhat.

Nuala mentioned that we needed to purchase Euros. Joe suggested that perhaps it would be better to buy their boots as soon as possible and start walking them in.

I noticed that the bowls of assorted sweets that Richard had prepared for us had barely been touched. As I stood to offer them round I remembered to tell Richard about the husband and wife, Chris and Angie, that had been invited to speak to us about when they had trekked this pilgrimage route last spring. 'It was very useful to learn firsthand from their experiences.'

'Such as?'

'Angie said that as they were setting out at eight-thirty on the very first morning, her husband, Chris, got stung. They had just walked down the hill from their B&B. Fortunately nurse Rita, was carrying EpiPen and checked that he was anaphylactic, removed the sting, washed the affected area with some of the water that she was carrying. It was then that they discovered all the first-aid remedies that others had in their rucksacks. Lotions and potions like Aveeno Anti-Itch Concentrated Lotion with Calamine, and Triple Oat Complex to prevent itching.'

'You get bitten very easily, Frankie.'

'And I can't take much sun on my sensitive, pale Irish skin either, Richard.'

I think the little midges know that it was covered up all those years.

I assured Richard that I would pack my Citronella lotion and my aloe vera factor 50 sun lotion, too.

We discussed whether we would make use of the various discount vouchers that had been included in our information pack and Angie reminded us that most of the trekking stores sell garments embedded with sun protection with practical design details such as integral drying loops, three secure pockets, and roll up sleeve tabs. She went into quite some detail about fabrics with polyester and wicking material, too. Essentially, she was stressing that clothes that dry easily are best. She talked about them taking as little as two hours' drying time. With these you just rinse them through and hang them out to dry in your room. Next morning, they'll be ready to wear. The less you have the better.

Nuala looked at her watch, realised she and Joe had better leave for home as they had an early start for school the next day.

After waving them off Richard suggested that we invite Karam over for Sunday lunch.

'Remember that he is a Sikh, Richard. He will most likely follow their diet. We will need to prepare appropriate food.'

Although we already have Sikh friends, it would be lovely to know more about their approach to life. He's Kenyan, too. I've heard that people belonging to other religions living there, mingle a great deal more than we do. It's good to remember that we have much to learn from each other.

14

LEARNING ABOUT SIKH CUSTOMS

'Come over here.' Richard invited Dante to sit next to him on the settee. 'I want to explain something to you about our friend Karam. He'll be arriving soon.'

'I know. He's a Sikh and he will be wearing a patka. My friend Tanvir wears a white hat around his bunch of hair.'

'Clever boy. You know so much. Now, because Karam is a man, he will be wearing a grown-up turban.'

'I know. I know. I heard Mummy saying that she wondered what colour Kar... K...'

'Karam.'

'Yes. It's white. He's just got out of his car. It's a silver car. He's got a dress on, Daddy.'

Sure enough, Karam was wearing a white turban, a long, white knee-length top over baggy white leggings. Dante followed Richard out to meet Karam.

'Good to meet you, Richard, and you too, Dante.'

Dante did a wiggly finger wave. Karam smiled back.

'You're welcome, Karam,' Richard said. 'You kept

your promise to wear your Sikh outfit.'

'Wait now. I'm going to greet you as Sikhs do, too,' Karam said, '*Sat Shri Akaal*.'

'What should we reply?'

'The same.'

'Sat tree… ah..'

'Good. You've nearly got it, Dante. But don't worry. I'll do as you asked and explain as much as I can later.'

'Of course,' Richard said. 'Follow us in and make yourself comfortable before our son starts to interrogate you further.'

I waited in the front room to usher Karam in. 'I'm delighted that you have come, Karam. You are very welcome. May I offer you a drink? Now, I know that Sikhs refrain from alcohol. But is coffee, or tea, or anything else okay?'

'You are so considerate, Frankie. I'd love a cup of coffee, please. But really, I don't want to put you to any trouble.'

'It's no trouble at all, Karam. We really want to learn about Sikhism. No doubt our son will ply you with questions. Go over there and make yourself comfortable on one of those armchairs, while I get each of us a drink.'

I was pleased that Richard had phoned a few nights before to ask him what kind of food he usually ate for lunch. He learnt that Karam adhered strictly to a vegetarian diet. That in Sikhism, only lacto-vegetarian food is served in the Gurdwara (Sikh temple). Sikhs are bound to be meat free because not doing so would harm another living being, he told Richard. Also, that Sikh family meals usually include sabzi, *cooked vegetable*, and or Daal, cooked pulse.

Richard had prepared a meal that was described as Sabzi. It consisted of cauliflower, cabbage, lady-fingers (Okra), aubergine, peas, green pepper, potato, carrot, turnip, gourd (bitter), spinach, green mustard. He included dishes of Bengal gram and black gram, moong (green lentil) and masoor (yellow lentils).

'I know it's not a dress that you are wearing,' Dante said, 'but what's it called, Karam?'

'Sorry,' Richard intervened. 'Dante, perhaps we should wait until we have settled before you start questioning Karam?'

'It's okay, Richard. It's good to be curious. Your dad's right. Let's wait until your mum returns from the kitchen. Is that okay?'

'Here we are.' Karam stood to help me as I laid the tray on the coffee table. 'Perhaps you would like to pour your own milk, Karam. Do you take sugar?'

Richard passed the biscuits round and settled Dante with his orange juice.

Karam seems to radiate peacefulness. There is a calmness about him that has already created a meditative atmosphere. I can't put my finger on it. He doesn't seem to be in a hurry. Even while he sips his coffee, his face is smiling. Dante has curled himself up on an armchair, quietly licking the chocolate off his biscuit. Perhaps Karam is a Guru? I feel reluctant to disturb the relaxed atmosphere by clearing away the crockery.

After a while Karam stroked his beard and cleared his throat before glancing over at Dante and asking, 'Now shall I answer your question, Dante?'

Dante moved himself to the edge of his chair. He circled his tongue round his lips and replied.'About your dress? Yes, please.'

'Well, let me explain. A kurta is traditional casual wear worn by both men and women. It can be made from cotton material, like your t-shirt, or from other materials too. Some kurta have long sleeves like mine, but they can be any length and any colour.'

'My friend's dad has one with lots of diamonds on it.

And he said that his trousers are called pyjamas.'

Karam smiled. 'You know a lot about Sikh dress, Dante. Although the top may look as though it is decorated with diamonds, most of the time they are not real ones. Did you know that the word *pyjama* was borrowed from another language used a long time ago by people who lived in countries like Persia and India? It means leg-garment. It's a lightweight, loose-fitting, pair of trousers with a drawstring at the waist. Much like what we call pyjamas.'

'May I butt-in, Karam?' Richard asked. 'What about the phrase that you used when we met? What does that mean?'

'*Sat Shri Akaal.* Yes. Sat means *truth*, *shri* is a word that we use to honour God. Akaal means *the timeless being, God*. So the entire phrase can roughly be translated as, *True is the name of God*.'

Dante raised his hand, presumably ready to ask another question, but Richard intervened. 'May I suggest that we eat now, before Karam is exhausted with all our questions? Shall we?'

We all agreed, but the questions and explanations continued while we ate.

'Do you have any other rules that you observe, Karam?' Richard asked.

'As with most other religions, we Sikhs have some that may not at first be obvious. The dastaar is an article of faith that represents honour, self-respect, courage, spirituality, and piety. Take, for example, the five Ks. They are:

• Kesh (uncut hair)

• Kara (a steel bracelet)

• Kanga (a wooden comb)

• Kaccha — also spelt, Kachh, Kachera (cotton underwear)

• Kirpan (steel sword)'

After stretching over the table to make sure that everyone was in reach of the dishes, I enquired, 'About not cutting your hair, Karam? I've wondered about that. Is that why you wear a turban?'

I love the way he gently laid down his cutlery, wiped his serviette across his face and glanced in my direction. His friendly, melodious voice seems to draw us into an amicable world.

'Precisely, Frankie. Since 1699, about two centuries after the founding of the religion, Sikh leaders have prohibited their members from cutting their hair, saying long hair is a symbol of Sikh pride. You're right. The turban covers the long hair. It also results in making Sikhs easily identifiable in a crowd.'

'Fine. What about the bracelet?' I asked. 'Many people wear bracelets, Karam.'

'Of course they do.'

'The last of the five that you mentioned, Karam. Something about a sword?' Richard asked.

'Here we are. See, a kirpan is a small sword.'

'The blade is quite long, Karam'

'Eight centimetres. But the ceremonial kirpans are the length of a standard sword.'

'I like it, Daddy. Lovely shiny handle. Could I have one?'

'No love, you are not a Sikh. It's part of their religion. Catholics have other symbols such as rosaries and medals.'

'Correct. It is an article of faith that Sikhs are supposed to wear at all times. It is worn in a sheath on a strap or belt. In this country the government has passed an amendment by which Sikhs are allowed to carry kirpans and use them during religious and cultural functions. It isn't sharp. Are you sure that you really want me to explain more of our Sikh customs?'

'We'd love you to continue, Karam,' I assured him.

'It's good for us to be aware and respect other people's belief systems. What are the rules about types of drink permitted?'

'The Sikh Gurus banned the use of intoxicants, including alcohol, on account of its damaging effects. It is thought to be physically and mentally disturbing. The body is considered the Temple of God. However, as in other religions, there are different sects in Sikhism: Akhand, Kirtani, Jatha, Akali, Nihang, Namdhari and so on. Our followers believe that since coffee does not contain nicotine, we may drink it. Does that explanation sound confusing?'

'Not at all, Karam. As you will be aware, there are many different types of Christians following differing observances. I expect there always will be differing understanding and sets of rules that people believe that it is good to observe.'

'Now can you tell us about turbans, please?' Richard asked.

'A young boy's hair is tied into what is known as a patka.'

'My friend Tanvir wears a patka,' Dante said.

'Does he? So you already know that it is basically a rectangular cloth tied around his head to cover his bun. Most boys will wear a patka until they learn how to tie the full turban.'

'Tanvir's dad sometimes wears a blue turban.'

'Good boy. That's because turban cloth comes in every possible colour and pattern. But the three most commonly worn colours are white, deep blue, and saffron orange. However, nowadays most men and women tend to co-ordinate the colour of the turban with their outfit and vice versa. Also culturally, there are some commonly regarded colour preferences for certain occasions, which are as follows:

• Saffron is associated with valour, and is worn during rallies.

• White is associated with peace, is worn by elders. Many Sikh men and women choose to don a white, off-white or a similar shade daily as part of their beliefs in keeping with the faith. It is also a common colour worn by Eastern Sikhs at events such as a funeral ceremony, or any event where a bright colour would not be considered appropriate. On the other hand, Western Sikhs commonly wear white as part of their daily Sikh garb. White turbans are worn to extend the aura and the person's projection. Pink and red, associated with spring, is worn during that season or for marriage ceremonies. Orange and navy blue are traditional Sikh Khalsa colours, also worn on days of religious observance or special commemorative events. The blue is the colour of the warrior, and of protection. Royal blue or navy blue turbans are common among Sikh ministers and Gyanis, especially in India. Orange represents wisdom. Black and navy blue are more popular with the younger generation, and also worn at more formal events. Camouflage pattern is worn by the military personnel.'

'Where do Sikhs worship?' I asked.

'Sikhs worship at home and in the Sikh temple called the Gurdwara. Food is cooked by the members of the community and served by members of the community, to all people at the Gurdwara. This system is known as Langar'

'Gosh Langar… is that what you said, Karam?'

'Correct, Frankie. In Sikhism, a langar is the community kitchen of a gurdwara, that serves meals free of charge to all visitors — without making a distinction of religion, caste, gender, economic status or ethnicity.'

'That is so very generous, Karam.'

'Where's the nearest Temple, Karam?' Richard asked.

I am surprised that Dante still is so attentive. He has

positioned himself on the carpet and is gazing up at Karam.

'The one that we have chosen to attend is Gurdwara Sri Guru Singh Sabha South-hall situated on Havelock Road and Park Avenue. That's in the London Borough of Ealing. It's the largest Sikh temple in London.'

'Who do you worship?' Richard wanted to know.

'Good question. Sikhism is strictly monotheistic, and believes that there is only one God. You are more than welcome to come along and pray with us.'

'Could we go to their temple, Mummy?'

'That might be a very good idea, Dante.'

'I could wear a turban like yours.'

'Your hair is cut,' Karam said. 'Sikhs don't cut theirs.'

'Oh. Is that why it stays on, Mummy?'

Karam replied: 'Yes. Exactly, Dante. To tie a Sikh turban, you pull your hair to the top of your head and twist it into a large coiled bun. Then tie on a patka, which is a small piece of cloth that helps your hair stay in place. Pick up the turban and hold one end, then begin wrapping it around your head from the back to the front.'

'Is it like a hat?'

Karam intertwined his fingers. His eyes twinkled. 'I suppose so, but we don't wear it like a hat. To put it on, I fold the cloth several times into a single layer that I then wrap concentrically around my head in four layers. More often Sikhs wrap turbans around five or more times.'

'May I ask the reason behind not cutting your hair, Karam?' Richard asked.

'In Sikhism, the practice of allowing one's hair to grow naturally is a symbol of respect for the perfection of God's creation. Most Sikh women and men do not to cut their hair from any part of our bodies, but then there are always exceptions.'

'Thank you, very much Karam. It's so good to know about other ways of living. We have a good deal to learn.

I hope that you are not too exhausted answering so many questions.'

We spontaneously clapped Karam.

'It's a pleasure, Richard. I'm delighted that you invited me here, and I want to thank you with these key rings. Just a tiny little present for each of you.'

'They're lovely, Karam. Really, we were not expecting you to bring us anything. Thank you, very much.'

'Is that a picture of a Sikh Temple?' Richard asked.

'Yes. The Golden Temple in Amritsar is the most important Temple. I would love to talk to you about it. But you've listened to so much already today. I'll just say this, the Golden Temple — we call it Sri Harmandir Sahib — plays an integral role in the rich history of Punjab, which makes this religious heritage the holiest pilgrimage site for the Sikhs.'

Dante had begun to dance happily around the room dangling his precious keyring.

'A huge thank you to you, Karam.' I said.

'My wife sends her regards, too.'

'Oh, Karam, maybe we should have invited her, too?'

'Not at all. Daljeet was busy helping our son, Yadvir, with his homework when I left them. Besides, they are well versed in our customs.'

It would be great if Joe felt free to let Karam know that he too had been steeped in religion. But I suppose he wants a fresh start in life. Still, they are both committed people. Both wore religious garb and observed rules. Joe has chosen not to abandon some that he used to observe. But can we really dispense with rules? How free are we to do so?

15

FINAL DETAILS

Richard popped his head round our bedroom door as I was inserting my name and travel details into my case tag. He crept over and rested his head on my shoulder.

Oh those mesmerising olive eyes. How am I going to cope without his love, his gentle touch, his beguiling smile?

'Are you any nearer to being ready for the off, darling?'

We kissed, then held each other at arms outstretched distance so that we could see each other's face.

'Almost. We have our final meeting at Oasis tonight, Richard. We've got 'til Monday before we're off. As is my wont, I keep taking things in and out of my case.'

'Not to worry. You've still got two days. I'm going to miss you terribly. I don't think Dante realises how long you'll be away.'

Richard sat on the bed and wrapped his arms around me.

Oh God, I am so lucky to have such a warm, loving and caring husband. Those doe eyes are trickling tears. He's not long back home from Florence, and now I'm going off.

But I opted to go on this pilgrimage to prove that I really care about his aunt, cancer patients, and his friend and, of course, we need to challenge ourselves while we are young and healthy enough to do so.

'Darling, is there anything I can do to help you?'

'Weigh my case again? I hope that I have not gone over the 20kg limit.'

'Well, you have put your walking sticks in there, too. You won't lose that case with the bright orange tags.' He chuckled.

'That's why I chose them. I'm delighted that we have managed to raise... have we reached twelve thousand, Richard?'

'Yes. Hurrah! And Joe has a total of six thousand already. Nuala gave him all the money raised from the music festival that they organised together.'

'Very kind of her.'

'We've traipsed up and down every hill and valley in Surrey in preparation. I've certainly worn my boots in. I have learnt how to adjust my walking poles, and all our fundraising events are over.'

'And you have managed to do this while you have been back at school. You are as fit as you have ever been. Deo gratias. You love a challenge, Frankie. You'll be fine.'

Because of my early convent training and the preoccupation with modesty, chastity and purity drummed into me, I worried about room-sharing even though I recognised that Catherine seemed to be reserved and respectful. But I am not going to allow my preoccupation about covering my God-given body ruin the trek.

'There's the phone ringing.'

Richard ran downstairs to get it, brought it up, and handed it to me to answer.

'It's yourself, Joe!'

''Tis indeed., Frankie.'

Joe had been checking the list of what we had been told to take with us on the Camino. He mentioned sunglasses, glucose sweets, Compeed, blister pads and a few other necessities.

'Compeed. Oh, I nearly forgot, Joe. Glad you phoned. Richard is weighing my case again. Compeed. Yes, those padded plasters that protect blisters, or coping with them. I'll pop into Boots.'

'Like yourself, Frankie, I'm mostly ready, but I think I'll check the list again. I'm not sure about packing walking poles. Mine are the folding, light kind. I will also look at the weather forecast. Mid October can bring changes.'

'Are you pleased with the person you're sharing your room with?'

'Karam. Couldn't be better, Frankie.'

I told Joe that when Richard and I invited Karam to our home to explain some of the Sikh customs we were impressed with his kindness and contemplativeness. Grateful that our fellow pilgrims would introduce us to a variety of races and their beliefs we looked forward to learning so much from each other.

Richard, who had been listening, pointed to our bed and sat next to me while I continued chatting to Joe. He reminded me to tell Joe about a Franciscan friend of theirs who recommended that we watch a film entitled Frances of Assisi and Al-Malik Al Kamil. It's all about Crusader armies being involved in the siege of Damietta and Francis meeting Al-Malik.

That set us off talking about how crusaders were involved in some dreadful things and how the saintly Francis of Assisi was taught a lesson or two by the Al-Malik, Al-Kamil, the Muslim Sultan of Palestine, Syria, and Egypt, when Francis set out to convert him to Christianity.

'We never seem to learn, do we, Frankie? It must be eight hundred years ago when those crusades set off. I'll have to look for that film.'

'Richard is next to me listening in to our conversation. He's nodding. I moved the phone piece so that he could join in. He's now miming himself drinking.

'Thank you, love. I'd love a cuppa.'

'Please Richard, I'd love one too!'

Richard leaned nearer to the phone and shouted back, 'If you still believe in miracles I'll see what I can do!'

'I'm not codding, I'm really thirsty… no chance of anyone making one for me, though.'

We laughed. Joe said that he had learnt that the leaders engaged a company that caters for pilgrimages to book cheap hotels for overnight accommodation. Also that we would be walking a minimum of thirteen kilometres on the first day.

'It's eight days, Joe. Nine if you are staying on a day at the end. You are, aren't you?'

'Of course, I am, Frankie.'

'Okay. We depart from Heathrow. Vueling VY7101 17.35 on Monday.'

'Yes. We arrive quite late at A Coruna. 20:10 and then we are transferred to Cebreiro. It will be dark when we arrive there.'

'Slan leat!'

'Ah sure, 'til we meet again, May God hold you in the palm of His hand.'

Just as Joe and I were bringing our conversation to a conclusion, Richard returned with mugs of tea and a KitKat bar. We split the bar, and I updated him on the parts of our conversation that he had missed.

I checked the list once again:

'Walking boots and socks. Some thinner inner socks, too. Liners. Compeed and scissors. A small medical kit. A tube of Voltaren gel. Antiseptic cream. Suncream. Continental plugs adapters etc. Euros. Maybe a Spanish dictionary. Camelback or Platypus to carry water inside your backpack. Camino passport ready to be stamped en route. Scallop shell to be attached to rucksack. Rainwear. Jacket and leggings. Two pairs of trousers, a fleece and four tops. Underwear, of course. A camera…'

Anxious to not to have to pack a big case, I decided to wear my big boots and follow the criteria of taking lightweight, easily packable, fast drying clothes that don't need to be ironed.

After I zipped up my case closed yet again, we sat facing each other and clapped the palms of each other's hands until I was relaxed enough to follow Richard downstairs.

I've always found packing difficult. I remember way back when I was still in the convent, on the occasion that I had managed to obtain permission to join a group who were taking young people who were deemed to have learning difficulties on a pilgrimage to Lourdes. At our training meetings, the team leader of the HCPT group constantly reminded volunteer helpers that our prime concern was to be for the welfare of the persons that we were caring for. We were therefore recommended to only take bare necessities with us. However, even though I was still wearing a religious habit, my interpretation of essentials resulted in tightly packing a large case full of… I cannot recall what. As we wore the same habit daily, what had I put into that case? I think now that I must have been full of fear, preparing to face an unknown journey outside the convent.

16

TAKE OFF

'Frankie, now that you have packed, you know that Dante is really going to miss…'

'Go early to the airport? Make a day of it?'

'You're a mind reader. That would be great. The only official viewing area at Heathrow is inside Terminal 4. We could apply to go through security. Dante would love that.'

Now that the day of departure has really arrived, I feel numbed. It's as though I've been mechanised. That's externally. Inside, I am a bundle of nerves. Am I behaving like a teenager whimsically following my own pursuits, shirking my responsibilities? Oh my God, guide me. No, I am going on this pilgrimage to prove my love for Richard… amn't I? Besides, cancer is an awful disease. I want to do my bit. Don't I? I bet that Richard senses my questioning myself. He must have had his doubts when he flew to Florence to be with his aunt during her cancer journey. Sure, any decision we make has consequences. I'm on my way now. I will be brave.

We did as we had arranged. We left early. Richard chatted to Dante as he drove us to the airport. All went according to plan. We tried to take Dante's mind off my going by encouraging him to count all the different types of aircraft. When the time for my departure neared, we made our way down to the lounge.

'Mummy, when will you come home?'

I must not cry. Hold back those tears. His little hand is so soft and dependant.

'Oh darling! Big hugs. Mummy loves you. I promise to speak to you every day.'

Richard assured Dante as he tightened his grasp on his little hand that they would talk to me every day. 'The days will fly past. We'll have fun together!'

'It's great that we can use WhatsApp to send photos free of charge, Richard.'

'Send lots, Frankie.'

Time is ticking. I'll have to make the first move. Let's do it.

'Now for the big, big hug. Come on, the three of us together!'

After I eventually managed to drag myself apart from Richard and Dante, with tears streaming down my face, I struggled to keep hold of my passport and ticket as I made my way through Departures. I just managed to dispose of my tear-drenched tissues, when I identified our Camino group by the scallop shells dangling from their rucksacks.

'Joe! It's yourself.'

'Poor little Dante. I saw you hugging him goodbye.'

'Oh Joe, don't start me off again. The little fellow… Well, yes, after lots of sobbing and weeping.'

Hugs over, we settled into our scattered seats on the plane. Memories of the time I flew to Lourdes when I was a nun were triggered off. The old fear of life outside the convent returned. *If only Richard was here to comfort me.*

Automatically, I started praying the rosary. One decade for him, another for Dante, and then more to ensure that the plane journey would be safe, that the Santiago pilgrimage would be successful, and that Catherine, my room sharing companion, would be compatible.

Praying set off memories of the convent, the convent reminded me of Marion, and that prompted me to unzip the pocket in my rucksack where I had placed a letter from her. As the postman had handed it to me just as we were about to set off on our journey to the airport, I had slipped it unopened into my rucksack. I slept on the plane, so it was not until we boarded the coach taking our group from the airport to our first night's accommodation that I managed to read this letter. As it was late evening, and the lighting was dimmed, I used my torch to read it.

How thoughtful of Marion. I wonder what she has to say. Probably a prayer or a holy thought. Here we are:

Dear Frankie I am sure that you will reap great benefits from taking part in the Camino.
You know that you are always in my prayers. I was delighted when you told me that you had decided to take part in the Camino pilgrimage.
I hope that you will not mind me letting you know what has helped me. You recall when recovering from cancer, I similarly joined a fundraising group climbing Machu Picchu. You were generous in sponsoring me then, in spite of the fact that having recently left the convent you were struggling financially.
I discovered the following on my pilgrimage:
1. There is an inner, as well as an outer, journey. Walking with others is not just the physical one of placing one foot in front of the other. Nor is it solely being conscious of God's spectacular creation. By listening to and learning from those who walk beside us we can gain a great deal of wisdom. Remember that

*we have more in common with others than that which
may be initially apparent.*

*2. A period of time spent alone each day helped me
to connect with something bigger than myself and to
ponder on what I was learning.*

*3. The daily practice of writing a brief note to myself
proved to be encouraging.*

*Buen Camino. Good Bless. Darling Amy has uploaded
WhatsApp on my mobile so, if you wish, we can keep
in touch.*

Marion xx

*How lovely. So very thoughtful of Marion. Three short
suggestions, but a lot to ponder.*

She's a wise woman. I will try to unravel what's behind
them.

When the coach arrived at our destination, each of us
pilgrims were welcomed to enjoy supper before finding our
rooms.

'You look pensive, Frankie.'

'Yes, Catherine. I suppose the reality of the Camino is
sinking in. It's a tight squeeze in this little bedroom. But
we'll manage, won't we?' *A bit too close, especially next
to someone that I barely know. But then, it's most likely the
same for Catherine.*

It was a long journey from the airport to O Cebreiro
however, we would only be sleeping in the accommodation
over night. Our hostess served us a typical Galician dish
of spicy vegetable broth with fresh crusty chunky bread. It
was past midnight by the time we climbed the stairs to bed.
We were scheduled to start our walk at eight. We left our
boots and socks outside our bedroom door and placed our
platypus next to them so that we would remember to fill
them with fresh water in the morning.

Next morning, Catherine's alarm woke us. We soon
realised just how small our bedroom was. We began to

negotiate its limits in order to dress, organise our rucksacks, and repack in semidarkness. Wearing our walking boots and carrying our cases down a narrow staircase we made our way down to breakfast.

It's a long time since I have been in a refectory. Of course, our convent was much quieter.

After breakfast we left the luggage that was to be driven on to the next destination ready to be collected and waited for the group to assemble outside. When I walked over to the wall so as to watch the sunrise I looked down over the sheer cliff drop and only then realised that last night our accommodation was not far from a cliff edge.

'Good job I wasn't able to see the road the driver took last night. Wow! What a drop, Joe. I'm going to send a photo of this to Richard. Then I will have to assure him that all is well.'

Looking round the group I recalled Marion's advice about the benefit of mingling and learning from others. I caught sight of Roberta coming out of the little chapel. The brim on her sun hat was shading her face. She was wearing a long-sleeved floral blouse and full length beige skirt and walking boots. You'd never have guessed that a person so stockily built could be riddled with cancer. A very brave lady.

Our leader, Karam began assembling us for a group photo in front of the house. I doused myself with Citronella to protect myself from being bitten. Bahis set about adjusting the height of the poles for those who found it difficult to do so by ourselves. Everyone was reminded to collect their lunch, fill their water containers and travel light, leaving what was not needed to be transported in the van.

'Waterproofs, Karam?'

'Not today, Joy. Sun hats and cream. Cover up if necessary. Up to you. You know your skin type. Insect repellant. Roberta, you have our Thought for Today.'

Joy's asking about rainwear and she's wearing a stringy top that exposes her arms to the elements. Weren't we advised to make sure that our arms were covered? Maybe I'm wrong. Surely she's old enough to know. Her ponytail hairstyle makes her look young and attractive, whereas I am covered up in a long sleeved top and baggy trousers.

We gathered round Roberta.'Our Thought for Today is simply: Smile and say *Hola, Hello!*'

'Thank you, Roberta. Short and genuinely delivered to whoever we meet.'

Karam issued instructions before we started walking. He reminded everyone that they would be facing the oncoming traffic, on the right-hand side. That we would walking at our own pace, following the yellow scallop shell signs and arrows leading us to the address of that night's accommodation.

Right I will begin to observe and learn from my fellow pilgrimage walkers. There goes Nuala sidling up to join Joseph.

I bet Nuala wishes that she was sharing with Joe. I overheard her telling him that she heard him having a shower. Their rooms must be near each other's. She looks lovely in green. Sensibly, her wide brimmed sunhat is protecting her neck.

I am grateful to Peter for helping me to make better use of my walking poles. He laughed before he told me that when I stuck my head out in front of the rest of my body I reminded him of a strutting chicken. Imagine! He suggested that it would be better if I straighten up and placed the right pole out, accompanied by your right foot, then the same for the left. I was to straighten my body and make the poles match my stride. Then I would avoid putting my pole too far in front. Catherine confessed that she feared that she was strutting like another chicken.

'Come on, Catherine. Let's strut our stuff, but not like chickens.'

Chatting to Peter, I learnt that he was a volunteer reflexologist at the Oasis Cancer Centre and he set up the Walking Group inviting patients to join him on a short walk around the hospital grounds. When I praised him he replied:

'Let me tell you that it's not one way. We therapists gain, too. We're kept up to date. Oasis looks after us. Courses cost a lot. There are other perks, too. Oasis organises Away Days, and of course I'm introduced to patients who might want to have private treatment later on.'

I asked him how reflexology helps cancer patients.

He explained that there is a foot map that shows the relationship between feet and corresponding parts of the body. For example, top left side of foot relating to lung. He added that some cancer patients who visit have never experienced the benefit of various healing therapies so reflexology is a good introduction. Men, especially, who are sceptical might eventually remove their socks, and once they have felt the benefits of reflexology, they often opt to try other therapies.

'Have you been volunteering long at Oasis, Peter?'

'Just two years, Frankie.'

'Is it predominately needy folk who avail of the support? Three free therapy sessions for cancer patients and their carers?'

'Define needy? Aren't we all needy?

'All sorts of people come, Frankie. One morning, a well-spoken, tastefully dressed, middle-aged lady, arrived out of breath requesting that someone help her get her yellow Porsche parked. Having reached frustration point in finding a parking slot, she'd had to abandon it.'

'Demanding sort, eh? How did you respond, Peter?'

'Phoned the parking people. She'd left the keys in the ignition. Sorted.'

'Cheeky!'

'You might well conclude that. However, when I brought her a cup of tea and started to chat to her, tears trickled and this self-sufficient looking lady revealed that she was struggling to cope with liver cancer.'

Peter appraised that situation very well. It's so easy to make snap judgements. People on their cancer journey are confronted with so many life-threatening issues. Marion admitted to me that she experienced so many different emotions. Sometimes she was angry and at others she deliberately busied herself researching the possible causes of this cancer.

When Peter moved on down the line of walkers so that he could speak to others in the group I chose to walk alone in silence. I marvelled at the sight of silver cobwebs holding hands, jewels in the glimmering early morning light. Tiny, chattering birds free floating; deciding where to go.

Is that what Marion meant? Being in the here and now.

After the group had covered another few kilometres someone in the group shouted out: 'Hurray! I spy a cafe ahead!'

As we neared, Peter reminded us to get our pilgrim passport stamped there. 'Present your passport to be stamped and say, *Sello, por favor* before asking for *Cafe con leche*. He added:

'You'll be lucky if there isn't a queue for the toilets. *Los banos*.'

When Catherine asked Peter what was best to do first he said that he intended on having his coffee with a slice of their wonderful almond cake, *torta Santiago*, then getting his stamp before queuing for the toilet.

Almost as soon as we reached the cafe, our fellow walkers started to queue for the toilets. Chairs vacated,

Catherine, Peter and I relaxed. But another group arrived by the time I joined the long toilet queue. Having befriended a group of retired Oxford Dons, undeterred I began entertaining the women in our queue with a poem that I used to recite when I was still in the convent:

'The swallow is a roving bird. Each year he flies to Spain. And when the summer comes once more, he flies back home again. But on the 'omeward journey he met a flipping hawk what whipped off all its feathers and said, now you 'ave to walk.'

The Ex-Oxford Dons seemed to be intrigued, so much so that I ended up walking with one of their members for some time. I asked Elizabeth, a retired, rather rotund lecturer of English Literature, to tell me one of the Canterbury Tales. She began by reminding me that the Canterbury Tales is a story told around other stories. That their pilgrimage to the shrine of St. Thomas Becket in Canterbury started at the Tabard Inn in London.

'I remember references being made to them when I was at university. Wasn't the shortest one The Tapestry-Maker's Second Tale?'

Elizabeth agreed with me. She really would have loved to relate that tale but unfortunately she had to catch up the others in her group. I thanked her for whetting my appetite.

'That's good. If I was to summarise I'd say that the tales are about love conquering all, lust only gets you in trouble, religion and morality is virtuous, and honour and honesty is valued. Although there are some contradictory stories, Chaucer kept to this set of morals through most of his tales.'

'Love conquers all, lust only gets you into trouble… religions and morality are virtuous and honour and honesty is valued.'

I think I'll need the entire pilgrimage to come to grips with that quote but this has given me plenty to ponder.

When Elizabeth caught up with her friends, their group donated twenty pounds to the Oasis Centre funds.

After all that chatting I re-entered a reflective mode walking alone in the heat of the midday sun. My supply of water was running out. I was further alarmed when I saw a herd of cows up in front blocking the road. My mind flashed back to when I was still a child and was cornered by a huge cow. A farmer was herding his cows through the street where I lived in Kerry. Fortunately, an old woman opened her door and let me take refuge in her home. Long after the cows had passed, this old lady allowed me to pick some sweet gooseberries from the many bushes that lined her long garden.

Now I stepped behind a low wall and waited anxiously. I was relieved when the farmer shewed the frisky beasts off the road, through a gap into a field, before they reached where I was hiding.

I WhatsApped Richard, attaching a photo of the cows. He had advised me to try and relax. Half dazed by the sun I ate my sandwiches under the shade of a willow tree before I continued my journey. But where were the Camino signs? Not a yellow arrow or a scallop shell sign anywhere. Hot, thirsty, longing for a toilet and alone, I began to pray that someone would emerge from somewhere.

'Hola!' An olive skinned, middle-aged lady appeared. 'Pies? Necesitas ayuda?'

From her accent and appearance, I assumed that she was Spanish. I hoped that my knowledge of Italian might helped me to understand what she was saying. Alas, it didn't. It was when she pointed to her boots and undid her First Aid box, that I concluded that her blisters had forced her to stop.

Through gestures we managed to communicate as we walked on together until we reached to a water pump. Maria waited while I filled my platypus. Then we continued on, singing The Lourdes Hymn. I in English and Maria's in Spanish: *Immaculate Mary... And bless, sweetest Lady, the land of our birth... Ave, Ave...'*

When Maria came across an older lady who was limping, she stopped to treat her. I noticed a yellow scallop sign. I also heard voices speaking English. Catherine turned round. Relieved and over joyed we waved to each other and walked on until we reached the place where we were staying that evening.

'Cold beer, Frankie? We are given a choice. Clock into our rooms and shower or collapse on the seats in the cafe in front of the hostel with a cold beer?'

'I'm exhausted, Catherine. A very long cold lemonade with lots of ice. Wash after.'

We almost fell onto the rickety seats and slowly unlaced our boots carefully extracting our tired, hot, smelly sock covered feet. We talked about the mixture of rocky roads, pebbly softer terrain and the streams and villages that we had walked through. An hour later, we carried our boots, rucksacks and poles into the room that we were allocated and showered. When Catherine showed me that the bottom half of her legs were very red we wondered what might have caused this. What could she do to remedy this irritation. Trying not to worry too much we decided that perhaps stretching our legs up the wall as we on lay on the bed would help to encourage the blood to flow back. After comparing and dabbing our blisters we lashed cream on parts of our necks that had got sunburnt. Catherine went first for a shower. That's when she saw the cubicle only had half a curtain and a merely a dribble of lukewarm water spurted from it.

Even though we were assured that Spanish drinking

water was fine, we joined most of the group in search of litres of water in a nearby supermarket. Later, spruced up, we assembled in a local restaurant for an evening meal. Tales were exchanged.

Once back in that night's accommodation we both WhatsApped home. Catherine told me that her son told her that she would soon be a granny for the second time. Dylan, their first grandson was three and called after Dylan Thomas.

Long after the lights were turned off I was awoken by a sharp cough and my name being called out. I turned over to face Catherine's bed.

'You're snoring. Sorry.'

'Sorry. I'll sleep on my side.'

But having been woken, I began to think over the day's happenings.

I wish that I could switch the light on. I feel an urge to write down my reflections on today. What have I learnt? I only managed to be silent twice. That was for such a short time, just after Peter showed us how best to use our poles. The second time was enforced. I was lost and had no choice. However, even then, although I was anxious, I was more observant of my surroundings. I am such an extrovert. Who else would dramatise a poem in a toilet queue? Is this type of behaviour helping me in my inner journey? I discovered that I am an extrovert when I was in the convent. It was at a time when personality testing became mandatory. I remember being delighted when my test result revealed that I was an extreme extrovert. That was until I was informed that a balanced person was deemed to score midway between an introvert and extrovert.

But then, had I not recited my poem, I would not have met Elizabeth and learnt more about Chaucer's principles. Of course, there is a balance to be achieved and I still have a long way to go on my inner as well as my outer journey.

Trying not to scratch or worry about red ankles I concentrated on my resolution to take time the following day to log my reflections and resolutions in my diary.

17

ROUTINE

*C*atherine's and my daily routine continued the next morning when Catherine's alarm sounded at 6:30. I remembered my resolve to find time to be alone so that I could follow Marion's advice and reflect on my inner journey. I made sure that I packed my notebook in an outside pocket of my rucksack in order to jot down some of my reflections.

Our group was required to have breakfasted and report at the front door within the hour.

As our shared space was limited we needed to avoid each other as we washed, visited the bathroom, collected the tops that we had rinsed and let drip dry overnight on a hanger in the shower. Before we zipped up our cases we agreed on a routine. We checked the weather, applied bite prevention and sun cream, dressed appropriately, packed our rucksacks accordingly, filled our platypuses and breakfasted.

It was still dark when Roberta faced the group to give us our spiritual Thought for the Day. She read the first verse of The Servant Song: *'Will you let me be your servant, let me be as Christ to you? Pray that I may have the grace to let you be my servant too.'* Then she suggested that we carry in our hearts all those we knew who were struggling with cancer.

When the group started to walk from our accommodation, short, blonde, Emma from Farnham turned to me. 'What do you think best, Frankie? Should I wear my jacket? I don't want to have to stop, drop my poles, and remove my rucksack after a few minutes.'

'My thoughts exactly, Emma. If you do that, you get behind and I'm not as quick as Joe, and certainly not Karam.'

Joe joined us. 'When you told me, Frankie about your panic when you felt lost yesterday, I'm keeping up the rear today.'

'That'll be hard for you, Joe. With your long legs you'll take bigger strides.'

'That's true, Frankie. But do you know what? I have decided to take in all the beauty in this lovely countryside today. We're not in a race, are we?'

I asked Joe if his leg was still paining him. He told me that after that scare he had when we were at the Sustainability Centre, he was advised that if he experienced any further pain he should take it easy. He might eventually need surgery, but as he was still young they would be reluctant to do that too soon. He has been allocated a physiotherapist. He was trying not to worry and keep going.

His blonde hair has begun to curl. Is it any wonder Nuala's attracted to him.

Emma shouted out as she reached the top of the hill that as expected she was hot and needed to take off her fleece. I told her not to worry. I would hold her poles while she unravelled herself.

'You're a darling. Thank you. Then I'll do the same for you.'

Remembering my inclination to chat instead of reflecting on my inner journey, I began to admire the Galician countryside. The rolling hills and undulating green pasture land reminded me of my childhood in Kerry. As I neared some fields, I noticed two farmers using enormous rakes to harvest the hay. By the time I reached that farm, a man had begun to haul some bales onto a big, old tractor.

I wonder what my life would have been like had I remained living with my aunt Nan on her farm in County Limerick? It must have been hard for my mammy to send me there after my father died. She most likely couldn't cope with me on her own. My older siblings had already left home. I don't think that I realised that I would never see my da again. I was fussed over at the wake and the funeral and then taken out to my father's aunt in the country. But, in spite of everything, that was a happy time. The men haymaking reminds me of the fun we enjoyed when my cousins and I sat on top of the bails of hay as the tractor was driven down O'Connell Street, Limerick.

I was still reminiscing when I realised that I was entering a small village. I quickened my pace to catch up with Emma.

'Un euro. Tortita.' A woman was holding a frying pan and tossing a pancake while calling out as they reached a series of stone cottages.

'Oh that smell of freshly baked pancakes, Frankie.'

'She might be dressed in a fifties style with an old fashioned, all-over-cover apron, but she knows how to hit the target.'

'I'm licking my lips, Frankie.'

'Could you root for my purse, Emma. I think it's in the bottom pocket of my rucksack. I don't want to unstrap everything again. And for that, you can take out two euros for the two of us.'

Emma supplied the tissues and we savoured our fresh

pancakes while we continued walking.

When I enquired about Emma's background she said that lived in Farnham, a fairly rural area of Surrey. In order to be close to her twins she worked as a Nursery assistant when her twins were beginning school. They'll be going to secondary school next year. She chatted to Emily, Eve, and her husband John every night on the phone.

'Today's the day that we're going to meet in the Octopus restaurant.'

'I noticed that you speak Spanish, Emma. Are you originally from Spain?'

'No. We have an apartment in Spain, so I have been studying the language in order to communicate better.'

I told her that Roberta was very pleased when she ordered her a taxi the day before when she was finding it difficult to continue walking. 'She seems to be so cheerful in spite of coping with her cancer. Is ovarian cancer curable?'

That prompted Emma to tell me that unfortunately, they lost their mother to ovarian cancer. She learnt a lot about its survival rate and prognosis. Her mother had Epithelial ovarian cancer, which is the deadliest of the gynaecological cancers. When I told Emma that I had heard that Roberta was suffering with the same cancer she enquired whether Joan, the lady who is supporting her during the walk, is she struggling with the same type of cancer.

'No, Joan had a germ stromal tumour. That has a much better prognosis, Emma. You probably know that people who have this type of cancer are often cured because they are usually detected at early stages.'

We went on to admit that the symptoms are not easy to detect. Abdominal bloating or swelling is one, and that people often feel bloated after a big meal. That a person who feels bloated might try to lose weight and weight loss is another symptom.

'Well, the symptom that Roberta apparently is coping

with now is that she feels that she needs to be near a toilet. Toilets are few and far between on the Camino, aren't they Frankie?'

Emma suddenly began to limp. At first I presumed that she was tired but when I asked Emma she showed me lumps that had appeared on her legs just below her knees. When she pressed them they popped in and out. They were painful.

I suggested that we stop and sit on a little wall for a while. Emma said that she was hoping that the lumps would not bother her. Her doctor thought that walking would help but that they have not discovered what causes them to appear. Just as we sat Catherine caught up with us. Emma asked her how she was coping with her leg problems

'They are still red but not raw, Emma. Maybe my socks are rubbing? I've kept my boot laces looser.'

'You should have seen Catherine and me last night, Emma. What were we like, Catherine? We decided to walk up the wall. Our instructions are to sit at the pillow end of your bed. Then turn round to face the bed board and stretch your legs straight up on the wall.'

'We had such a laugh, Frankie, didn't we?'

'You've got blisters too, Emma?'

'Two so far. That and my lumps. But I'm hungry so let's… oh no! Sometimes these lumps really hurt.'

I tried to console Emma: 'Here, I've tissues. Wipe those tears. You are so brave, Emma. Bubbly, happy Emma. All the time you're in pain. Looks like a restaurant ahead. Come on, lean on the two of us.'

Emma struggled to be cheerful. Then suddenly she cried out: 'Hey. Can you see what I see? Cyclists. Men in lycra!'

The three of us laughed. I joked: 'Pain's gone, Emma?'

Catherine and I watched Emma instantly transform from a distraught pilgrim into a bubbly, fluent translator for the men in lycra. Exuberant, before long, she bounced into the lap of a cyclist in this apparently highly rated Wagamama-style octopus restaurant.

Catherine drew our attention to the noticeboard: This large and popular restaurant specialises in tender and delicious octopus and other local Galician food. Service is friendly. The standard of food is good. Servings are generous. This restaurant located on the Camino de Santiago is popular with pilgrims as well as locals.'

I joined the rest of the group watching the cook boil the octopus.

After we had enjoyed a delicious meal, Bahis put fresh Compeed on Emma's blisters before we continued our journey. He congratulated those he had helped to use our walking poles efficiently, rhythmically and had therefore succeeded to establish our own pace.

Bahis started off walking beside us so I availed of this opportunity to question him about the reasons why he does not wear the short rounded cap that many Muslims seem to wear.

'The taqiyah. That cap is made from a coarse cloth that is known in the West as a Muslim prayer cap. It's brimless so as to allow the man's forehead to touch the ground while he's praying to Allah. It's quite attractive, and it fits close to the head. Am I selling it to you? It can be plain white or crocheted with intricate geometric patterns.'

'It does sound attractive. So why aren't you wearing one?'

'Really ideal when trekking! No. I made sure that my hat has a wide brim. Anyway, I choose when I wear my taqiyah. That's what I mean by the Dutch approach.'

'So observance of rules is voluntary. No different to most people's opinions on religious adherence.'

'Agreed.'

'I overheard a pilgrim back along the road saying that

there is going to be rain tomorrow. Have you been checking on the weather forecast, Bahis?'

'Gosh, yes, Frankie. Rain. More like a deluge all day. You'll need all your wet gear.'

I have a lot to write in my diary tonight. When I have prepared all my rainwear, I will update my account while Catherine is taking her shower. There will be more time when she phones her son. I'll phone later. I must tell Richard about Joe's leg. I noticed that Nuala stayed behind with him. So he will be okay should he fall behind.

Listening to Emma today, and being reminded of Marion and Joan's cancer, makes me realise just how fortunate I am to be healthy.

Both of us were confronted with the death of our parents early in our lives. When Richard's aunt was diagnosed with cancer, he had to face the fear that cancer can bring. When I left home to enter the convent, maybe I didn't fully realise that my mam drank and smoked in order to cope with loss and loneliness. She was depressed and had always been jealous. Perhaps, subliminally, I knew something was not right, and that is why I opted to leave her. Dear God, please help Richard and I to take stock of our lives and be aware of the messages that we are giving to our son.

Before I retired to bed that night, I also sent Marion a photo of haymakers with the caption:

I too have begun to make hay while the sun is shining.

18

A PONDEROUS RAINY DAY

'Good morning, Frankie!'

'Oh. It's still dark. Ah... when the alarm rang I thought you mistook the time, Catherine.'

'So did I. It is lashing down outside. Didn't you hear it? I had to close the window in the middle of the night. Rain was forecast, but it sounds like a storm.'

I switched the light on. We followed what had become our routine and after breakfast, donned our rainwear. When we assembled, once again Karam invited Roberta to give us our 'Thought for the Day':

'When I saw that it was going to be a hard day walking through the rain, I decided to offer you two quotations to spur you on your way. The first is taken from Isaiah 55:10, *'The rain and the snow come down from heaven, and do not return to it without watering the earth and making it bud and flourish.'* Then there is a lovely rhyming, anonymous quote: *'Everybody wants happiness, nobody wants pain, but you can't have a rainbow without a little rain.'*

Karam thanked her. 'Very apt. Thank you, Roberta.

There is little need for me to remind each of you that this is going to be a challenging day. The weather forecast predicts wind-driven rain. Persistent precipitation. It seems that there will be no letup. But let's look out for the rainbow that Roberta spoke about.'

'Thanks, Karam. Shall I lead the way?'

'Okay, Bahis. Off you go.'

'This is what I dreaded, Frankie. I checked the forecasts before leaving home. This weather was to be expected. I read a remark somewhere saying that the weather is the only negative thing about Galicia.'

'Bit like Ireland then,' I replied. 'On the plus side, it wouldn't be as green without it.'

'Same goes for Wales. Come on, Frankie. I'm going to be first to push open the door.'

'Oh. Gosh,' Catherine warned. It's lashing down. Keep behind me, Frankie. I'm being sheltered by Bahis.'

With my head down, as I struggled against the full impact of the rain and the wind, my poncho blew up and out. I struggled to keep pace while grasping two walking poles in one hand and trying to tuck the flapping overcoat into my armpits. Preoccupied with that, I nearly toppled off the kerb.

I could use the belt on my trousers to put round my poncho. But how can I do that while I am walking? I'd have to lift my poncho up, unzip my jacket so that I can undo it, and pull the trouser belt through the loops. Oh, great. Now that we've turned the corner, the wind is behind us. I'll just keep walking. Just as well Bahis is following the shell signs indicating the route. My eyes are on the puddled, asphalt road. We seem to have reached an open road on a hill where the gullies are flushing away excess water. I'll move nearer to the camber of the road.

Someone called out. 'Car coming. Move in!'

Someone else is tugging at my poncho. I can't turn

to see who it is. Car horns blaring. Splash! There are no pavements. I can't hear anyone. Neither can I communicate with the others. I don't know how high this hill is. Sheet water is creating a curtain of mist. I'm drenched, and even though the wind is behind me, the rain is relentlessly bucketing down. Water is dripping from my hood and trickling down my face. The tissue I managed to pull out from my jacket pocket is soaked. I'm perspiring. Too many clothes. Leggings on top of trousers. Gaiters over walking boots. Two pairs of socks: woollen and boot liner. Poncho protecting jacket. Tightly clasped hood. Rucksack under poncho. Platypus streaming through from the rucksack. I need to keep sipping my water through my platypus. Everything's so heavy. Oh. Why have we stopped?

We're crossing the road. Catherine's crossed. Two way traffic. Just as well I looked round to see a bike approaching. My turn to cross. Now we're on stony ground. Uneven, slippery and sodden. Difficult to manipulate my poles. Hanging trees and undergrowth. Thorny bushes. Oh, one is snagging my poncho. Pull. Can't stop. Queue behind me. Must keep going. This is a narrow road.

When will we come to a cafe? I'm being pushed against the bushes. Why? Clip-clopping. The nostrils of a snorting, skittish horse spewing his nasal discharge into my face. Is this spirited horse expressing contempt for the atrocious weather conditions? Good for him. I'm laughing aloud as his swishing tail bids us good luck, I'm enjoying my own nasal discharge. Oh well, there's nothing I can do. Better make the best of this struggle. After all, I wanted a challenge.

We're off the road, and out in the open onto a muddy, puddled path. Oh, here comes a quagmire. A huge puddle extending to both sides of the path and continuing as far as I can see. Catherine is an experienced walker, and she has chosen to walk through the middle of it. I'll follow suit. Oh no… down I go.

'You alright? Hold on to our hands. Up you come. Are you alright?'

'Thank you, Bahis and Catherine. My pole slid off a stone. The puddle is so deep I didn't see…Sorry. I'll be alright. Really. I'm holding everyone else back.'

Bahis encouraged: 'That's the spirit, Frankie. And the good news is that according to my map, there is a cafe marked as we exit this field.'

That horse has jerked my thinking. I wonder what it was like for pilgrims travelling to Compostela in earlier times? Knights with retinues riding high, sending others ahead to clear paths through overgrown woods and fields.

Had they set out to do penance for their failures? Even Henry VIII is reported as having walked barefooted from London to Walsingham in order to attain a place in heaven. Long before his time, the Crusaders tramped a path to Galicia, some say, to rid Spain of Muslims. I wonder what Bahis thinks about that?

Nobility, Royalty, Crusaders travelled over this ground on horseback. But what about ordinary folk trudging along unmade paths, repenting for their failings and in fear of damnation in the next world? What must it have been like for them? Perhaps the noble horsemen hired them to serve their needs? Would there have been thieves and robbers out to exploit their naivety and fear of God's punishment? Thank God there are cafes in our lifetime.

'Praise the Almighty,' Catherine wiped rain from her face. 'Hot drinks at last, Frankie. Are you really okay? You're covered in mud. I'll ask the chap for some tissue paper. How do I say that in Spanish? Oh, there's no need, there's a roll on the counter.'

'Thanks. Luckily, I was able to break my fall by grabbing hold of a sturdy tree stump. I bet I'm not the only one who fell.'

'Look at my boots. They're coated in mud. They were heavy enough before I managed to squelch out of that big puddle on the very muddy path.'

'Here, Catherine. I've removed a good lot of mud from mine. Take the rest of the tissue to do yours.'

The tarpaulin gazebo cafe was being buffeted by the windswept rain. The hanging side-flaps swung as our group queued for hot drinks and a slice of Torta Santiago. The rain was trickling off the steel garden chairs and tables, but what did that matter to this group of dripping pilgrims? When I eventually made my way to the toilet cubicles, I realised that the person in front of me would need time to undo layers of rainwear before they were able to use the facilities. Mindful of that, I shook off excess rain water from my outer clothing, only to realise that the rain had seeped in through to my underwear. Not only that, but my poncho was torn where the thorn had snagged it.

I should have invested in a proper rain overcoat instead of a poncho. Never mind, someone will surely have tape to repair it. Besides, since I realised that I can use my trouser belt to hold it in place, it's no longer billowing as much.

Revived after our refreshments, and resolved not to let the inclement weather dampen our spirits, once again our group found ourselves back on an asphalt road. The traffic had increased, so had its speed. When Bahis reached the junction, he was confronted by arrows and shell signs pointing to Santiago by two different routes. He grouped everyone under a flyover while he consulted Karam, Peter, and other leaders in the group. An eerily whistling wind accompanied slanting rain seeping from above, and splashes from passing traffic had to be tolerated by the group while the leaders consulted their maps.

A decision has been made. The route to follow has been selected. I am going to make a decision, too. I want to return to the mindset that helps me to reflect on who has walked this route before me. I'll walk at the back of the group.

We're back to slithering along another muddy lane. Some of the group have begun to climb up onto a grassy ridge along the side of the path. I'm joining them. I am now near enough to breathe in a minty aroma from the eucalyptus trees that line this lane. We'd call it a boreen in Ireland. Gosh, these tall, slim ladylike trees are so elegant. The rain has eased off enough for me to be able to admire their blue-grey bark. On the trees where the bark has peeled off in strips, there are yellow patches. What a lovely contrast.

I wonder if back in the time, earlier pilgrims who trod these lanes, discovered the oils that are distilled from this plant. I know that antiseptics, repellents as well as flavourings and fragrances can be extracted from the leaves of eucalyptus trees. Maybe these early pilgrims knew this and delighted in their use? Perhaps the fragrances helped them to depress the unpleasant bodily odour that must have resulted from the effort that they had to make in order to persevere on their pilgrimage? I'll try and pull off a few leaves. There we go. Lovely fragrance.

I am walking on holy ground in the footsteps of thousands of pilgrims throughout past ages who have gone before me. From the mighty to the lowly, with differing intentions. Countless feet must have trodden this part of the Galicia. An old barefooted woman with a shawl round her shoulders, carrying all her worldly possessions in a bundle on her back. Was she alone? Did she have her children with her? How did she feed them? Did she forage, turning over a rock or log in search of termites, ants, slugs, snails, earthworms in order to survive? They would have used their ability to search out and collect food in the wild, including herbs, plants, fruit, nuts, mushrooms. They probably killed animals like rabbits, hares and of course birds. Would there have been deer and other animals? Possibly richer folk used them to hunt for their food. Everyone would have needed to sustain themselves.

Preoccupied with these considerations, I nearly bumped into Nuala pushing Joe up the hill in front of us. She had her hands on his bottom while she issued instructions about keeping his back straight and leaning on his walking poles.

'Is that leg of yours giving you trouble again, Joe?'

''Tis, Frankie. But sure it's a hard day for us all. With Nuala's help here, I'll eventually get the hang of things. Perhaps it's better if you overtake us. Don't worry. We'll get there. Peter is keeping an eye on us and on you too. There he is turning round to check.'

'Okay, Joe, Nuala, Frankie,' Peter turned to ask. 'Good news, we're coming up to another cafe.'

Oh, for a hot drink. Now that Joe has pushed back the hood on his rain-mac, I notice that his cheeks look flushed. He's holding on to the edge of the table as he collapses onto the attached wooden bench-like seating. I suppose we all look hot and bothered after all that trudging. I wonder what I look like? Nuala is really taking care of him. First in the queue in spite of being last in. How did she manage to get to the front of the cafe queue? Anyway, there are two mugs and pieces of Torta Santiago on the tray that she's placing down in front of Joe.

'Attention everyone. Congratulations to each of you. We've managed so far. Three more kilometres and we'll be at tonight's accommodation. We've walked together today, and I think it's best if we register at our destination together when we arrive. Well done!'

'Thank you, Karam.'

The rain was still pelting down when our group resumed battling on for the rest of our walk.

Is that thunder rumbling? Oh, I hope not. We're heading back onto a tree-lined path. Trees and lightning could be killers. No, that noise must have been signalling a cloud burst. Or is all that rain coming from the branches of the overhead us? Mud concealing stones again. My poles will help me find the stones before I put my weight on them. Don't want to slip again. Once more, the rain water is dripping down from my hood to my face. I'll have a lot to tell Richard tonight.

That hymn. What was it called? One more step along the world I go. *If only I could remember the words. There's the other hymn: Walk with me, oh my Lord... I remember the air of that well. Thank God for that. I'll sing that one. I'll change the words to suit the occasion:*

> *Walk with me, oh my Lord,*
> *On this boggy road*
> *Be at my side, oh Lord,*
> *Stop me before I slide*
> *Oh God this road is long,*
> *My energy is spent.*
> *Oh Lord, give me strength*

I sang, satisfied that I was composing my own lyrics to fill the gaps. My spirit was raised as I pounded out the beat with my boots. Eventually we arrived at our accommodation. We huddled round Karam as he opened the door into the entrance. We faced the proprietor. He ordered:

'Botas fuera! Boots off. Remove boots. Shake wet. Before enter.'

Karam replied: 'Sir, excuse me. We need to enter before we can remove our boots.'

But the chap repeated: 'I repeat. Boots off. Floor is clean.'

'Sorry, señor. We need to sit in order to remove our boots.'

Karan rested an arm on Bahis's shoulder as he struggled to untie the laces on his boots. Our group moved nearer to see who was shouting commands to Karam. We were astonished when we saw that it was an arrogant little man wagging his pointed finger at our group leader. His grimaced, angry face was threatening us not to enter without removing our boots and shaking off the rain dripping from our clothes.

Joe was leaning on my shoulder, said, 'Sure aren't our boots almost glued to our feet after all that walking. Not an easy job removing them.'

David, the slightly older Scottish man in our group, realised that the señor at the desk did not seem to understand that it was senseless issuing us impossible commands. After all we had just emerged from the deluging rain. Until we were seated, it was physically impossible for us to unlace and remove our boots. Observing this angry fellow's contorting facial features as he continued to shout instructions while pointing to his highly polished floor, David smiled and with his boots squelching he approached the reception desk. But the chap, instead of realising that it was impossible for the group to obey his orders, started to demand our passports. *Pasaportes!* He kept shouting as he thumbed the desk.

David shook his head, and must have decided to pretend that he did not understand the señor. Karam signalled the group to enter the room and pointed to stools just inside the door. We unlaced our books and tried not to shake off the rain from our soaking clothes on to the polished floor. Then David held up a key hoping that the proprietor would see sense and provide us with keys to our rooms. Fortunately, at that point a kind faced smiling woman entered from a door across the room, grabbed a bunch of keys and signalled us to follow her. But she had to wait, because she realised that we needed to put our boots back on before she could lead us outside into a rainswept courtyard in order guide us to our apartments.

After this genial lady handed Catherine the key for the apartment that we were to share, we shook off our excess water before entering.

'I don't know how you can laugh, Frankie. What an idiot!'

'A proper ejeet. What else can we do, but laugh? I've never seen the like. If that kind lady is his wife, she has a lot to put up with.'

'Feel the radiators, Frankie. They're lovely and warm. This room feels snug and cosy.'

We bounced on the mattress and examined the shower

'I might as well have been walking in my pelt. Even waterproofs have their limits, Catherine.'

We showered, washed some of our clothes, placed others on radiators, removed the mud from our boots, compared and consulted each other about our blisters, stretched our legs up against the wall, and got ready to assemble with the others near the end of an indoor corridor. When the last person arrived to the group, we followed each other along ambulacrum linking our accommodation to a restaurant.

'There's Roberta at the entrance. Of course she must have bused it here today. Oh, she's pointing to—'

'A rainbow! Look through that window!' shouted Catherine.

Everyone stopped and clapped and joined Sonia's outburst as she sang *Somewhere over the rainbow*, while swaying her arms in time. We all delighted at the sight of the promised rainbow.

Over the dinner that night, pent-up emotions and accounts of individual struggles were shared.

When I phoned Richard that evening, I surprised myself when I told him that I had had a Damascus experience.

'That's rather dramatic, darling. According to the weather bulletins, it was lashing down in Galicia all day. So, in spite of that, suddenly a light from heaven flashed around you and Jesus called out, Frankie, Francesca, why do you persecute me…? Well, not persecute me, of course?'

'Really, Richard, I am being serious. Like Paul, I felt some sort of a conversion. But instead of being blinded and falling off a horse, my eyes seemed to be opened, and I became aware of the earth beneath my feet, the soil, the richness of my surroundings, the path I was treading. It's hard to put into words.'

'Wonderful, Frankie. It sounds like you reaching the real meaning of pilgrimage. A journey to a sacred place.'

'More than that, Richard. I am beginning to realise that it is the journey itself that is important. It's… it's travelling through life's pilgrimage. That's it. Even if I find that Compostela is not all that I hope it will be, I don't think that will matter as much as the importance of being stirred by the impact, and being aware of where I am at this point of my life.'

'Gosh, you really are benefiting from this experience, Frankie. And that on what was a really bad weather day.'

'Was the stormy day serendipitous? Maybe. Let me fathom that out while I sleep. I'm off to bed now, Richard. I'm sure that you're tired too. Kiss our darling for me, and may the deluge of my love drench you.'

I'm not surprised that it sounds as though Catherine seems to be fast asleep. Thank goodness I brought my torch outside in the corridor with me while I spoke to Richard. I'll slip past her bed and into mine as quietly as possible.

I am beginning to realise what my friend Marion meant in her letter when she suggested that I connect with something bigger that myself, while on this pilgrimage.

19

SEEKING ADVICE

*R*oberta, dressed in shades of yellow, stood on a raised platform to give her Thought for the Day. It was the morning after we had all struggled through the awful rain.

'What a difference the weather can make. Today with the promise of sunshine, we are blessed. I am going to read an excerpt from the Song of Solomon, to cheer us on our way:

> *Get up, my dear friend,*
> *fair and beautiful lover, come to me!*
> *Look around you: Winter is over;*
> *the winter rains are over, gone!*
> *Spring flowers are in blossom all over.*
> *The whole world's a choir—and singing!*
> *Spring warblers are filling the forest*
> *with sweet arpeggios.*
> *Lilacs are exuberantly purple and perfumed,*
> *and cherry trees fragrant with blossoms…'*

'Thank, you Roberta. Let's hope that, although it's autumn, we will still be able to marvel at the fauna and flora along our paths today. So off we go. Follow Mark,' instructed Karam.

'The top of the morning to you, Frankie. Mind me traipsing alongside you for a while?'

'You're more than welcome. Aon sceal? You look as though you're brimming with a story.'

'My story? I hope that you won't mind, but I'm looking for advice, Fran. I'm getting confused messages from Nuala. What was it in that Roberta has just quoted from the Book of Wisdom for us today…? Something about a beautiful lover.'

'You both looked as though you are enjoying each other's company, Joe. Yesterday I saw Nuala getting your coffee and even pushing you along up the hill in that dreadful weather.'

'Nuala has been really kind and caring. She couldn't be more understanding about the struggle I have in hauling this leg of mine up, down and along everywhere. But I am confused. She gives me mixed messages. Well, I think she is. That's why I wanted to check with you. Only you know that I have never experienced what it's like to be touched by a woman before.'

'I'm no expert, Joe. But if you don't mind, you'd need to give me an example.'

'Of course. Well, last night after we returned from our dinner we kissed and hugged… I feel so embarrassed. I'm not used to this.'

His eyes are cast down. Now he's combing his hand through his hair. He's scratching his forehead. This must be so embarrassing for him.

'Okay. Still hugging, she dragged… well, I didn't need much encouragement. I ended up in her room. But all we did was sit next to each other on her bed. This is what I didn't understand. Nuala then began to say that relationships have consequences. That close friendships are not always easy.'

'Do you think that she might be frightened of becoming too close or even becoming pregnant, Joe? I mean if you… well if… but you haven't?'

'Oh. No. No. We haven't. She… Sometimes her hands are all over me, and then she'll abruptly turn away. I know that I have to be careful. I wouldn't go too far. We haven't known each other long enough. In fact, I haven't told her that I was training to be a priest.'

What advice can I give Joe? If only Richard were here. He could talk man-to-man. It doesn't seem right to question Joe about the extent of his arousal. That's all too intimate. He may not even have the vocabulary to express that.

'Relationships are all so different, Joe. You know that. I admit that I would find the description that you gave me of Nuala's behaviour disconcerting. But then I don't really know her. Perhaps she has experienced a traumatic relationship. She may even have been engaged. Has she told you about… well, I suppose she probably wouldn't discuss past lovers. As you say, you are reluctant to tell her about your past.'

'You're right, Frankie. That's it. We're both being cagey. I'm not ready to reveal all yet and maybe, neither is she. Thanks. Talking about it has been very helpful. Maybe there's a way around this? There must be. If you don't mind, I'll go off and walk by myself while I try to puzzle this one out. I'll try St Jude, too. He deals with hopeless cases, after all.'

'You're far from hopeless, Joe. You're on a journey of discovery. We all are. You're not alone. Surely you and I have more reason than many to share with each other. Be careful of that knee of yours. Remember that you can ask for transport if it gets too painful.'

Might it be a good idea to get Richard to phone Joe? I'll ask Richard when I contact him tonight.

Now to continue the inner journey that Marion

recommended in her letter. That's a stork up there in the church tower. It looks as though she is guarding her nest. They're often associated with bringing babies. I wonder why. My mam used to say that. One certainly didn't bring Dante. It must have been hard for women like my mam. Saying that the storks brought a baby probably prevented women from talking about the pain involved. Men were not allowed to go into the labour room. They would be handed a washed and cleaned baby bundle, so how would they appreciate all that was involved?

Come to think of it, women were encouraged not to aspire too high, anyway. Mam taught me the poem that every Irish girl recited at school.

An Old Woman of the Roads, by Pádraic Colum
O, to have a little house!
To own the hearth and stool and all!
The heaped up sods upon the fire,
The pile of turf against the wall!
To have a clock with weights and chains
And pendulum swinging up and down!
A dresser filled with shining delph,
Speckled and white and blue and brown!
I could be busy all the day
Clearing and sweeping hearth and floor,
And fixing on their shelf again
My white and blue and speckled store!
I could be quiet there at night
Beside the fire and by myself,
Sure of a bed and loath to leave
The ticking clock and the shining delph!
Och! but I'm weary of mist and dark,
And roads where there's never a house nor bush,
And tired I am of bog and road,
And the crying wind and the lonesome hush!
And I am praying to God on high,
And I am praying Him night and day,

There we are. That was all women were led to expect in life. But thank goodness that we are 'out of the winds and rains way', today.

Catherine sidled up to join me as a cafe came into sight. She playfully tugged at my soggy socks drying, tied to my rucksack. But my attention was drawn elsewhere.

Out of the corner of my eye, I saw Sonia hurtling towards us. *There is a man too. Is he smirking? Here she comes.*

'Listen up, everybody. Hi. Can I have your attention, please?'

'Such a shrill voice,' Catherine said. 'I wonder what Sonia wants.'

Before I could answer Catherine, Sonia began, 'Okay. When I was walking along quietly, I heard a beautiful bird song. Fortunately, Tom, my new friend, is an ornithologist. He has volunteered to help anyone who wishes to identify birds. He very kindly let me peer through his binoculars. What was it we saw, Tom? Oh yes, a finch.'

'Thank you very much Sonia and, of course, Tom,' Karam said. 'If Tom doesn't mind, some of you may wish to consult him.'

'Oh, dear, Karan has replied diplomatically, Catherine,' I whispered. 'I hope that Sonia's loud voice doesn't frighten all the birds away.'

'I'm surprised that Sonia was quiet enough to hear a bird sing,' Catherine replied. 'Poor Tom.'

At this stage of the pilgrimage, I noticed that many of us had chosen to walk alone. That suited my intention of following Marion's suggestion of 'connecting to a higher self'.

I can be so critical. Sonia has extrovert qualities that

*register off the scale, but I am an extrovert too. Who am I?
What a philosophical question. How far back do I go? Oh,
what about the poem that I wrote many moons ago:*

> *A Child
> Was I ever a child
> Careless, carefree
> Beginning to be?*
>
> *The facts are there
> The date, the year.
> I was little and small
> But did I play at all?*
>
> *Little fingers and toes
> tiny ears and a nose.
> Utterly needing
> feeding
> teething
> constantly growing
> more and more
> conscious.
> Listening
> hearing
> babbling
> crying.
> But
> Was I ever a child?
> Really a child?*

*Being the youngest of three — two had flown the nest, and
my father had died — so I tended to look out for my mam.
I must have sensed that she was failing. Maybe she was
drinking and smoking her hopeless feelings away? Why
else would I have opted to enter the convent aged sixteen?
I had been deprived of my childhood. I was never a child.*

    The routine, timetabled life in the convent provided

me with the stability and security that I lacked. When she visited me, I was delighted to see that my mam seemed to be content to be free of the responsibility of rearing me while struggling to tend to her own worries.

I was happy for many years until I realised that the Holy Rule stated that we were not permitted to form close friendships. Given what I have learnt since about sexual misconduct in religious orders and other institutions, I suppose the nuns wanted to prevent this happening. But by the time that we were instructed about that, I had already formed a close friendship with a girl who had entered on the same day as me. In fact, we met before we entered and consequently shared a good deal with each other. So strong had our dependence on each other developed, that we devised methods of communicating between ourselves despite the imposed ruling.

But disaster set in after we had made our full commitments to the Order and Margaret was sent to South Africa while I was to remain teaching in England. Breaking this friendship proved painful because the nuns had prevented our letters to each other from being delivered. Of course, not knowing that, I could not understand why Margaret eventually committed suicide. That was bad enough, but the nuns tried to deny that she had taken her own life.

Religious Orders seem to find the reputation of their institutions and that of the Catholic Churches, more important than admitting that their members often fail to live up to the standards expected of them. That was evidenced when Marion suffered sexual abuse by a priest when she was recovering from cancer in one of our houses in Sicily. That issue took over twenty years to be admitted. Of course, the consequences were never really resolved. The hierarchy of the Catholic Church constantly reiterates that it is one united family. However, it appeared to revert to being under a separative jurisdiction when the abusive incident that took place in Sicily was reported.

So scared of men, Marion has never married and instead spends money and effort on making sure that her niece has all she needs. She lives on her own, and the rest of her family expect her to care for them rather than the other way round.

I'm so fortunate. I received a good education that set me up for life in the convent. I wouldn't have received that had I not entered religious life. I need to be positive, count my blessings. Richard is so kind, caring, and full to the brim with love. We both are making every effort to teach Dante by example to live a good life.

'I hope that you won't mind me catching you up, Frankie. You are progressing at a fair speed today.'

'You're more than welcome to join me, Joe. You look a lot happier. Is it the good weather that's cheering you along?'

'That too, Frankie. But it's more that Nuala is her generous and friendly self today. I wanted to ask you, if you think that Richard would mind if I phoned him tonight? Just to chat. Nothing serious, you know.'

'Of course, Joe. He'll be glad to listen to your account of the Camino so far.'

It's great that Joe has taken the initiative to chat to Richard.

20

EVENING NEWS

When Catherine and I examined the room that we were to share that night we were delighted to find that the accommodation was better than had been elsewhere on route. After deciding who was going to sleep near the window, bouncing on the mattresses we rushed to release our aching feet from our boots.

'My feet. How are those legs of yours?'

'I don't know what to think, Frankie. They are still red but the skin's not broken. Maybe the heat and the rubbing is caused by the thickness of the socks. Perhaps if I pull the sock liner up as far as I can tomorrow that might help. Thankfully the socks that I washed and pegged to my rucksack are not only dry, the fresh air has improved their smell.'

Tired out after walking fifteen kilometres I stretched out on my bed while Catherine showered. I was dozing when I heard Catherine moving around as quietly as she could on her bed so that she could stretch her legs up the wall. When I was roused we rejoiced because the shower had two shower curtains, a bigger nozzle and hotter water.

After we had both completed our washing and sorted out what we needed for the next day we chatted while we rested. We discussed the fact that once we became confident we could rely on the arrows and shell signs to point us in the right direction, we felt that we benefitted from the experience of walking alone. That led us to comparing our new found freedom to that of birds flying wherever they like singing lovely songs. When Catherine asked my opinion about Sonia's new friend, Tom, the ornithologist, we agreed that Sonia appeared too enamoured with this friendship but the test would be in he joined us when our group went for our meal that night.

I'd love to talk about Joe to Catherine. She's so accommodating. We've had no problems sharing the various bedrooms that we've found ourselves in. Each evening we consult each other about which bed we'd prefer. She's taken charge of the alarm to arouse us each morning, and I mind the keys to our rooms. However, I am aware that I must respect confidentiality. Besides, I would have to divulge a great deal about myself before I could even hint at what Joe has entrusted me with. Ah well, while Catherine and I often walk side-by-side, our lives travel on different tracks. Sure, that must be the same for most of us.

Another thing I have noticed is that Catherine does not seem to have brought many clothes for evening wear. But she always looks smart. Again, tonight, she's wearing the same blue long-sleeved top that she wore two nights ago, with a darker blue scarf. But tonight she's draped a light blue patterned shawl over her shoulders. So far she has only worn two different pairs of matching earrings and necklace. She certainly has taught me a lesson about not packing my suitcase with non essentials. I suppose that having spent so many years in the convent, I still haven't fully adapted to some things. But maybe this is also a sign of insecurity? However, why shouldn't I make up for lost time and wear as many different styles of clothes in an array of colours?

Our group was seated around an oval shaped table in the restaurant that evening. Catherine and I decided to separate and mingle with others in the group. Joe and Nuala came to sit next to me.

'Hi, Frankie!' hailed Joe. 'Dante sends his love.'

I laughed. 'The cheek of you, Joe. I promised that I would phone Richard later on. Of course I spoke to Dante earlier on before he fell asleep. Did he tell you that he has been to Hastings? He swam again. He loves the sea.'

Just as Joe was about to answer Sonia seated herself on the other side of me.

'Mind if I join you, Frankie?' Sonia asked.

'You're welcome. Are you saving a place for your new friend, Tom?'

'No, Frankie. I don't know why, but he texted me a few minutes ago to say that another friend had already booked them into a different restaurant. I'm so disappointed. I'll try and arrange to see if I can meet up later. '

Ting! Sonia has started tapping her wine glass and calling out in order to attract the attention of the waiter. How rude.

'Waiter! Waiter! My glass. Can you see how stained it is? Let me hold it up to the light. Dirty marks. Not been washed properly. Surely you can't expect me to drink out of that? A clean one. I need a clean wine glass.'

'In the name of the Almighty,' Outstretching his hands, Joe said. 'What's got into her head? Look at the haughty way she's holding that glass up to the light. And the tone of that shrill voice of hers. She's a disgrace.'

'Whisht, will you, Joe. She'll hear you. She's probably disappointed that that ornithologist fellow, Tom, has abandoned her.'

'But she's so loud, Frankie.'

'I know. Let me try and calm her.' I turned to Sonia. 'How are you finding the pilgrimage so far, Sonia?'

'Wonderful. It's such a privilege to have time to meditate and reflect. We are a chosen people. I am fortunate in sharing with lovely Emma. Each morning, I wake her up with my Christian mediation CD. It's our means of soaking up God's overflowing grace. We can hear his voice and receive the joy of His presence in our room. Then, later, when we are relaxing after a tiring day, I share my guided relaxation through instrumental music, scripture, and even nature sounds. We benefit immensely by this God-given wrap around.'

'Oh. What does Emma say about the CD sharing?'

'She seems to carry on sleeping in the morning. I expect that she is mediating. In the evening, she very kindly offers to go the supermarket to buy some bottled water for us both.'

I expect that she pulls her duvet over her head while she screams inwardly in the morning and makes a dash out of the room in the evening. Poor Emma. Sonia appears to be a typical over-enthusiastic, zealous convert.

'Sonia, have you ever thought of asking Emma if she likes being woken up early with your meditation playing? She might prefer you to wear earphones and listen to it on your own.'

'She never complains. We are on a pilgrimage, after all.'

While Sonia chatted to Bahis, I managed to report on the conversation that I had with her to Joe. He found it hard to understand how blinkered Sonia appeared to be. Undeterred, Sonia's voice grew in volume the more wine that she drank. Eventually, Catherine tapped me on the shoulder indicating that she was going back to our accommodation.

'I'm coming too,' I replied. 'Lovely meal tonight. I'll go down to the common room to phone my hubby first, though. I'll be very quiet getting back to bed. I didn't drink much wine, so hopefully if I sleep on my side I won't snore.'

As Catherine and I walked from the restaurant to the hotel, she was aghast when I told her about Sonia's imposition of her piety on Emma first thing each morning.

I was looking forward to Richard telling me how he dealt with Joe's confusion about his relationship with Nuala. So I phoned him. He began by telling me that it was just as well that I had spoken to Dante earlier because he was fast asleep. The sea air must have knocked him out. He had tried to keep his eyes open but he had to carry him into bed. What Richard then said aroused unsettling feelings that I struggled to conceal.

'I have just had a phone call from Angela. She's flying into Heathrow tomorrow morning at ten. She's planned to meet her sister in London. They've booked a Travel Inn apartment near by.'

'Oh. Has she asked you to drive her in to join her sister?'

'I offered to pick her up, Fran. I know that Dante will be delighted to see her, and I thought that maybe I could act as their guide and introduce Dante to the London Eye.'

Why am I feeling awful? Has that sneaky green jealous snake coiled itself around me, again?

I said that I hoped that the weather would be good and that Dante would be very excited on seeing Angela. 'Enjoy yourselves, and give my love to Angela and her sister, Ursula, isn't that her name?'

'Yes, Ursula. Yes, I will of course, Frankie. I was delighted that Joe phoned me, too. We discussed women and their mysterious ways. Such a lot to fathom, especially after a life training to be a priest. No joking aside, Joe was glad to talk man-to-man.'

'He's even more fragile than we were when we met, Richard. But slowly, bit by bit, I am sure that between us we can support him.'

As Richard and I concluded our phone conversation, I realised that silence had descended all round me. When I looked out of the window, it was so dark that I could see myself reflected clearly in the glass.

I'm glad that Richard can't see how distraught I feel on learning that he and Angela will spend tomorrow together. I really need to ponder on what is causing me to be jealous. Am I insecure? Richard loves me. Why do I feel this way? Have I inherited this tendency from my mother? Surely not.

I tossed and turned as I tried to get to sleep. I put my restfulness down to the fact that I had drank too much wine. One drink often results in disturbed sleep. Little did I know that I was talking in my sleep about Joe.

21

ANOTHER DAY

'*W*ell done! You're quicker at assembling for our *Thought for Today*. What's it to be today, Roberta?

'Praying for unity and peace in our world, Karam. '*From the tenth to the sixteenth century, Santiago de Compostela was one of the most popular places of pilgrimage. In fact, it was as well known as the roads to Rome. Nowadays, Compostela enshrines the hope of Europeans for unity and peace transcending nation boundaries.*'

Grateful to Roberta and her invaluable helper, Karam thanked them both on our behalf before we started climbing yet another hill. Damp socks were pegged to many a rucksack.

Catherine and I noticed that Roberta seemed to have less energy and looked flushed. Someone said that the heat was getting to her, and that she only managed to walk a very short distance the previous day. We were concerned that her poor health was showing signs of further deterioration. We were discussing this when Bahis joined us.

'Frankie, I'm curious about your bulging rucksack. Are you carrying more than you need?'

'Maybe, Bahis. All the usual, and a map, and two books, rain gear and—'

'Two books. Why? What are they? Sorry, that's your decision. Only—'

'No. You're right. One book was for when I rest in the afternoon, and the other one is about the route. Packed full of useful information. But honestly, I usually become too tired to use either en route. Besides, I am more conscious of my surroundings now.'

'That book. John Brierley's *Camino de Santiago*. Excellent, but heavy.'

I agreed with him. He offered to carry my rucksack for a while as his was very light. He put his in front and mine on his back. He said that he did the same for his sister when they went on the Hajj pilgrimage to Mecca in Saudi Arabia, the holiest city for Muslims. He explained that Muslims aim at travelling there at least once in their lifetime. 'That applies to all adult Muslims who are physically and financially capable of undertaking the journey, and can support their family during their absence. They are advised to carry essentials only on that journey, so that we are free to fully engage and soak up the new environment. This is in order to learn what we can from the local culture. You know; live in the present moment.'

That's what Marion advised. This young chap who's probably in his thirties is a wise guy. So generous, too. He is carrying my rucksack as well as his own.

Bahis then spoke about the Quran, the Muslim holy book. He explained how it is the central religious text of Islam, that Muslims believe to be a revelation from God. It's a textbook designed to meet all our needs. In one volume is included the basic history of the Prophet Muhammad, the teachings of Islam, the history of the ancient Prophets, the study of the Quran, the Islamic philosophy of the world, and life within Islamic law.

'Like the Christian Bible. You also believe that there is only one God.'

'Yes Frankie, Muslims believe that there is only one God, and there are 99 names of that one God. All these names refer to Allah, the supreme and all-comprehensive God.'

'Yesterday, I saw you kneeling and, I presume, praying. Facing Mecca?'

'Facing Mecca is important because Muhammad was leading the prayer when he received revelations from God instructing him to take the Kaaba as the Qiblah. *Turn then Thy face in the direction of the Sacred Mosque.*'

'How do you know the direction of Mecca?'

'A Qibla compass is a modified compass used by Muslims to indicate the direction to face to perform ritual prayers. The qibla points towards the city of Mecca, and specifically to the Ka'abah.'

'Do you carry a prayer mat too, Bahis?'

'Yes. Let me show you. Here it is. Fortunately, the pouch for my portable pocket prayer mat has a compass with Qibla finder, which makes it easy to find my prayer direction in an unfamiliar place. The mat conveniently folds down into a postcard size zipped carrying case.'

'Compact. It was about midday when I saw you praying. How many times a day do you pray?'

'Five times:

• Salat al-fajr: dawn, before sunrise.
• Salat al-zuhr: midday, after the sun passes its highest.
• Salat al-'asr: the late part of the afternoon.
• Salat al-maghrib: just after sunset.
• Salat al-'isha: between sunset and midnight.'

I explained that when I was a child growing up in Ireland, the Angelus Bells rang out three times a day. Six in the morning, midday and six in the evening. That was to remind us that Jesus was born of Mary, the mother of God. In Religious Orders, there are also fixed times of prayer. Matins and Lauds, Prime, Terce, Sext, None, Vespers, and Compline.

'Our call to prayer is called out by a mu'azzin from the mosque five times a day, traditionally from the minaret, summoning Muslims for prayer (salat). Do the Angelus bells ring out? Are they actual bells?'

I recounted that in most places in Ireland bells no longer peal from church towers. However, on the national television, Radio Telefis Eireann, still show a scene that hopefully leads people to stop and pray, while recorded sounds ring, mimicking the bells.

'Why were they stopped, Frankie?'

'Apparently they caused a lot of discussion and controversy. The devotion was traditionally recited in Roman Catholic churches, convents, and monasteries three times daily. This call to prayer, to spread goodwill to everyone, was also used by some Anglican and Lutheran churches. The angel referred to in the prayer is Gabriel, a messenger of God who revealed to Mary that she would conceive a child to be born the Son of God. There is a hymn too. I'll sing it for you if I can still remember the lyrics:

The bells of the Angelus
Call us to pray
With sweet tones announcing
the sacred Ave.
Ave, Ave, Ave Maria,
Ave, Ave, Ave Maria.
I can't recall the rest of the lyrics.'

'You've got a lovely voice, Frankie. But what caused this custom to transfer to the television version?'

I explained that I heard that RTÉ appointed Roger Childs, a British man with a background at the BBC, as the new head of religious programming. His job was to reconcile the old broadcasting traditions with the new cultural and media landscape. In his opinion, the problem was not the Angelus itself but rather its outdated presentation. When it was shown on the television the bells were accompanied by short clips of Irish people pausing to reflect, interspersed with religious iconography.

Bahis replied that Muslims have the crescent moon and star and that although Islam has no symbol doctrinally associated with it — the symbol of the crescent moon and star are sometimes controversial in the Muslim world — they are now widely used to symbolise Islam.

'I understood that Muslims don't have images of Allah. Am I correct?'

'Muslims believe that Allah can be understood through his attributes. That Allah is beyond our limitations. He cannot be put in any shape, form or image.'

'Getting back to the Angelus being shown on TV. Many people were beginning to recognise that the country was growing in cultural and religious diversity and that while Catholics there perhaps number maybe eighty per cent, Muslim and Hindu populations are on the rise. That was probably why RTÉ attempted to reflect religious and cultural diversity.

'That seems a shame. I'm sure the people of other faiths weren't put out.'

I agreed, pointing out that Ireland remains the only country in Europe that continues to broadcast the Angelus daily. I heard that it was the head of Clonskeagh Mosque who wrote to say that he liked living in a country where the news and weather have to wait, because it shows that Ireland is a country that values prayer and religion. There were no complaints from other faith groups either.

Apropos of changes I began discussing the fact that women used to wear hats or mantillas when they went to church, but nowadays no one does. My old aunt Annie was a milliner. I remember her telling me that the word *milliner* came into English in the mid-15th century, it was sometimes spelled Milaner and meant "a person from Milan, Italy, who sells fancy wares.

Talking of head gear led me to ask Bahis why Muslim women wear a hijab. I said that some sources said that rules concerning women's clothes was a means of men controlling women.

Bahis was not phased by this comment. He suggested that there are many opinions on this subject. That many women who wear a hijab see the veil not as a symbol of control by a man, but rather to promote their own feminist ideals. For many Muslim women, wearing a hijab offers a way for them to take control of their bodies.

Bahis and I were focused on this discussion as our route took us on undulating countryside past fields of wheat, maize, apple orchards and old farms. Shaded from the afternoon sun and feeling very tired we suddenly emerged from a stone strewn road lined with tall boxwood trees to face an exceedingly high hill. We both stopped to rest on a huge stone.

'WOW! That hill's so steep I almost can't see the skyline, Bahis! You've carried my rucksack for miles. I insist on carrying it before we tackle that hill.'

I don't know why I think that I can manage to carry my rucksack now. This seems to be the greatest gradient on the road that we have climbed so far. Would it be one in ten? The sky is just peeping narrowly across the top of massive incline. Thank God Bahis has ignored my suggestion and is continuing to carry my rucksack.

'Look at that girl, Bahis. Her shoes. Any wonder she's struggling. Is she crying? Glorified flip-flops. Well, not much more.'

'There's the other couple that we saw this morning, Frankie. Didn't he say that they are Argentinian? They've got a dog, too.'

'Oh that's lovely, Bahis. What a lovely girl. She's getting down from her horse and… oh, he's lifting the girl with the flip-flops up on the horse. Lovely, caring young people. My eyes are filling up. So kind.'

'Lovely to chat to you, Frankie. I hope that you won't mind, but I need to take some time on my own for a while. See you further along the road. Not far to go now.'

That was a very informative conversation with Bahis. This pilgrimage has provided us with time to learn from one another. Now I should reflect on why I felt disturbed last evening when Richard told me that he and Dante would be spending the day with Angela and her sister today.

Why do I feel jealous? I can understand my mother succumbing to a period of depression. After all, judging from what she told me, she was squashed in the middle of thirteen siblings. There must likely have been rivalry, deprivation and possibly neglect experienced within the family. The older children being forced to take responsibly in rearing those younger than themselves. Those at the top and the bottom of the family received better education and more attention. Probably the money ran out to pay for the education of those in the middle. When I arrived home after leaving the convent, I recall Mam encouraging me with, 'Would you ever cop yourself on and stop acting like an ejeet? Haven't you received a good education? Not like me, who barely scraped through school.'

She was right. So what happened? Can I blame my time in the convent?

Oh, why don't I sit under that lovely grandfather oak tree just coming into sight along this wide path? Oak trees are said to be a storehouse of wisdom and strength. I can see its acorns sheltered by rich, ochre leaves. Autumn is such an abundant, fruitful season. On one side, the tree has spread its huge, gnarled roots, clinging on to a hillock overlooking meadowland. If I sit with my back to the tree, I may not be disturbed by anyone walking along the path, while I try to puzzle why something sometimes appears to diminish my sense of security. Surely that's what is at the root of jealousy?

During the sixteen years that I spent in the convent, we were all encouraged to strive every day to become humble. To distrust ourselves. We learnt that every sin we commit is the result of our pride and self-reliance. If we completely distrusted ourselves and relied only upon God, we would never sin. We were to acknowledge our nothingness. We meditated on the grandeur and greatness of God, while simultaneously acknowledging our own nothingness in relation to Him. We were to think better of others than of ourselves.

We often joked about the impossibility of achieving the recommended forty degrees of humility. But even if we did, there was a danger inherent in that too, because a person could become proud of reaching that state. However, we were encouraged to keep striving to attain this goal. Failure to do so was not taken lightly. For example, when, as a young aspirant, I was called in to the sewing room to try on a second-hand school blazer, so that I would be able to join the day girls at the beginning of the school year, I happened to smile at the image of myself that I could see reflected in the glass window of the cupboard. When Sister Superior entered the room, she noticed me admiring myself, and immediately reminded me that the reason that we did not have mirrors in the convent was precisely to prevent us from self-admiration.

Much later, when, as a qualified as a teacher, I handed the brown, unopened envelope containing my salary to Sr

Superior, I was reminded not to consider myself any more important than other Sisters who were engaged in house work.

There were many other instances such as these, purposefully aimed at lessening my self esteem. No wonder then, when I left the convent, I felt like an egg without a shell. I recall that I found it difficult to actually see. My eyes were strained, and people used to remark on me being wide-eyed and always seeming to be on the alert. I was compelled to show off and be proud of my achievements when I had to compose my Curriculum Vitae. Far from hiding my talents, I was made aware that if I didn't list my skills, education, and work experience, I would not be considered for employment.

Dear God, I have managed to revert back to my former, confident self. Thank you for granting me precious time under your mighty oak tree to rejoice in the gifts and talents that you have helped me develop. The entangled roots of this tree must occupy a great deal of underground space, and they surely absorb all the water and minerals, and send them circulating through the rest of the tree. The branches stretch out and the light seeps in. So, too, I have examined my intertwined growth and drawn on my inner strengths as I become aware of the light helping me to see my way forward in life. I am happily married with a delightful son. I do not need to be jealous of anyone. I no longer believe in self-effacement.

Oh, I thought I heard drumming. That must be a woodpecker flying off. Black and white feathers and a lovely red patch on its breast. Was he trying to drum good sense into my head? Well, I think he succeeded.

When I emerged back onto the path, I saw Joe walking a little further on in front of me. He was alone. I called out to him, but he didn't turn round. So I resorted to banging my two walking poles together and shouting out his name.

I succeeded. He stopped to let me catch up with him.

'All alone, Joe? Maybe you wanted some time to yourself. I shouldn't have intruded.'

'No, Frankie. I needed to...'

'Is it your leg?' I asked. 'Is it paining you?'

''Tis a bit, but Nuala—'

'Where is she? Is she on in front? Joe, have you been...'

Crying? But it might be better not to ask.

'Frankie, I'm glad it's you that caught up on me. I don't know what has happened. It's hard to explain. I'm not sure.'

Should I intrude? He's a grown man. But then, given his seclusion from ordinary life, he's probably never had to fathom out some things before.

We walked on in silence for a while. Then Joe asked me if I would mind if we slipped off the main path into a side lane. A few steps along the path we saw what looked like a small picnic area. Joe looked from a conveniently positioned tree stump, to me, and back to another stump.

'Good. Will we rest here, Joe? That leg of yours needs refuelling.'

'Yes. That's grand.'

I watched Joe collapse down onto a tree stump, bend his head onto his knees and wrap his hands round his head. After a while, he raised his head.

'Frankie. Frankie, I am making a mess of this friendship with Nuala. I don't seem to catch onto how I should react. Self-control, purity, familiarity and oh... I could preach a sermon on them and deal out any amount of advice...'

'Joe. I hate to see you torture yourself like this. There's nothing wrong with you. It's just that you... we have lived other kinds of lives. I've said too much. Who am I... I have no intention of delving into...'

'But I need you to, Frankie...'

'Joe, Richard and I will always be there for you. We

might not have solutions, but we promise to try and support each other. Now, I realise that there might be some things that you may wish to discuss man-to-man with Richard.'

'Okay. Thank you, Fran. It's already a great relief just to say that Nuala and I have fallen out... well, not really. You see, Nuala arranged that we both stop at a Wellness Centre today. A sort of spa. Nothing posh. She thought it would be good for me. We went into this small bungalow building with a couple of rooms. It was a help-yourself set up. No attendants. All you had to do was to insert payment into a slot for the amount of time that you wished to spend in a steam room and a sauna. Nuala and I had carried our swimwear with us.'

'I can see what's coming, Joe. Was it a mixed spa?'

'Exactly. We had separate lockers in the same changing room. But we were provided with disposable underwear and a separate locker. With the help of a large towel, we both undressed modestly. But it was when we entered the steam room that we realised that there was another couple in there,'

'In the nude?'

'At first, because of the steam, I didn't realise. But... and... touching... although I was embarrassed, I realised that this might happen. It is Nuala's reaction that I can't understand.'

'Oh. Surely she knew what was involved. Did she do the booking, Joe?'

'Yes. Exactly. It was she who suggested this special healing experience. To tell you the truth, I was excited. Intimacy at last. I was curious too, of course.'

'So... what happened... I don't want to pry, though.'

'Frankie, it was Nuala who left me in the room with the couple and didn't return. At first I thought that perhaps she had gone to the toilet. But when she didn't come back after about ten minutes, I went out to find her, only to discover that she had left the building. Her locker was empty. I dressed and went out, and walked along the road in search of her.'

'Gosh, Joe. That's strange. Did you catch up with her?'

'No, but she texted me. All she said was that she hoped that I would understand that something had compelled her to leave that place immediately. She would talk when we met up.'

'Honestly, Joe, I don't know what to make of that. All I can think of is that it might have been for feminine needs. What we women call 'the time of the month'. Our periods. That can be embarrassing if it happens when we are not prepared.'

'Oh. Maybe that's it. She thought that I would not necessarily be aware of that happening. That's grand, Frankie. I needn't worry. See, you have been a great help. Thank you.'

Strange why Nuala didn't give some sort of explanation to Joe. I would have whispered some kind of excuse. At least she should have said that she was leaving him alone while she continued her journey. Something is not right. I'll talk to Richard later.

Joe and I continued our journey until we reached that night's accommodation. As we approached the hotel, we saw that most of the group were sitting at the bar outside in the street. Nuala jumped up with her arms outstretched and shouted out, 'There's a space here, Joe. Sit there and I'll get you a cold beer. And you too, Frankie.'

Later, when I phoned Richard to recount what happened between Joe and Nuala we both remained puzzled. While Richard accepted that it might have been the explanation that I offered Joe, neither of us understood why Nuala had not informed Joe that she was leaving him behind while she continued the journey. After a long discussion, we concluded that perhaps the situation in the spa might have triggered off a past trauma in Nuala. Richard said that this sort of thing can cause a person to feel overwhelming sadness, anxiety, or panic. Potent flashbacks or a negative memory may appear without warning.

'Well, whatever it was Frankie, it looks as though we need to support both Joe and Nuala. I might phone Joe in the morning. But we haven't enough time for you to tell me about the rest of your day. I hope that you are keeping up to date with your diary. We'll have a lot to discuss when you get home. I'm counting the hours now. Love you, darling.'

22

YOU'VE COME HOME!

I held back when the group started off walking next morning. I wanted to be near enough to Joe and Nuala so that I could see how they were getting on with each other.

'How's the leg, Joe?'

'Okay. It takes a while to get going, It's like that most mornings. I'm hoping that it will last out for the rest of the pilgrimage.'

Nuala then began to demonstrate how she helped Joe when they approached a hill and he started lagging behind.

'When you're ready, Joe, straighten your back. Place your poles in front, at a distance that suits your pace. Then, I will push into the centre of your back and propel you ahead. Is that alright?'

I watched Nuala go through the same process that I had witnessed before. Nuala pushed Joe forward first by using the full force of her strength into the small of Joe's waist, and then followed that up with lifting his bottom up, and propelling him forward.

I wonder what sensation that gives to Joe? They're laughing. They are obviously enjoying touch and intimacy. It seems that there is no need to be over concerned with what happened between them yesterday.

At the bottom of the hill we reached a magnificent church sitting on the bend of a vibrant flowing river. When we approached, we discovered that the whole complex included a Benedictine Monastery. We marvelled at the overwhelming sight of the architecture. A simple and pleasing style. Not too dramatic. We wondered if it might be a classical Greek or Roman type. There was a little bridge over a gentling flowing stream, too.

As I watched Joe's eyes flicker I wondered if he was thinking of the Carmelite monastery where he has spent a number of years training for the priesthood. Was he reevaluating the time he spent there? He caught me looking at him. He started reciting the Irish Blessing. Nuala and I joined in:

> *May the road rise to meet you*
> *May the wind be at your back*
> *May the sun shine warm upon your face*
> *May the rain fall softly on your fields*
> *And until we meet again*
> *May you keep safe*
> *In the gentle loving arms of God*

Another group of pilgrims must have heard us. A lady stepped forward and offered to take a photo of the three of us. We happily handed over our mobile phones in acceptance.

Watching Nuala and Joe walk round the abbey church and the monastery grounds together I wonder if Joe reveals anything about his former life to Nuala?

I felt overwhelmed by the medieval atmosphere in this ancient church. When I discovered that the monks in the adjoining abbey followed the Rule of St Benedict, I was pleased, because this way of life was the basis of the regulations of the religious order that I had belonged to. I was even more delighted when I read a notice stating that in the ninth century, the remains of the Apostle St James were discovered here. The pilgrims who came to visit the tomb of Santiago were welcomed by the monks, who offered them this special Benedictine hospitality. I was lost in mediation, seated near the front of the church, when Joe tapped me on my shoulder.

'Sorry to disturb you, Frankie, but Nuala and I have decided to continue walking. Do you mind if we leave you here, or do you want to join us?'

'No, no. You two head off. I'll probably catch you up later on.'

Just after they had left, I was astonished by voices of a choir of monks singing Gregorian chant. I looked around the church, searching to see where the music was coming from, but I couldn't find the source of this mystic, monophonic sacred plainchant.

How wonderful. Maybe it has been set to come on automatically at this time every day?

As I listened, I recognised the chant as the Deum Verum. It was sung in Latin, Spanish, and finally in English.

Mesmerised, I felt rooted to my seat as I listened:

We praise thee, O God : we acknowledge thee to be the Lord.
All the earth doth worship thee : the Father everlasting.
To thee all Angels cry aloud : the Heavens, and all the Powers therein.
To thee Cherubim and Seraphim : continually do cry,
Holy, Holy, Holy : Lord God of Sabbath;
Heaven and earth are full of the Majesty : of thy glory.
The glorious company of the Apostles : praise thee.
The goodly fellowship of the Prophets : praise thee.

After this extraordinary experience I went outside to telephone Richard. I sent him a photo using WhatsApp and related what had happened. I also updated him on how Nuala and Joe were acting today as though nothing worrying had occurred between them the previous day.

'Dante is longing to speak to you, darling.'

'I love you, Mummy. Please come home. I want a cuddle now. Please.'

It took a long time before Richard and I managed to console Dante. Cuddles, kisses and promises were exchanged, and eventually I finished by repeatedly saying 'Love you' several times.

I did not catch up with Nuala and Joe. Instead I stopped a few times to jot down some recollections in my diary. Alone, I was glad to savour the events of the day as I walked to our next accommodation. On arrival, I assumed that they had all retired to their rooms.

'You've come home, Frankie!' said Catherine. 'Those arrows and shell signs take us safely to our next accommodation.'

'Ah, what a lovely welcome, Catherine. That's a lovely thing to say. Our rooms seem to be getting better, too.'

After we had decided who preferred the bed nearest to the window that night, Catherine began to tell me about the unusual graves that they had stopped to see. They were fortunate that Emma was with them because she was able to translate the information given. They learnt that each municipality has a cemetery. Spanish cemeteries have a system where a coffin is inserted in a recess, or niche, rather than buried in the ground. The burial service takes place very quickly. What they found strange is that a niche can be rented for a pre-determined number of years. The remains are interred in there, but once the period expires the body is moved to a common burial ground. The stone recesses were different. Each with their own decorations pictures of Saints and flowers, prayers and photographs.

When I enquired whether they had cremations there too, Catherine said that a Spanish man who happened to be there told them that when the Catholic Church permitted cremations, most people opted for that.

Catherine then went on to tell me that Peter was taking photos of grain storing structures called *hórreos*, that are a very common construction across rural Galicia. He explained that these interesting rectangular structures are close to most homes in rural areas. They are what we call granaries. They are used to store grain and other food crops for the winter, keeping them dry and safe from animals, hence their slatted panels.

'Peter is keen about these, Frankie. He showed me some photos of them yesterday. He explained that these hórreos seem to be made of different materials. They can be of wood, carved granite stone, thatched, tiled, or slate roofs. He said that it depends on the area. Some hórreos also include roof decorations, from simple pointy carved stone, to crosses or more elaborate figures. Peter is very good at explaining. He took some good photos and appeared to be really enthusiastic.'

When Catherine told me that it was rumoured that romance between Joe and Nuala seemed to be in the air, I quickly changed topics and immediately began to describe the wonderful Benedictine Monastery and church.

I'm restricted in what I can tell Catherine. If I confide in her in what I am learning about them, I would betray Joe's trust in me. Maybe it is better just to listen to what others observe?

Catherine must have realised that I did not wish to discuss the rumours. We both lay on our beds reading for a while. I eventually asked Catherine for her opinion on the DVD, *The Way*, that we had watched at one of our preparatory gatherings, pointing out that we all have a different purpose for walking the Camino.

'I loved the character that James Nesbit played in it,' Catherine said. 'A writer eager to use every incident for his novel. It's hilariously funny, isn't it?'

I pointed out that the film also has a serious side relating the story of an American father who travels to France to retrieve the body of his estranged son, who died while attempting the pilgrimage to Santiago de Compostela. Martin Sheen portrays a sceptic who resolves to take part in a pilgrimage, in an effort to understand both himself and his son. We recalled that the reason why the woman character took part, was so that she would give up smoking and that there was a chap who just wanted to lose weight so that he could fit into the suit that he longed to wear for his daughter's wedding.

'Frankie, I might be wrong, but I don't suppose that each of us is really aware of what propelled us into taking part in a pilgrimage such as this. Obviously it is to raise funds for our cancer patients but—'

'Correct, Catherine. The more I progress on this pilgrimage the more convinced that… wait, I wrote it down. Yes, here it is inside my diary. 'It's your road and yours alone. Others may walk it with you, but no one can walk it for you."

We both noticed that we are increasing the amount of time that we are spending on our own. Catherine said that she saw me sitting under that sturdy oak tree on the edge of a lovely pasture.

'Gosh, yes, Catherine. I must have been oblivious to those passing by on the path. I am beginning to treasure these times when I can relax and reflect.'

'Me too. I am no longer fearful of walking alone. Any pilgrim that I have met seems to be on a mission of their own. Come on. Let's don our glad rags and join the others for dinner.'

'Great. I'm nearly ready. But would you mind it if I join you after I have phoned home? I phoned earlier and my son was upset, so I want to speak to him again before he goes to bed.'

'Hola! I'm going all Spanish, Richard.'

'Mummy! I love you! We went swimming. Daddy caught me. He threw me up. I landed in his arms. Whooo! Splash!'

'You had a good time.'

'We ate ice cream. We're having chips now.'

'He's being a very good boy, Mummy,' Richard said. 'Haven't you, Dante?'

'Yes. Can I play with Paddington?'

'He's off. So how are things, darling?'

I told him that I was able now to spend some quality time reflecting but I also had come to realise that often I seem to spontaneously react to things. 'I don't know, Richard. It's hard to explain. But as I am on a pilgrimage I have time to reflect on these things.'

'Deep, soul searching, Frankie. Sounds like serious stuff.'

'True. As long as you are happy, darling, that is what matters. But I am curious. That's if ever you want to share… I just want to tell you that I love you as you are. How about the actual putting one foot in front of the other? I bet that you are a wiz at that now.'

'I love you even more if that is possible, Richard, for… everything and I miss you so much. And I no longer walk like a chicken. I can use my walking poles much better now.'

I added that Catherine told me that quite a few of the group have noticed that love is in the air between Joe and Nuala.

'How was your day, Richard? Did Angela's plane land on time?'

'It was a strange day, Frankie. When I collected Angela, Dante was so excited. It was lovely meeting again. But she asked to be dropped off at Wimbledon Station so that she could travel by tube into Waterloo, where she had arranged to meet her sister. They had planned to enjoy a girlie day together. I was glad that Dante didn't mention my promise to him to go on the London Eye.

It was a lovely warm day. An Indian summer, so I drove down to West Wittering. Remember, there's plenty of sand there. I only wished that you were with us, Frankie. We both missed you a lot. We're counting the days until you come back to us.'

After that conversation, I hopped, skipped, and even did a little jump. As I joined the group for their evening meal, I continued to revel in Richard's expression of his love for me.

After the evening meal, as I walked along the corridor back to my bedroom, I noticed Nuala and Joe kissing each other good night before they separated and made their way upstairs.

Catherine was still awake when she quietly crept into our bedroom.

'No use, Frankie, I can't get to sleep. I'm wondering if it's the coffee that I drank after our meal tonight? I should have remembered that when I drink coffee in the evening, I find it difficult to get to sleep.'

I offered to let her borrow my radio and a spare pair of earplugs. 'Listen away, and you'll drop off.'

Catherine accepted. 'Everyone else must be fast asleep by now. But tell me first about your little son. How is he? I was very happy when my daughter-in-law told me that she feels her little one is kicking. Only a few days to go. I thought that I would be home before the birth, but the hospital informed her that she miscalculated the date. It's great being able to keep in contact so easily by mobile phone now, isn't it?'

'Maybe they're wrong, Catherine and you'll be home in time. I was so happy when I listened to my little darling. Both darlings. Son and husband.'

I refrained from telling Catherine that I had seen Nuala and Joe in a warm embrace again. I continued to hope that they would be happy in their love for each other. The next thing I knew was that I was being shaken. Startled I sprang up into a seated position. I rubbed my eyes and stared into Catherine's bewildered looking face.

'Frankie….sorry. You're talking ….a nightmare?'

Catherine wrapped me in her arms. I was shivering and rubbing my eyes. What had happened? Now I was propped up with pillows and tucked in with a warm blanket. Catherine handed her a cup of tea and was seated on a chair beside me telling me that this was maybe the result of being exposed to too much sunshine.

What is the result of sunshine? What has happened? What did I do to disturb Catherine? I must have been talking in my sleep. What if?

When Catherine began to reassure me that she respected my privacy and that what I had spoken about was safe with her I worried even more. I realised that I would have to ask Catherine to tell me what had happened and of course what I had said in my sleep. At first Catherine said that she could not really remember but eventually she admitted that she was not surprised that I was worried about Joe and his relationship with Nuala.

Dear God what am I to say? I am not at liberty to declare Joe's celibate journey in training for the priesthood to learning how to form a loving relationship.

Catherine noticing utter bewilderment on my face immediately tried to reassure me that what she had heard would be safe with her. She promised not to divulge any-thing adding that the fact that we shared the same sleeping accommodation meant each of us had to respect each other's confidentiality.

Okay. Confidentiality. Whatever I spoke about in my sleep concerned Joe. In order to draw attention away from him maybe it might be best if I disclose something about myself. I'll have to wait for an appropriate moment. Perhaps there will be one tomorrow.

23

A DIFFICULT STAGE

Our group assembled around Karam as he stood on the second to last step on the stairs leading down to the entrance of the hotel. He wanted to address us before we were ready to begin another day walking the Camino.

'The thought that I offer you on your pilgrimage today, is to remember those who struggle to cope with physical and mental illness. I'm sure we all know someone.'

'Thank you, Karam,' Joy interrupted, 'No Roberta?'

'No. I'll explain. Two things. Most of you will have heard that Joseph here is wisely going to take things a little easier. His left leg is failing him.'

'Sorry guys,' Joe jumped up on the step to say: 'It's just that I don't seem to be able to keep up. I'm not sure what is wrong. I thought that the physio that I had been having would do the trick, but...'

'The good thing is that Nuala has volunteered to keep Joe company,' Karam said. 'We have allocated transport for this purpose. You've also noticed that Roberta and Joan were not at breakfast. Unfortunately, Roberta's condition has deteriorated. We're looking after her. As your leader, I feel it's right that I stay with her today. Mark and Peter, our faithful father and son duo therapists and stalwart walk leaders, will be our guides today. Mark will start you off, and Peter will be a back-stopper. You have each other's contact numbers. It's a beautiful late autumn day, not too hot, not too cold. Not too many people on the Camino this time of year, either. After watching the video last night, you know that the Galician landscape takes on a Celtic feel. Enjoy the lovely verdant countryside. You'll see ancient grey granite stone buildings. You'll come across a picturesque little church en route, too. Most of the day's walk is a long, gradual uphill climb. However, you will be able to warm up on the paved flat terrain of the lush valley. The gentle ascents on the paths are bordered by moss-covered stone walls and shaded by chestnut trees. Tonight, if you are not too tired, we can chat about our progress so far, and perhaps also other things to look out for on our pilgrimage.'

'I see you are keen to be at the front today, Frankie?'

'Oh yes, Mark. I was thinking about what Karam said about Joe. But yes, my walking poles are at the ready. I'm determined to increase my pace. See!'

'Very good.'

Catherine was just poking her platypus tube through from her rucksack pulling it near to her mouth.

The group were sorry to learn that Roberta's health was declining. Somehow, although we hoped she would cope we were aware of her poor health. Catherine and I discussed the fact that Roberta might have been helped by sticking to the Sikh diet that Karam followed. While we were offered a good deal of vegetables, the Galician diet seemed to consists of dairy and meat products from cattle, sheep and pigs. Sikhs adhere to a diet that excludes meat and fish. Neither do they eat eggs. They consume food that does not harm another living being. Galicia brings in more fish, shellfish and crustaceans than any other region in Spain and the Galicians regard it as their staple diet.

'I read somewhere, Frankie, that Galician agriculture products such as potatoes, maize, and wheat are also in their diet.'

'I'm sure that you're right there, Catherine. However, I've noticed that very few of the cafes that we snack in provide these and very often the hotels don't serve lacto-vegetarian food. Even their delicious soups often contain chorizos, beef, gammon and other meats. I'm so forgetful. I remember that when we invited Karam to a meal in our home he explained that Sikh family meals usually include sabzi, vegetable, and or Daal, rice and pulse.'

'He's so caring. Big responsibility too, making sure that the rest of us are okay. Thank goodness he's sharing with Joe.'

'I'm sure Joe will be glad of the company, Frankie. He and Nuala seem to already have developed a close friendship. I'd like to think that we have too?'

Maybe this is an opportunity to find out what I have revealed when I talk in my sleep?

'That's very kind of you. Friendships are so important, Catherine. I learnt that a few years ago when a close friend of mine died. Margaret. God rest her soul. I miss her. I always will.'

'I'm sorry. Some friends become so close that we consider them to be members of our family.'

If I tell Catherine about my friendship with Margaret, I'll have to explain too much about my past life. I don't know if I'm ready for that yet?

'I was talking to Joy last night. We sat next to each other at dinner. She's a counsellor. She is becoming a little concerned about the relationship between Joe and Nuala. I noticed that she sighed this morning when Karam announced that they were going to be excluded together.'

'I was wondering, Frankie, but I didn't know if I was being perhaps a bit prudish? With my Baptist background I sometimes feel that maybe I am excessively concerned with sexual propriety.'

'It's exactly that, Catherine, that Joy was talking about. I mean she wonders if Nuala is the driving force in their relationship. Well I suppose someone is bound to take the initiative.'

'Yes. Joe appears to be somehow naive. I don't know. There is something unworldly about him. Little boy lost.'

If only she knew. Should I really be revealing Joe's background? Don't think so. I need to divert Catherine's attention. Good. I spy a church.

'Look, Catherine, there's a lovely little church coming into view. I wonder if it's the one that Karam mentioned? It looks like a priest's opening up.'

'Are you thinking what I'm thinking, Frankie? A chance to get a sello.'

'We'll have to be quick. If it is a priest, he may be intending to spend some time in prayer. We don't want to disturb him.'

The heavy door creaked. The priest was walking quickly up the aisle towards another other door. I tried to catch up with him.

'Leave it to me. My Spanish is limited so I'll try speaking Italian,' I said. 'Padre. Padre. Sello, per favore. Scusi.'

While I was calling out to the priest our group were entering the church witnessing me running up the aisle and between the pews, waving my pilgrimage passport, determined to get my stamp. Just as the priest was about to disappear through the door, I tapped him on his shoulder. To my surprise, his smiling face turned round to greet me.

'¡Peregrinos! ¿De donde son?'

Equally surprised, I replied, 'Si, pilgrims from Ingli-terra… e Irlanda.'

'Ah. You want stamps? Come. Mi nombre es Padre Francis.'

'Oh. Same. La stessa, Francesca.'

'La misma' means the same in Spanish. You speak Italian,' Fr Francis questioned. Then he reached in behind a statue of an angel in an alcove to retrieve a wooden stamper. After that, he opened wide his arms, and beckoned to the others in the group to come nearer. When I held up my passport to show everyone that it was stamped with a picture of an angel, everyone clapped. The priest continued to smile as he stamped each person's passport. Then he waved the group goodbye. Sonia, with her blonde curly hair and baby blue eyes, angelic Sonia, began to clap her hands and sing the hymn *Rejoice in the Lord always and again I say rejoice*, as the group made their way out of the church.

'Well done, Frankie.'

'Thank you, Catherine.'

The church was small enough to be called a chapel. Romanesque. Ancient stone. The altar was stone too. There was a bell tower and a stone arch structure over the front of the church.

'If the stones could talk, imagine what they could tell us, Catherine. Perhaps some poor pilgrims arrived here at nightfall and slept the night. While those on horseback were accommodated in a local hostelry.'

As Catherine and I left the church we noticed that most of our group were already seated in a cafe further up the hill.

'Hola! Buen Camino. Torta Santiago and caffe con leche per favore. Oh, I forgot. Por favor, again sello, Catherine.'

'Me too, Frankie My pilgrim passport has been stamped

sixteen times now. The stamp before the one we got just now in the chapel was in the Hostal Restaurante San Paio. Look, it has an armoured knight on horseback.'

'I'm jealous,' Catherine said. 'Mine was a green arrow. They must have run out of ink because I can't see the writing on it.'

Mark read out another joke sent from Ann, a volunteer back in Oasis as we were about to queue for the toilets.

'That was a quick decision, Frankie. Were you avoiding listening to the joke, by any chance?'

'Yes, Catherine. I… well…'

'Me too. They're a bit too crude for my ears.'

Ann probably means well, but I would prefer not to hear that kind of joke. Certainly too offensive for a person with my background.

By this point on our journey nearly all of us had blisters. We waited for each other while we untied the double knots on our boots took off our smelly socks and put on a Compeed. The redness of Catherine's ankles appeared to be worse today. She still did not know what caused that.

That night, when we went out for our evening meal, there was a Galician family of twelve seated round a nearby table in the restaurant. As soon as our group entered the restaurant, Joe and Nuala went over to speak to two lads who appeared to be about the same age as them. From the way they greeted each other, it seemed that they had met earlier. When Joe and Nuala returned to the group's table, Mark seated next to Joe asked him if they were a local family. Joe told him that when Nuala and he were coming out of the Supermarket the two guys were keen to speak in English to them. 'That's when we discovered that they would be dining here tonight. Lovely family. They're celebrating a birthday. Apparently it's the lady seated at the top of the table.'

Our Camino group ate, chatted, and exchanged information as usual throughout the meal. As expected, a member of staff carried in the lighted birthday cake, and the party group sang the Galician style Feliz Aniversario, Happy Birthday. That seemed to be the cue for Joe and Nuala to join two of the men and ladies from the party group. Joe pulled out a mouth organ from his pocket, and Nuala was handed what looked like an Irish musical instrument, a bodhran, much like a small drum or tambourine. Joe shouted out, 'Let the hooley begin.'

'Come on, guys. Get to your feet,' I stood and waved my hands. 'The festivities have begun.'

'What do we do, Frankie?' Catherine asked.

'I don't know about ye, but I can't keep still listening to that jig music. The Galicians must have reels and jigs, just as they do all over the Celtic world.'

Soon the staff removed the dishes and pushed back tables, providing space for people to dance. Guitars, a violin, castanets, and other percussion musical instruments guided the dancers. Then, to the surprise of our group, Joe and Nuala accompanied a beautiful lady soloist singer and a guitarist. Joe playing his mouth organ, and Nuala performing small dance movements while rhythmically clicking scalloped shaped castanets. Nuala's orange bolero and skirt accentuated her sunset red hair, and her naturally upturned nose gave her the haughty appearance that sometimes is adopted by flamenco dancers. Next to Joe, she looked petite. They contrasted beautifully. He being much thinner, with blonde hair, bewitching blue eyes, and dressed in black.

A tremendous applause erupted as this performance concluded. When Joe and Nuala eventually returned to our group, they were congratulated and questioned.

I asked Joe how he knew those tunes. He and Nuala told us that they had spent most of the afternoon learning and practising with the Galician musicians.

When I phoned Richard before going to bed that night, he was amused by my success in obtaining Camino pilgrimage stamps for the entire group in the church. He was very happy to learn about Joe and Nuala's musical performance.

When I laid my head on my pillow, I prayed:

Dear God, Our Heavenly Father, thank you for looking after Joe and Nuala.

They looked so content to be together tonight. Sharing music with a person surely is a form of intimacy. I wonder if they have disclosed more about their backgrounds to each other.

'If music be the food of love...' Was it a Duke in Shakespeare's Twelfth Night who uttered this?

24

HOW FAR, SO FAR?

*A*fter the day's walking, our evening meal, and watching a video, the Camino group gathered in a hall in our hotel accommodation to listen to Karam's announcement.

'First of all, what another lovely meal we enjoyed tonight. Galician food can be so good, they even catered for my diet. But what about the night before? We won't forget that, will we? Thanks largely, if not entirely, to Joe and Nuala.'

Karam led the clapping and everyone joined in. Joe and Nuala bowed their heads in acknowledgement.

Karam continued. 'Congratulations, too, on completing the fifth day of our pilgrimage. I'm sure like me that, while you are very tired, walking has become more natural. Not easier. I doubt if anyone is blister-free.

'Now, an update on Roberta's condition. As you know, she is in hospital in Santiago. I won't go into detail. Suffice it to say that we have been speaking to her brother back in England. Emma accompanied me to the hospital last night. With her knowledge of the Spanish language, she was able to translate exactly what Roberta was saying. Of course, the doctors and nurses also speak English, but we felt that it important that Roberta should be able to voice her opinion on every detail of her treatment. She must maintain control of all that is happening to her. Spanish hospitals seem to be excellent. I can assure you that she is being very well cared for.'

'Thank you very much, Karam!'

'Thank you, and each one of you. I appreciate the tenacity, generosity and sheer determination that each of you has shown. I hope that the video we watched tonight reminded you of just how far you have trekked over different terrains during the last five days. Up hills and down valleys from O Cebreiro to Triacastela. Sarria, Portomarín, Sierra Ligonde to Palas del Rey. reaching Arzúa! Today, you'll reach the edge of Santiago. WOW!'

The group clapped Karam at the end of the announcement, and then we broke into smaller groups.

'That video was a lovely reminder of all the wonderfully interesting places we have travelled through, wasn't it Frankie?' Joy remarked.

'Indeed it was,' I replied. 'Passing those concrete milestones with the number of kilometres to Santiago decreasing, was great encouragement.'

'The milestones are so different, aren't they?'

'Some are really worn. I loved it when someone had planted a worn-out boot on top. I just hoped that they had a spare pair.'

'Joe and Nuala are missing this part of the pilgrimage,' Joy continued. 'I hope that Joe's leg is not too painful. But he is certainly a skilled mouth-organ player.'

'He is a music teacher and Nuala is musical too. They seem to have formed a close friendship, haven't they?'

'I wish I could use my counselling skills, Frankie. I don't want to jump to conclusions without evidence, but on the surface it would seem that maybe their closeness could benefit with scrutiny. I'm sorry, but I don't seem to be able to switch off my counselling skills.'

'Really, Joy? Their friendship makes me recall the delight and pleasure of falling in love with my husband. Somehow though, I must admit that most of the time we preferred to share our intimate demonstrations of our love when we were alone.'

'Precisely.'

'But times have changed and people differ, don't they, Joy?'

What has Joy tapped into? She possibly just sees Joe's vulnerability. She won't know that, like Richard and me, he will have been deprived of romance while he was training for the priesthood. He might well feel intoxicated now by the abundance of tactile love satisfying his hungry body. After all, Nuala looked lovely again tonight in her long-flowing, green polka dot, low-necked dress. Those auburn curls framed her beautifully tanned face.

'Hello!' Catherine said. 'You're miles away, Frankie.'

'It's been a long day, hasn't it?' I said. 'Have you phoned home?'

'Yes. No baby born yet. I'll shower and get ready for bed while you phone your hubby, shall I?'

'Thank you, Catherine. I won't be long.'

Richard was interested in what counsellor Joy had to say about Joe. He told me that when Joe contacted him, they had discussed that maybe it would be good to reveal something about his previous seminary training to Nuala. That was in the hope that it might prompt Nuala to disclose more about her own background.

Before we started walking the next morning, Karam introduced David, the Scottish, older member of the group, to address us. 'Today, I have asked David to provide you with something to ponder on as you walk.'

'Thank you, Karam,' David said, 'I suppose that some of you will recognise the following invitation taken from psalm 150.

> *Praise the Lord.*
> *Praise God in his sanctuary;*
> *praise him in his mighty heavens.*
> *Praise him for his acts of power;*
> *praise him for his surpassing greatness.*
> *Praise him with the sounding of the trumpet,*
> *praise him with the harp and lyre,*
> *praise him with timbrel and dancing,*
> *praise him with the strings and pipe,*
> *praise him with the clash of cymbals,*
> *praise him with resounding cymbals.*
> *Let everything that has breath praise the Lord.*
> *Praise the Lord.*

Shakespeare in Twelfth Night appears to agree with these sentiments. 'If music be the food of love, play on; Give me excess of it...'

That's the exact quote I remembered last night. Must be appropriate, then.

'Enjoy your day.'

'Military precision attained, Frankie,' Catherine said. 'Up, weather checked, dressed accordingly, breakfasted, platypus filled, luggage down by the front door to be transported to next accommodation, Thought for The Day delivered, and off we go.'

'Now that we have become so familiar with the routine, we won't know what to do when we go home,' I said. 'Such a lovely autumnal day. I noticed that your ankles are still red but that you have fewer blisters than me.'

'Oh, I am okay really. I hope that Roberta is not suffering too much.'

'Yes. Her condition must be serious to merit her brother flying over to be at her bedside.'

'As the psalmist says, *Let everything that has breath, praise the Lord.* Roberta is a reminder that it's a good idea to live each day to the full, isn't it, Frankie?'

'I love the reference to all those musical instruments. Harps, lyres, trumpets and cymbals. Dancing, too. Should we add the mouth organ and guitar? Joe and Nuala are so musically gifted. What a pair. Good to see romance blossom, is it not, Catherine?'

'Do you play an instrument?' Catherine asked. 'Being Welsh, I grew up singing in the Chapel.'

'I used to play in the...' *I nearly said the convent!* 'Yes, I attempt to play the guitar and sing with the children whom I teach in school.'

Then I saw Sonia.

'Oh hallo, Sonia. I didn't see you creeping up on Catherine and me, just as we have reached a cafe.'

'I have been absorbed in admiration of the countryside,' Sonia replied. 'Beautiful. Wonderfully constructed bridges spanning seemingly clean, unpolluted rivers. Such a variety of churches, and so many shrines. I prayed the fifteen mysteries of the rosary every day. At midday, the various chapel bells reminded me to recite the Angelus. The power of prayer. We're so fortunate to have faith in Christ, Jesus.'

Here we go! A convinced convert out to enmesh all in her faith.

'That young woman is showing us to a table over there. No queuing for a change. Shall we follow her, Catherine?'

'I'll join you,' said Sonia.

'Of course, Sonia.'

'I'll sit in the middle between you two. Just in time. Here comes the server.'

Server? Servant? Surely this young lady is a waitress? But in Sonia's mind?

'Hola. Sit here. I take your order. You pay and I bring your order to you. Okay?'

'Oh no. I don't seem to have packed my purse,' Sonia exclaimed. 'Could I repay you tomorrow, Frankie? Do you mind?'

'That's fine,' I said. 'Go ahead and order.'

So I am the victim today. If the rumours are correct, I shouldn't expect repayment.

'Hola! Café con leche. Tapas. Torta Santiago.'

Such a loud voice and a commanding attitude. No 'please' and such a lot of food at an early morning stop.

I felt myself being nudged.

Sonia stood as she said, 'I think that I will join the toilet queue while I wait.'

'I see you have succumbed, Frankie.'

Uncertain that Sonia might hear her, I responded to Catherine, 'Yes. That Tarta de Santiago indeed looks delicious. I love the delicate almond flavour and the characteristic cross of Santiago, on top.'

'She can't hear you now,' Catherine said. 'Let me know if she ever repays you. Miracles might happen.'

'We can but hope.'

'I looked forward to having a slice of that torta with my coffee each day,' Catherine said, 'but the cake served in some cafes seems to be a bone dry version.'

'When I chatted to my husband last night, I promised him that I would most definitely bring at least three cakes back with me. I'm determined to search Santiago for them on our final day.'

'Me too. Mine will be for my son and his expectant wife. My lovely daughter-in-law.'

'Children are so precious. My darling little boy. I miss him so much. My husband has been looking after him so well. I look forward to recounting all that we have seen and done each day.'

'I hope that I am at home in time for the birth of my new grandson.'

After we finished our break, Catherine and I decided to start off on our own. We wanted to enjoy time to reflect as we walked. We aimed to have lunch before the arrival of the midday sun.

Alone, I reflected:

I am glad that I still carry the crochet badge that my dear friend, Margaret, gave me all those years ago, before the nuns parted us for ever, sending her off to Kenya. If only we had each been given the letters that we sent to each other. She would not have taken her own life if she knew how much I missed her. Life can be so short. I really must make the most of it. On this pilgrimage, I have time to evaluate what I have achieved and try to make some sort of plan. But then I don't want to be rule-bound again. I want some goal to aim at. Not a structure. More organic. Nothing imposed. Whatever I decide should be based on the growth of my personality. I am a free spirit. When jealousy rears its head, I want to keep Richard for myself. But he is a free spirit, too. He would never be happy locked away from his friends and family. We might play the same song while being different instruments.

What kind of instrument am I? An Irish harp, perhaps. I must ask Richard if he were a musical instrument what would he choose to be. A clarinet. A cello, or a piano.

At midday, when I arrived at another cafe, I was delighted to see that Joe, Nuala and Karam were seated with most of our Camino group. I wondered if they had arranged to be dropped off there in order to meet everyone. Karam welcomed me with open arms:

'Come on, Frankie, join the celebrations. It's Joe's birthday.'

'I'm so excited,' Joe said. 'I couldn't wait to celebrate until the meal tonight. Anyway, it's only us here. Besides, we're out in the open air on a fine autumn day. I don't want a lot of fuss. It's just good to be able to rejoin the group again.'

Everyone was very happy that Joe was footing the bill for each person to order tapas and drinks of their choice. Karam had organised the celebration with the cafe.

The group had not realised that Karam had texted each one so that they all arrived at the same time.

A party streamer hung over the cafe, and two birthday balloons were attached to tables that had been joined together for all the group to enjoy each other's company. The two members of staff joined in when we sang Happy Birthday/Feliz cumpleaños a ti. Were his flaxen curls tickling his scalp as he beamed a huge smile all round.

'You look so young, Joe,' David said. 'Perhaps all the music that you teach keeps your spirits refreshed?'

'Thank you,' Joe replied, 'but looking around I'd guess that at thirty-six, I am not the youngest among us. But I suppose you're right about the music. Sure, my da was always encouraging the four of us to take part in the feis.'

'Oh, I think I have heard of that. Is a feis an Irish dance competition?'

'Too right, David. It's another word for festival. It is loud, crowded, exciting, exasperating, exhilarating, fun, and tiring. Keeps me fit. Most likely wore the bones in my leg down, too.'

'So many ways of celebrating lives,' David said. 'I was thinking as I was walking along today, that the thousands of pilgrims who trod the ground that we are treading must have lightened their journey by playing various kinds of musical instruments.'

Catherine asked, 'Is that what you were referring to when you gave us that quote from Shakespeare's Twelfth Night, this morning?'

'Yes,' David replied. 'After enjoying the music the

other night, I was wondering if I had to choose to be a musical instrument which one would I like to be?'

I found myself clapping. 'I can't believe it! That's exactly the question that I was putting to myself, David.

'Gosh, that's fun. What did you decide?' I asked.

'Really?' David said. 'Great minds and all that. Something must have prompted us. Well, I haven't come to a conclusion yet, Frankie. Being a Scot you might except me to choose the bagpipes, but although I love them, I'm not too sure that I would be too keen to be blown into, and tugged at, and make such loud music... but we'll see. I wonder what instrument each of you would like to represent you? Many instruments accompany flamenco dancing; castanets, classical guitar. Like other nations, they will have played a style of flute. I believe that they had a type of larder drum called the macho, and a smaller drum called the hembra.'

'Very interesting,' Mark said. 'I play the harp. I often wonder why I was drawn towards this instrument. That'll give me something to think about as I walk to our next destination.'

'Good luck,' David said. 'I'll be doing the same.'

I would never have guessed that Mark was a harpist. I associate delicate ladies, wearing beautifully flowing dresses, plucking the taut strings of a harp. But why can't stocky men with stump-like fingers choose this instrument?

I think that the instrument that I love is my capacity to sing. At home in Ireland, we sang many a rebel song. I recall my uncle Tim telling me that they used to delight in giving gusto to a song like the Four Green Fields, *because English folk listening, or even joining in, would not realise its meaning. Of course my mam's songs were* This is my lovely day, If I were a blackbird *and* I'm forever blowing bubbles. *Then there was the Gregorian Chant and the motets that we sang in the convent chapel. I taught the children in my class how to play the descant recorder, primarily so that they could read music. But the psalms were often accompanied by a lyre or harp. Psalm 50 that David spoke about this morning mentions so many instruments. Maybe the song that fits in most with this part of my journey is* Laudato Sii *in the Damian Lundi collection of hymns. This echos St Francis of Assisi in his praise for all God's creatures.*

I continued my walk, singing this hymn for the rest of my journey that day. That night, as I was going off to sleep, I wondered if it might be a good idea to write a plan that I hoped to live by.

I certainly do not wish to revert to convent rules. Over the years, since I have left the convent, I have been contacted by other ex-nuns from the same Order. One in particular, before she left, learnt that the younger nuns were living a very different, freer life. Some no longer wore their religious habit. A few had been permitted to live in flats outside the community. Others had become involved in social work. This particular ex-nun had been ignored when she attended the funeral of one of the sisters. She felt like a persona non gratis. She failed to understand why those who professed to be followers of Christ could behave in such a non-Christian manner.

25

DAY SIX

'*B*uenos días, everyone! Tomorrow we walk into Santiago.'

'Hurrah! Hurrah! Thanks, Karam.'

We were all so excited.

'Firstly, an update on Roberta. She is hoping that the catheter procedure together with the enema will help her. Maybe, most of you are aware of the reasons for these. Of course, we must maintain Roberta's privacy. Bahis is going to read us the Thought for Today.'

'Yes,' Bahis said. 'Here it is: *Write a blessing for the places that you have travelled through, the people that you have met on this journey, the villages, the chapels, shops, cafes etc. Include a blessing for the people who have walked with you*. Of course we will remember Roberta, too.'

Karam continued:

'Sonia has decided to opt out today. The strain on her back is increasing. She is saving her strength so as to be able to walk into Santiago on our last day. So Sonia replaces Nuala, who will be joining us today. Sonia will

189

travel by car with Joe and me.'

What's Sonia up to now? Maybe she has back problems? I wonder, though, if she has other intentions? God forgive me, but is she jealous of the relationship between Nuala and Joe? But then she is a good looking lady with an outgoing personality. True, the way that she inflicts her piety on others is very unfortunate and off putting. However, I did my fair share of proselytising when I was a nun. It's a typical reaction of converts, too. We've discovered something that we consider worthwhile and of course we want to share the good news. I still do it. Not with religion, but, for example, when I discover a salad dressing that is delicious I will recommend it to my friends. Oh, Karam is still talking.

'Peter, would you like to tell us something about our walk today?'

'It should be a lovely one,' Peter began. 'Up and down over gentle, rolling hills to Lavacolla on the edge of Santiago. A mere sixteen miles to walk. Ascent of 200 metres and descent of 250. Easy peasy!'

Karam thanked Peter and encouraged him to continue. 'Let me read this to you: As the name suggests, Lavacolla, a village close to the city outskirts, is a place of cleansing. It's cited in the Codex Calixtinus as a place of ritual washing. In medieval times, at this river, pilgrims would cleanse their bodies and clothing after the long, arduous journey.

This custom echoed the ritual bathing at the end of the pilgrimage to Jerusalem, when the faithful would immerse themselves in the River Jordan. This cleansing of the body was associated with the elimination of sin, in the same way that baptism symbolises cleansing the soul through the purifying power of water. Likewise, on the Camino de Santiago, in preparation for arriving at the Cathedral, it was customary to wash before entering the holy place.'

'I'm glad I brought my bathing togs, Karam. Just joking. But seriously, I hope that river will be shallow and warm enough for us to have a paddle.'

'Let us know, Frankie. Better still, if you succeed, take a photo.'

The group began the day's walking. Joy joined me. *Those penetrating eyes and that taut facial expression. She looks so earnest. Ready to scrutinise me. Yet the jazzy rainbow coloured stringy top that she's wearing belies her ardent evasion of small talk. What a mixture.*

'Buen mañana, Frankie!'

'Fair dues to you, Joy. I am impressed with your Spanish. And the top of the morning to you, too!'

Have I misjudged her?

'Just curious. Did Sonia ever repay you for the wine?'

'Alas, no Joy. But then I wasn't expecting her to. Poor crater, she's probably needy.'

'Of love? She's staying behind with Joe.'

'Well, I suppose Nuala wants to walk.'

'Maybe, Frankie. But the best way to find out is to talk to each of them. I find that very often people honestly can't recognise their own motivation.'

'You're right,' I said. 'I often wondered why some of the children that I taught sometimes seemed determined to break up friendships, only to discover that their home life deprived them of love. No hugs or cuddles.'

Denial of friendship! She'd hardly believe the effort that the nuns demanded to keep us from forming so called 'particular friendships'. What were they afraid of?

'Correct. Like me, Frankie, as a teacher, you'd have studied psychology. You know as well as I do that all our body parts work together. Take Roberta, for example. Last night I pleaded with Karam to let me go and speak to her. My training and, indeed, my instinct prompted me to think that a little counselling might help her in the state that her body has reached.'

'And did he permit you?'

'He did. I held her hand while I whispered positive thoughts to her. She managed to smile before it became obvious that she was too fragile and weak.'

I was right. Joy takes life seriously. She probes and she cares.

'At last I have caught up with you two.' It was Bahis, 'You're really speeding along now on those poles, Frankie.'

'Sometimes I am conscious that I still forget and stick my head out chicken-like, Bahis.'

'But you have succeeded wonderfully. I wanted to tell you about the beautiful drinking fountain that we are coming up to soon. Make sure that you top up your platypus there. I am off down the line to tell the others.'

'Thank you, Bahis.'

'Oh, here we are, Joy. Wonderful. What a huge yellow scallop on a radiantly blue shiny background.'

'Photo call. We'll have to take a photo. The shell covers the whole of the back wall, Frankie.'

'Oh good. Wait, Joy. Here come Catherine, David, Bahis and Peter too.'

'Okay, Frankie.'

Photos were taken in various groups in front of what we named the scallop fountain. Scallop shells had become synonymous with the Camino by this stage on our pilgrimage.

David had come prepared with a photo of a pair holding a scallop shell in front of this water fountain that was taken many years ago. He was eager to share information about these shells that he had discovered. He said that some claim that the scallop symbol is a metaphor, in that its lines represent the different routes travelled by pilgrims from around the world, that all lead to one point, the tomb of St James in Santiago de Compostela.

'This pilgrimage is a real eye opener into the lives of many people, isn't it?' I remarked.

'Well, yes, Frankie. Even within our comparatively small group, it seems to me that we each appear to adhere to a set of beliefs or customs.'

'We could say that we are indeed a motley lot,' Catherine said, 'or that maybe unconsciously we represent a cross section of belief systems.'

David suggested that we continue our discussion while we walked on.

I said that I felt privileged to get an insight into Sikh customs when Richard and I invited Karam to our home. Joe, who shares rooms with him said that he is a devout Sikh. 'He keeps to their diet and even at night when he removes his turban, he does so discreetly, replacing it with some other material. He's very competent, too. He's really doing a great deal for Roberta ill in hospital. Of course, that means that he is missing out on part of the pilgrimage.'

Catherine said:'I'm a Baptist. You're a Catholic, and so is Sonia. Bahis is, of course, a Muslim. It seems that he is somewhat selective in some of their practices, though. For instance, while he carries his prayer mat and faces Mecca at the hours stipulated, he often takes off his headgear, and he is clean shaven.'

I asked David if he is a member of the Church of Scotland. He told us that initially he was and added there have been fascinating developments in the Kirk of Scotland. Over the years he learnt a good deal about the inception of Christianity in Scotland. That there are references to St Columba who lived somewhere around 521. Apparently he was known as *Colum-cille*, or *"Dove of the church"*. He was from Donegal.

'We studied him at school,' I said. 'Columba was an Irish abbot and missionary evangelist credited with spreading Christianity in what is today Scotland at the start of the Hiberno-Scottish mission. He founded the important abbey on Iona.'

'That's correct, Frankie. There was also Calvinism and Luther. Discussion about predestination and the no-frills approach with regard to icons and images in their Kirks. Many Scots say that they are Christian, some are stricter than others. Then of course immigrants will have enriched us all with their beliefs, David.'

As we neared the river we met other groups joining together. Emma pointed to men who were on horseback and wearing cowboy hats. I teased Emma: 'Emma! More handsome men. Trust you.'

'Lavacolla! We'll have to wait until these horses stop splashing about, though,' I said.

'Spoilsport,' said Emma. 'Don't they paint an inviting picture in the shade of those overhanging trees? Will someone take a photo of me with them?'

'Oh course, Emma,' Joy said. 'We'll send it to your husband. Oh, I don't believe it, if it isn't that the Argentinian chaps who got a taxi for Roberta when she had almost collapsed by the side of the road?'

Joy told us that she met those men yesterday when she was alone in a cafe. She said that she discovered that they were both doctors.

'Come on,' Emma said. 'Let's get cleansing. Rid yourselves of all your faults. If only.'

I laughed and said: 'Sheer sweat you mean, Emma. I'm longing to get these boots off and at least dangle my smelly feet. It's so hot today.

'This is great. We're nearly all here together,' added Catherine.

'Shall we say the Angelus prayer? *The Angel of the Lord declared unto Mary...*'

'Maybe privately, Sonia,' I interrupted. 'Not everyone is familiar with that prayer.'

'Those of us… oh, okay. Maybe not, Frankie.'

As our group sat dotted around in pairs and began to eat our sandwiches, Nuala sidled up next to me. 'Thank God you intervened, Frankie. As soon as she was dropped off, she starting reciting decades of the rosary along the way. I succumbed because, having been apart from the group, I wasn't sure if ye'd agreed to that.'

I agreed. 'Stuffing religion down the throats of folk is not on. Besides, we're a mixed group of believers, and maybe none. Did you notice how Bahis has discreetly wandered off with his prayer mat? He'll be facing Mecca without having to intrude on the beliefs of others.'

'I think that Joe is feeling guilty,' Nuala said. 'He's saying that people sponsored him to walk and—'

'I'm sure he'd walk if he could, Nuala. I heard that he is going to join us all the time tomorrow, so that we can all walk into Santiago together. All except Roberta, that is,' I assured her.

Once in our shared bedroom that evening, Catherine and I were very pleased that there were lovely bolsters at the foot of each bed. Catherine really needed to rest her legs over them and ease her pain. Her ankles were still red.

While we rested we talked about the little shrines where people rested stones on top of the milestones and the shrines where prayers written on pieces of paper were left surrounding statues of Mary and of St James. I showed Catherine a t-shirt that I bought en route that had the names of all the places that we had walked past written on it. Catherine showed me hers that she bought with a big scallop shell design. We decided to find our way to the supermercado to buy our drinking water to fill our platypus for he next day.

'Our final trek! Can you believe it, Frankie? My son contacted me to say that I will probably be home before my grandson will be born, too. Delighted.'

'Brilliant, Catherine.'

When I phoned Richard that evening, he told me how much he had struggled without me. That although he was always aware of how much he loved me, my absence had made him realise that he couldn't do without me. That we had become one in so many countless ways. He said that Dante could think of nothing else but giving me a huge hug as soon as I came through those doors at the airport. He enquired about Joe and of course, Roberta.

I need to send a WhatsApp message to Marion. She'll enjoy the photo that I took of us washing away our sins in Lavacolla, the place of cleansing and ritual washing. But I wonder what she'll say about all the chatting I was engaged in today. I miss the quiet times when I was able to mediate. But then again, we learn a good deal from listening to others. That brings me full circle from the physical washing in the river to pondering on whether it's possible to wash sin away. Surely the one is a metaphor for the other. What is sin? A mistake. A learning process. Deliberate intent to harm. C'est la vie.

26

ENTERING SANTIAGO

*B*ahis clapped his hands. 'Hurrah! We'll be in Santiago today.'

'Well done, everyone!' Karam joined him. 'We're on our last lap. Under ten kilometres, and more down than up.'

'Wonderful, Karam! But what about Roberta?'

'Unfortunately, Frankie, Roberta is still struggling. She sends her love and good wishes. Her brother has flown over to be with her. She'll stay in the hospital here until she's well enough to fly back. She's in good hands. Spanish hospitals appear to be well run. This one certainly is. Joan plans to join us later, too. At present, she's taking turns being near Roberta while Roberta's son, Matthew, finds out more about her prognosis.'

I caught Catherine's eye. She winked a knowing wink. I pursed my lips.

Gosh. Matters must be serious if her brother is flying over. What are we not being told? Looking around at the others' faces, their wide open eyes portray their acceptance that what we are being told is significant. Roberta would have been aware of her prognosis and suspected that her condition would eventually deteriorate. Another reason that I should seize the day. Carpe diem… every day is precious. Roberta was a constant reminder that cancer patients and their relatives need our support.

'Bravo for taking care of her in our name, Karam,' I said. 'And to Emma with her translating, and Joy with counselling skills, too.'

'Thanks, Frankie.' Everyone fell silent for a few seconds. 'Now, as you can see, Joe is joining us on our last lap. And we have asked him to give us our Thought for Today.'

'Begorrah! Oh… that's not swearing, It means "by God!" Well, as I have been on my tod for a good part of the pilgrimage, I've availed of that opportunity to ponder, to reflect. You know, there is something familiar with my homeland and the Galician countryside. Not a lot of rain during this season… well, most of the time, except for that thoroughly soggy day, but sure there's evidence of it. So I offer you a Celtic blessing:

> *May the friendships you make,*
> *Be those which endure,*
> *And all of your grey clouds*
> *Be small ones for sure.*
> *And trusting in Him*
> *To Whom we all pray,*
> *May a song fill your heart,*
> *Every step of the way.'*

Joe must have kissed the Blarney Stone of eloquence. He's had a way with words throughout this pilgrimage. Well, eloquence is one of the many talents that we Irish are gifted with. Even the nuns made sure that we enhance that facility when they took us to kiss the Blarney Stone. That was when I was over on retreat in the Irish Provence of the Religious Order. At that time, visitors had to be held by someone as their heads were lowered over the battlements to kiss the stone. Of course that was not really practical, nor advisable for nuns wearing veils. Needless to say, mine fell off and had to be rescued before I was permitted to leave the battlement.

Catherine tugged at my sleeve. 'Here she goes, Frankie. Nuala's made a bee-line for Joe. He's giving her a big hug.'

'Ah. Lovely, Catherine.'

Karam clapped his hands to gain attention in order to inform the group, 'Just before you start off, I forgot to remind you that we'll take a group photograph outside the Cathedral. You assured me that you're each carrying your own special blue T-shirts. Sorry, David, we got your size wrong, so yours is a slightly lighter shade of blue. And I'm told that we'll meet many more pilgrims as we near the city, so keep an eye out for each other. We must remember that it's Emma's birthday tomorrow. 'Gosh, there are more folk coming on either sides of us. Differing languages being spoken. Was that Portuguese or maybe South American Spanish just now?'

The group had moved off, and we were mingling with many other pilgrims following the route into Santiago. Karam was beside me.

'You mentioned Emma's birthday. She's invited us all to indulge in a special cup of hot chocolate in a really upmarket hotel. I think she said that it is called the Parador now, but I understand that originally it was a kind of hostel. I have some information stored on my phone. When we stop for coffee, I'll look it up.'

'That sounds good,' I said. 'How generous of her. I hope that the chocolate is not sickly sweet, though.'

Gradually the route became crowded. Everyone was friendly, and we engaged freely in conversation with whoever we found walking beside with:

'Buen Camino!'

'Buen Camino!

The Polish group seemed to be taking the religious aspect seriously. They were praying the rosary. Sonia should join them. We tried to decipher the various accents. The American accent was easier to detect. A tall fellow in front of us slowed down to speak to us. 'Hola. Buen Camino. Are you with that Irish guy and his girlfriend back there?'

'I'm Frankie. This is Karam. I think that you may be talking about Joe and Nuala who are in our group. I guess you're from the States.'

'Pennsylvania. Philadelphia, to be exact. Translates as the city of brotherly love. Good name for this journey. Right?'

'All creeds and none, today we're all treading the one path,' I said. 'Same in everyday life, isn't it? We're a mixed bunch too.'

Karam tapped me on my shoulder to alert me to the cyclists spinning down the road. They were followed by the chaps that we met yesterday on horseback.

'Oh, look down there, Frankie. That huge…. The spires. That's the cathedral.'

'Wonderful, Catherine. One, two spires. It's still too hazy to be able to see properly. It's really getting crowded now. Oh, there's David.'

Bahis was waving to us. We tried to keep closer to the others as we descended off the paths onto proper pavements leading into the town. Just as we did we saw Bahis waving his arms about gesturing for us to go back to him. Our Camino group gathered together around David. Karam invited David to address us:

'As it's our first time seeing the Cathedral de Santiago de Compostela, David is going to explain a little about this wonderful place.'

'Thank you, Karam. You will all know that Compostela comes from the Latin "Campus Stellae" literally, *Stars Field* or *field of stars*. Latin to Galician-Portuguese. The Cathedral combines styles such as Baroque, Gothic, Neoclassical, Plateresque or Romanesque.

'They began building the Cathedral in the ninth century. The story goes that Pelayo, a Compostela hermit, was resting in his home, when heavenly lights caught his attention. According to legend, the lights began to call from the depths of the forest.

'Pelayo related this to the Bishop of the area, called Teodomiro. When they investigated further, they are said to have discovered the remains of Santiago the Apostle. What is certain is that King Alfonso II had a basilica built. Pilgrims began to visit this holy tomb, the small basilica was found to be too small to accommodate them. So another, more modern, temple was built in 829. Finally, in 1075, a new Romanic cathedral was erected. However, it was not finished until the year 1211. Its construction followed the original design of the Church of Saint Sernin of Toulouse. Over the centuries the cathedral has undergone many renovations, although it retains much of its medieval style. Baroque etc. Neoclassicism has left its mark with the Azabachería façade.'

Karam thanked David, before leading the way to a nearby restaurant. Karam said that after we'd eaten, we would take our group photo in the Plaza de Obradoiro, in front of the specular Cathedral. Following that, we will go to our accommodation and change into our special T-shirts ready for the photo. Karam added that after the group photo has been taken, it's up to each of you to get your Compostela:

'When we reach the Cathedral, I will show you where you take your credentials, the card that you have had stamped en route verifying that you have walked the required hundred miles. As we calculated ours in miles rather than kilometres, we have walked for longer. There will most likely be a queue. Of course, you have the opportunity to enjoy the interior of the cathedral. We'll join the other pilgrims at the celebration of Mass tomorrow morning. We've booked our evening meal for eight o'clock this evening. Bahis has texted you the address of the restaurant. Make your way to the restaurant over to your right now. Be careful not to get separated from our group, at least until we eventually walk down to the Cathedral. After the meal, I'll try and lead the way through the crowds still going down there.'

Once our group had finished our meal and changed into our special T-shirts and many other groups of other pilgrims had moved on, we walked down to the Cathedral. By the time we reached there, more crowds were gathering. Karam signalled to us from between the two flight of stairs leading up to the cathedral: 'Tall ones at the back!'

'I'm middle-sized so I'd better move past you, Joy, and position myself in the centre.' It was Sonia.

I might have guessed. Sonia has positioned herself between Joe and Nuala. Was this intentional?

'Okay, Sonia. I'm sure that we all know our height and will position ourselves accordingly. But it's better that you remove that lovely hat while we take the group photo.'

'Oh, I thought it would be okay. It's got a big yellow shell sign… Okay. Maybe not. Sorry, Karam.'

'Hello. Would you like me to take one that includes you?'

'What a lovely chap,' Catherine said, 'offering to take the second photo, with Karam in it, Frankie.'

I recognised him. He was one of the Oxford Dons that I met way back when I stopped for coffee.

There were hugs and tears of joy all round.

'We're here,' Joe said. 'We've done it, Frankie!'

'Congratulations, Joe.'

'Back there, I was so worried that I wouldn't make it. Thank you, Nuala, for all your love and support.'

Why do I feel a strange feeling? I can't seem to fathom it. Nuala's smiling, but her eyes have that far away look. I wonder what's preoccupying her?

'What were you saying, Peter?'

'Well, you know already. I was reminding myself that this Cathedral has been here since the Middle Ages. According to what it says here, it's a predominantly Romanesque structure with later additions adding both Gothic and Baroque features and that there are four impressive plazas in front of each of the four doors of the cathedral.'

'David said that this big square is called the Plaza del Obradoiro.'

'Yes, he said that the main plaza was given that name of Obradoiro, meaning workshop in English, because, for nearly ten years, around the middle 7000, the Obradoiro, was where the stones for the Baroque facade were cut and carved.'

27

THE CREDENTIALS

'Oh, how wonderful to only have to pack once more, and that's to go home, Frankie.'

'I can't wait to unlace my boots. I wonder, will my blisters hurt when I put on my sandals? What about your red ankles, Catherine? Show me.'

'Red, but less so. I'll be fine. I don't care, anyway. My blisters are healing. Come on, shall we go down to join the queue for our certificates?'

'Good, Catherine. I'm going to wear my special t-shirt with all the places that we have walked through listed on it.'

'Off we go to the pilgrims' office of Santiago de Compostela, and we pass our magnificent Cathedral en route.'

'I'm really looking forward to peeping into the Cathedral, too, Frankie. It's huge. There are four entrances. I never thought it would be so imposing.'

By the time Catherine and I joined the queue at the bottom of the winding stairs leading up to the pilgrims' office, there were many pilgrims in front of us. Some looked as though they had just arrived in Compostela. All shapes and sizes, young trendy types and older grey-haired folk with ruddy faces and unkempt hair, clutching on to the bannisters with one hand, and the other holding their passports. Many differing languages were being spoken. One and all friendly, smiley, satisfied looking people.

My God, how fortunate am I to be numbered among these pilgrims. I feel as though I have completed something special. I can't name it. There are tears of achievement welling up inside me, and a sense of peace, too. Hard to describe. Helping others, while helping myself. Something like that.

'Let's see how many stamps, sorry *sellos*, that you've got on your passport, Frankie.'

'Oh yes, Catherine. Let's check. Credencial del Peregrino. That's their proper name. It's written over there on that poster.'

'You're right, Frankie. As we often walked and stopped together, mine will have many of the same stamps as yours, starting with Casa Carolo O Cebreiro. Soon after that, I have one with a lovely pastoral scene. Of course, lots of St James.'

'Scallop shells in abundance, too,' I said, 'yellow arrows, and the symbol of the distinctive Santiago cross. I've a church tower, and a knight on horseback. I've counted thirty-nine in total, Catherine.'

'Look, up there nearing the top of the stairs, Frankie. I'm sure that's the German man who was determined to make it, in spite of struggling with a terrible cold.'

'He's waving to us, Catherine.'

Catherine and I read the instructions as we moved nearer to the office:

As you approach the Pilgrims' office, you need to find a ticket machine located in the waiting room. This ticket has a number to be attended, and a QR scanning code.

You can stay in the pilgrims' office waiting room, and look at the screen to check the number that has been called, and the number of the counter where you'll be attended.

I noticed Joan, the lady who was caring for Roberta just leaving the office. Her head was down. She did not seem to be very happy. We'd reached the top of the queue. I was next. The fellow at the desk welcomed me and then asked:

'Do I detect an Irish accent? D'you mind me asking you, where do you hail from?'

As usual, I chatted away with the Irish official who was stamping my passport. I discovered that he was from Dingle, that he lived in Surrey, and that many of his golfing friends were regular visitors to Ireland.

Catherine and I were delighted to receive our Compostela Certificate. The actual certificate is free, but it was just another €2. for the beautiful Credencial written in Latin. The man who was serving me translated it:

The Chapter of this Holy Apostolic and Metropolitan Cathedral of Compostela, custodian of the seal of the Altar of St. James, to all the Faithful and pilgrims who arrive from anywhere on the Orb of the Earth with an attitude of devotion, or because of a vow or promise, make a pilgrimage to the Tomb of the Apostle, Our Patron Saint and Protector of Spain, recognises before all who observe this document that: ...{Name}... has devotedly visited this most sacred temple with Christian sentiment.

'I assume that the official who interviewed you, was Irish. You seemed to have enjoyed a long conversation.'

'Indeed, Catherine. Sure, we Irish are everywhere. Itchy feet. That's what we've got. Always on the move, or you could say, well-travelled.'

I suggested that we catch up with Joan. She looked sad as she walked in the direction of the Cathedral.

Joan explained that when she had gone to the Pilgrims' office to try and get a certificate for Roberta, she had been refused. The reason given was that because Roberta had not satisfied the requirements, she was not eligible. I was furious.

'How could she? She would have done, had she been able to. Bureaucracy. How I detest it. She should have been congratulated for the supreme effort that she made.'

Catherine read out the Rules: To obtain the Compostela you must fulfil the following premises: The pilgrimage must be done for religious and spiritual reasons, or at least in the pursuit of these. They are required to comply with the following requirements: 100 km/62 mi on foot or on horse, or 200 km/124 mi for those on a bike.'

'Rules, my eye! What would Christ have done?'

My whole body feels as though it is about to explode. Memories of religious regulations. Rule books, obligations, and sinfulness make me angry.

I asked Joan if she would give me Roberta's details. Her date of birth, and address, etc.

'Yes. Why?'

'Because I am going back to the Pilgrims' office to get her a certificate.'

'You can, but they won't give it to you.'

'Even if I impersonate Roberta? This is all wrong, unfair, unchristian. Roberta could not have done more. She's so ill, that she might even die.'

'I'm coming with you,' Catherine said. 'I won't go in, of course. I'll queue with you. Even though I doubt that you'll succeed. Remember that you had a long conversation with that Irish man? He'll recognise you.'

'Thank you, Catherine.'

When my turn came, fortunately, the officer who interviewed me was an Italian woman. The Irish man must have gone off duty.

Telling lies does not come easy to me. I'm shaking inside. I can feel my blood rushing to my cheeks. Trying to speak with an English accent is such an effort.

I was successful. I was handed Roberta's certificate.

'Well done. You looked scared as you went in.'

'I was so frightened. But it's worth it.'

'Hola. You look happy. Good to see you again. You've got your Credencial del Peregrino.'

It's the Oxford Dons that we met early on, near the beginning of our pilgrimage.

'Yes, Elizabeth.'

When I told the Oxford Dons what I had done, they said that I would have to confess to a priest. Jokingly, they offered to find me a confessor. Then, John, a member of their group, told me that their group would like to contribute more money to the Oasis Cancer Centre that my group and I were fundraising for.

'That is so kind of you. They will be delighted, John.'

'Our pleasure, Frankie. But, we have one proviso. We would like at least two of you to meet us in Canterbury Cathedral on the feast day of St Thomas a Becket on 29th December.'

'That will not be a problem. We'll make sure that a few of us will be there, John. Now that I have experienced the benefits of pilgrimages, I am hooked.'

'Pilgrimages for good causes is what our group do,' John said. 'We will be starting out from various locations on or after Christmas Day aiming to be at the Cathedral to celebrate the great man. Why not exercise ourselves after consuming rich Christmas niceties? Seriously though, we try to fund-raise for different charities each year. At our age, we mostly have all we need, so our families are happy to sponsor us instead of struggling to think up an appropriate present.'

'A huge thank you, for your promise,' I said. 'Along

the way, I have been wondering if I should write an account of this pilgrimage. What title should I give it? This sponsorship has helped me to decide. Most folk know about the Canterbury Tales, so why don't I keep to the title that I first thought of and call my account, The Camino Tales?'

At the meal that evening, everyone congratulated me for managing to obtain a certificate for Roberta. They were overjoyed to learn of the donation promised by who they now referred to as the Canterbury Group. Joe and Nuala vouched that when Joe had recovered from, possibly, a knee-replacement operation, that they would return not only complete the last hundred miles of the pilgrimage, but to continue on to Finisterre.

When Catherine and I returned to our hotel that night, I was surprised when a small sized man was waiting there to greet me. Taken aback at first, I didn't recognise him.

'You don't remember me, Sister, do you? I'm Tom. From Wimbledon. Sean's dad.'

'Oh, I'm sorry, Tom. Of course I do.'

'But you wouldn't have been expecting to meet me here.'

'That's true.'

'Well, I'm a volunteer in one of the information centres for the Camino. After I had walked it a few times. I fell in love with the place.'

I was glad that Catherine had slipped away. I hoped that she had done so before Tom had addressed me with 'Sister', the title that I had used when I was still a nun.

'You didn't walk the entire route, Tom, did you?'

'I did. I suspect that you must be tired, but I was hoping that we could chat? Am I asking too much? I'll understand if—'

'No, Tom. That's okay. But, how did you know that I was here?'

Once seated, Tom explained that by chance he met Karam a few days earlier when some of the group stopped for coffee. As they were talking, he thought that he recognised me just as I was about to resume walking. Since he had access to information about where the group would be staying when they reached Santiago, he was determined to renew acquaintances.

'Sean often talks about you, Sister.'

'Tom, I'm Frankie now. But tell me, how old is Sean?'

'He's married with two healthy sons, Sis Fran…'

Tom reminded me that the French route to Santiago Compostela on average took 30-35 days, walking between 25-27km each day. That it began in St Jean Pied de Port, a beautiful bustling French market town in the foothills of the Pyrenees.

'So you started from St Jean Pied de Port, Tom?'

Although I was interested, I was also aware that I wanted to phone Richard, and I still had to complete my packing. Besides, Catherine would be asleep by the time Tom left me. Nonetheless, I considered that since Tom had taken the trouble to find me, he deserved to be welcomed, at least for a short time. He explained that he had become so convinced of the good that can result on the Camino, that he decided to become a volunteer.

'Some of the pilgrims that I met were inspirational, Sis… Frankie. One of our group suffered from severe depression, another was recovering from chemotherapy. A lady in the group had recently been widowed. You know the story. People choose to take part in this pilgrimage for various reasons.'

'No need to remind me, Tom. I met Ann from Drogheda, who had become a member of the third Order of Francis, and was following their spirituality guidance as she walked. Then there was Maria from Rome, a couple from Ohio who were great fun, and young Joe and Henry from Brighton, but they had started from Pied-de-San Jean. So many from everywhere.'

'What really inspired me to do something about the Camino flashed into my heart when a group of us visited a church.'

'You had a vision?'

'Well, you're not far off the mark, Sister.'

'Frankie.'

'Yes. I don't know if you know that I am a Salesian past pupil. Do you know about that religious Order? Their founder, St John Bosco?'

'Great Italian priest. His motto, Da Mihi Animas, Cetera Tolle: Give me souls and take everything else. The salvation of especially the young was the ultimate purpose of the life of Don Bosco. A truly inspirational saint.'

'Well, can you imagine what came over me when I saw his picture hanging in an alcove in that church that night. I knew that I was meant to see it. I just knew that John Bosco wanted to educate young people so that they would mature into decent, kind human beings. So, inspired by him, I decided that I was going to stay and volunteer to help out in one of the Camino offices. My goal has been to try and follow St John Bosco's approach. Another axiom that I find inspirational, that Don Bosco adopted from St Francis of Sales is, 'A spoonful of honey attracts more flies than a barrel full of vinegar.''

'Lovely. Kindness works much better than giving suggestions or worse still, issuing punishments.

'Well, Tom, it's been a lovely surprise to see you tonight. Thank you for finding me. You are indeed enthusiastic. I am delighted that you are engaged in helping pilgrims on the Camino. You've certainly found your niche here. Please give my wishes to your son, his boys, and of course your wife, Mary, too.'

When I phoned Richard that night I was very surprised

when Richard told me that Joe had phoned, and that they had a long conversation about Nuala.

Joe said that when he started to tell Nuala that he had been training to be a priest, she said that she had assumed that long ago. Certain phrases and incidents that he used led her to suspect that was the case.

'Really. Gosh. I suppose in some ways that was obvious. Did she give Joe any examples, Richard?'

'Apparently they laughed a lot when she pointed out that he had let slip phrases like 'in one of our houses' and often said 'we' when relating some past incidents. Lots of examples. But in general it's his shy, reserved, demeanour, innocent remarks, and his piety and knowledge of scripture that betrays his previous life.'

'That's good. That must have been a relief for him. Nuala accepted him as he is. She knew all the time. Did she reveal anything about her own background, though? I noticed that she often has a glazed, far-away look. What about the way that she left the spa without him, too?'

'Frankie, that's the important thing. I suspect that there's still something that she is not saying. All she gave as way of explanation is that she is is not ready for a proper relationship, yet.'

'I suppose it is the 'yet' bit that Joe is holding onto. With his, and indeed our own backgrounds, we tend to turn to prayer and are always seeking to save souls!'

'There is still a day left on the pilgrimage, Frankie. You never know. Maybe Joe's prayers will be answered and we will understand Nuala better?'

'Oh, I hope so, Richard. I'm so happy that we did not have a hot and cold blowing relationship. Love you. Love to Dante.'

'Amore!

'Grá go leor! Love galore! There you have love in abundance in the three languages, Richard.'

28

MASS IN THE CATHEDRAL

*T*oday was the day of the Pilgrims' Mass in the Cathedral. It felt very special to be able to celebrate our arrival with this special service.

'I have been to Catholic services before, Frankie. Sadly to say, it's usually been at funerals, but I'm not sure about Mass. Oh, I know it will be fine but—'

'No buts, Catherine. No doubt it will be a little over the top, even for me, but sure it'll have some flavour of Baptists' services, too. Imagine what it will be like for the Sikhs and Muslims among our group. Then there are those who are members of the Church of England, and David who probably attends the Kirk of Scotland. I suspect some among our group may not even be church-goers.'

Karam warned us that there would be a multitude of pilgrims there so it was advisable to arrive at the Cathedral by eleven at the latest for the Mass beginning at twelve noon.

We had been reading up about the Cathedral in preparation. We learnt that it is a hundred metres in length, seventy wide, seventy-five high, two spires and a clock tower. Another fact that we were delighted to discover was that on special occasions when there were big groups an enormous thurible was used called the Botafumeiro. As we were joining a large number of pilgrims we were hopeful that would be used at this Mass. According to John Brierley in his Pilgrim's Guide, the swinging of this giant incense burner was originally used to fumigate the sweaty, and possibly disease-ridden, pilgrims. It is huge, needs a dozen strong men using ropes to haul it up and consumes a great deal of incense.

Catherine and I decided to set out at 10:30. We locked the doors of our rooms and after carrying our room keys down to reception, we waited for anyone else who would be setting off for the Cathedral.

En route we met David.

'Gosh, David. All those sticks. Lots of them stacked in that alcove over there.'

'When I came across them yesterday, Frankie I was curious, so I asked a priest who happened to be passing by.'

'Oh, David. What did he tell you?'

'He said that the staff, or walking poles, as we call it nowadays, long ago had a practical and a spiritual use. As you can imagine, in the early days of the Camino, pilgrims often had to protect themselves from wild animals, and possibly robbers, especially when they walking through rocky passages.'

'It must have been a risky journey in those days, David.'

'The spiritual aspect attached to the staff was that it reminded the pilgrim of their humble position, relying on supernatural blessing to arrive secure at the threshold of Saint James.'

'A far cry from the collapsible walking poles that we use today, then,' Catherine said.

'Yes indeed. There was even a religious ceremony through which the medieval pilgrim, stick or staff became a tangible representation of the help of God and submission to the Church.'

'Nowadays, I'd imagine that most walkers opt for a pair of trekking poles on the basis of their practicality. Ones that are lighter, smaller, that collapse into themselves and, most importantly, fit into our cases,' said Catherine.

'Another piece of information that I recall this priest telling me,' David continued, 'is that many items get left behind by pilgrims along the Camino. So much so, that in the pilgrims' hostel at Roncesvalles, there is a 'leave and take basket', for all the items that pilgrim abandon.'

Karam was standing at the entrance of the hotel when we were about to go to the Cathedral. He said that he, too, was anxious to get there early. When Catherine and I joined Mark, Peter, and Bahis, Karam WhatsApped those who had not come down from their rooms, informing them that our group decided to begin walking towards the Cathedral.

When we reached the Obradoiro square in front of the Cathedral, we were sent to join crowds at one of the entrances on the other side. The ushers were instructing Pilgrims carrying rucksacks that they had to leave them outside. Uncertain when the rest of the group would arrive, we joined the queue and proceeded into the darkness of this huge building.

We saw Bahis signalling to us to join him on the steps at the right hand side. We noticed the rest of the group struggling in and out between other pilgrims in order to be able to be with us. When I saw the sun shining on Joe's smiling cherub-like face, I remembered the morning when he appeared on my door step, and I recalled my conversation with Richard the night before. I wondered if Nuala would tell him more about her past history, today. I was pondering on that when Catherine remarked, 'It's difficult trying to make oneself heard over that organ music, especially when people are speaking in so many different languages. Did you hear me, Frankie? You're perhaps more familiar with that kind of music?'

'Yes. Actually no, Catherine. I prefer orchestral, choir, traditional and modern. Different types. The organ seems to be all pervasive.'

'Now that more lights have been switched on, I'm noticing the ornate mixture of architecture.'

'I don't know if I like its fussiness though, Catherine. I appreciate that it's been changed and added to throughout the ages. Oh, there are some of the clergy coming in.'

'All robed in bright red, Frankie.'

'I wonder if that contraption at this side of the altar, is the botafumeiro. We have a very good view over the heads of people from up here.'

We watched the procession of clergy advance towards the altar and move to their seats, accompanied by playing of traditional organ music. A man moved towards a microphone. When I heard *Gran Británico* and *Irlanda* mentioned, I whispered that he must be welcoming pilgrims from various countries.

Karam, who was standing next to me, passed this information on to the rest of the group.

Having met pilgrims from many nations en route, we were not surprised that so many had arrived in Santiago and had claimed their Compostela within the last twenty-four hours.

Karam asked me if I could distinguish the language that the service was being conducted in.

I replied that I was puzzled, because with my knowledge of Italian I had expected to be able to understand a little Spanish.

I asked Emma. She replied that she had concluded that

they were probably speaking the Galician language that is more like Portuguese.

I realised that the priest approaching the lectern wearing a mitre was a bishop. I hoped that he would not speak for long in a language that I surmised that most of the congregation would not be able to understand.

'Frankie, Peter has just whispered that Joan feels that she needs somewhere to sit.'

'There's nowhere. She's looking faint. How is she going to get through the crowds? Here.' I passed her my flask.

Peter signalled to indicate that a young fellow had provided her with a folded seat and had passed it up the line.

'The service seems to be moving on,' Catherine said. 'That nun has a lovely voice.'

'I wore a habit like that, Catherine.'

'Whatever for? You weren't a… were you a nun?'

'I was going to tell you, but then the time passed. Yes, I was in the convent for sixteen years. Hearing that nun singing evokes many memories.'

'I must admit that I am not completely surprised,' Catherine remarked. 'I did wonder. I don't know. Now I am curious, though.'

Maybe I should have kept my past in the past? Now I have become a curiosity. But then I don't know what I revealed when I spoke in my sleep.

A woman fainted. The guards carried her out.

Then we noticed that one of the altar servers has started to push the huge thurible. The men begun to pull at the ropes. The huge thurible started to swing backwards and forwards throughout the length of this big cathedral and clouds of incense permeated the entire building.

'I want to get hold of it and swing… whoa…'

'Irreverent, Frankie?'

'Wearing my habit, I'd look like a swinging witch.'

Karam heard and tapped on my shoulder. What kind of habit?'

'A nun's habit, Karam.'

'Like the lady who sang during the service?'

'Yes, Karam. Duck down. It's gathering momentum. WOW!'

Eventually, when Mass was over and our group managed to reform on the step leading down to Plaza Obradoiro, Karam reminded us that we were invited to celebrate Emma's birthday with a special cup of delicious chocolate at four that afternoon in the Parador Hotel.

'Eat, and then hunt for a present for Emma? I noticed some lovely scallop shaped earrings in a shop that we passed on our way to register our Compostela credentials, Catherine.'

'Me too. And Emma has pierced ears.'

Most of our group began to follow David. He confidently led the way to a spacious restaurant where we were seated together. Menus were distributed in English and Spanish, and included Galician dishes. He collected the orders, the dishes were served and, after efficiently collecting our payments, the bill was paid.

At half past three, most of the group were waiting for the others in the Parador Hotel. When Emma was chatting on the phone to her husband John, we were unobtrusively passing round a birthday card for each of us to sign. It had been agreed that we would celebrate her 43rd birthday at our evening meal.

When Emma finished her phone call she told us that her ten year old twins and her husband longed to join us in celebrating her birthday. When I asked her what her husband said about the lumps that had developed on her legs she replied that she didn't tell him. He'd only worry. He might have insisted that she took the next plane back. Besides, the lumps come and go and she would make an appointment to see her doctor when returned home. She reminded us that it was her husband John who is treating us to a special chocolate drink in a prestigious hotel.

'I am in no doubt that you are all grateful and well deserving. It only costs just over two euros per person. So the price of the drinks doesn't amount to much.'

David told us that this Parador Hotel had started off as a hostel way back near the end of the fifteenth century. It was called the palace of kings. Everything is really beautiful, it has an imposing entrance and is carpeted throughout and is comfortably furnished.

'I wish that my clothes were more in keeping with this elegant ambiance, Karam.'

'Me, too, Frankie.'

'David, was it always called the Parador?'

'I read that it was in 1954. It's really elegant and their brochure claims that the bedrooms are luxurious, Karam.'

'Here comes the chocolate served in what seems to be china cups.'

'Of course, Joy,' I remarked

'It's passed its test, Frankie. Try it. Spoon stands up in it. The aroma...'

'It's like nothing else. I was dreading it tasting sickly sweet, but this is simply delicious. Thank you, Emma.'

Before we were about to depart, Karam reminded us that our last supper had been arranged for eight that evening, and that Bahis had texted us the necessary instructions. He added that we would be departing for the airport at 4pm, and that he had been advised we might be better to shop around if we were intent on buying Torta Santiago cakes, because there were a variety of different types to choose from.

We all departed in separate directions. Catherine and I purchased a pair of gold scallop earrings as a birthday present for Emma. I also bought three different types of Torta de Santiago, and a bottle of Orujo liquor that the proprietor convinced me was one of Galicia's most traditional drinks. I bought matching tan coloured t-shirts for myself, Richard, and Dante decorated with yellow scallop rays that resembled the signs that had guided us throughout the Camino.

Oh, I must buy a gift for Marion. A book, maybe.

Eventually I bought a book on the life and meditations of St James and a smaller Torta de Santiago for Marion. I kept looking out for Joe and Nuala, and eventually I saw them together in a cafe overlooking the piazza. Again, I hoped that they were revealing more about their lives to each other.

29

CELEBRATIONS

*O*ur last supper! Our final meal together before we returned home. But what had we left to wear? What was clean? All things considered everyone looked remarkably smart. Ladies' scarves might be concealing the folds in their tops and skirts. The men mostly likely were wearing drip-dry shirts. Joy had even found a hairdressers to restore her hair to her multi-layered bob. Fortunately, I had kept a medium-length, non-crease blue dress for this occasion, however, my nylon pop socks left a gap between the top of the socks and the hem of the dress. Left with the dilemma of either hoping that no one would notice, or exposing my flakey pale legs that had been covered throughout the trek, I opted for the former. Catherine, of course, like a girl guide, was prepared. She wore a beautiful brown animal print jumpsuit over which she placed her cream lacy shawl. As we seated ourselves for dinner, I sensed the feeling of satisfaction coupled with achievement emanating from each member of our group. I guess, although we had not become intimate, we had mingled and shared some aspects of our lives with each other, and we had come to accept each other's idiosyncrasies. So, when Sonia arrived in an off-the-shoulder bright red flowing long dress, no one remarked on its inappropriateness. Quite the contrary. She was clapped. No doubt that was because she looked stunning with her blonde hair and fair complexion. Far from flouncing in to join the group, she looked flummoxed as she placed her hand over her mouth and stood in silence. In silence! David had to call her over and invite her to sit next to him. Another miracle! Maybe this extrovert had not up until now realised that she had been seeking attention throughout the pilgrimage. Is this what she had been doing, or was she just being herself? Everyone was smiling. Nuala winked at me, and I felt Catherine's leg touch mine. I suppose in order to bring attention back, Catherine intervened, 'Oh it's just wonderful to enjoy our last meal united round this table tonight, Karam. Thank you so much for being a brilliant guide throughout.'

'No, Catherine. If you all had not been so cooperative, this task would have been very difficult. Every single one of you contributed. Emma seems to be very happy with all the presents that she has received. She's already wearing the scallop shell shaped earrings and matching necklace. And the turquoise blue and yellow match the colour of her long flowing dress.'

'Who chose the delicious birthday cake, Karam? It's so moist and delicately decorated. Sumptuous.'

'That was recommended by this restaurant, Frankie. I agree. It melts in the mouth. The portions seemed to be large, but because it's so light everyone appears to be pleased.'

'I hope, Frankie, that you won't mind, but I have a request.'

Oh, God, no. I hope that I am not going to have to reveal all about my convent life to everyone.

'How can I refuse you on your birthday, Emma! I hope that you are not expecting me to sing. You'll regret it if you are.'

'No. I would have requested that too, but my request is a little more delicate. I hope you won't mind me asking. But it's being rumoured that you were a nun. Is that true?'

Will I regret outing my background? What will be the consequence? I'd better be careful.

'Okay Emma. It's just that the image of a swinging nun on the huge, Cathedral thurible seemed hilariously funny. I was longing to be up there with the stelle... the stars shining over the fields... the Compostela. The great Italian poet, Dante says, 'Heaven wheels above you, displaying to you her eternal glories, and still your eyes are on the ground'.'

When everyone clapped, I hoped that I had escaped furthering questioning.

David stood and tapped his glass to gain our attention. He thanked each of the leaders and then presented them with a voucher that can be used in many stores and for multiple products. Members of the group had contributed to these. Initially, he said that he was going buy bottles of wine, but he was reminded that Sikhs, and possibly Muslims, don't drink alcohol.

The music started. A group of Austrian pilgrims, seated at a nearby table, began to sing. Their conductor led them on his guitar. They were a happy, cheerful group, and everyone clapped rhythmically. Then Joe rose to join them. As he didn't have his mouth organ with him, he must have asked one of the group if they had a spare tambourine. He succeeded in playing it much as he would have done with an Irish bodhram on a previous occasion.

Music really seems to set Joe on fire. Lovely to witness his gorgeous smile.

Tired and happy, reluctantly everyone eventually

walked back to our hotel together. On the steps of the hotel, Karam reminded us all to have our luggage ready at the airport bus stop the following day.

'Frankie, did you hear Joe inviting Nuala to meet him in the Parador at ten tomorrow morning?'

'I did, Catherine. I was thinking of going up there for coffee, too. It's such a lovely place and really the coffee is not much more expensive than elsewhere. Fancy joining me?'

'Around ten? Yes, that would be very good. I'd like that. It's a majestic hotel.'

'You may have gathered, Catherine, that I have a soft spot for Joe. He is a friend of my husband and me.'

'You brushed off the nun enquiry. Well done.'

'Do you think so, Catherine? I wasn't ready for complete exposure. Besides, I don't want to be labelled. Although a comparatively long time has elapsed since I spent sixteen years in the convent, no matter how hard I try, memories still return when I least expect it.'

'Don't worry, Frankie. I respect your privacy.'

'I appreciate that, Catherine. I realise that you are trustworthy. We've shared a lot throughout this pilgrimage. So, if you wish, I'll tell you a little more as you drop off to sleep.'

I then proceeded to relate a brief outline of my convent story. After that we both marvelled at the change in Sonia's behaviour. Catherine said that, at the supper that evening, Joy told her that David had to persuade Sonia to let him buy her a drink.

I sent a photo of the group birthday party to Richard and Dante, and informed him about Joe and Nuala meeting for coffee the following morning.

Catherine seemed very interested in what I selected to tell her about my life in the convent. On reflection, I noticed that I omitted relating incidents that might demean the nuns. I don't know why, after some of the awful occurrences that I endured, that I continue to present a perfect image of convent life. Is it because I don't wish to reveal the warts-and-all in what became my family for many years?

30

REVELATIONS

*T*he following morning, as Catherine and I made our way to the Parador hotel, we caught sight of Joe entering through the huge ornate doors. Then we noticed Sonia following on behind him.

'What on earth is Sonia doing here, Catherine?'

'Maybe she overheard Nuala talking to Joe? Nuala could even have told her. She shares the same room.'

'I noticed her joining Joe and Nuala yesterday when they were shopping together. She seemed to impose herself on them. Last night, she appeared to quieten down. Has she reverted to her former self today, Catherine?'

'Maybe, Frankie. Nuala must have found some hidden corner to wait for Joe. Where is she?'

'Over there. Come back. Let's keep a safe distance, Catherine .'

'Incredible. Would you believe it? Sonia is going over to them.'

'She's turning away. They must have told her to. She's heading our way.'

'Buenos días! May God bless us. Isn't it luxurious? Too palatial for pilgrims, don't you think?'

'You're right, Sonia. It's very grand,' I said. 'However, we're told that way back when the devotion of the Camino reached the ears of Monarchs they decided that this pilgrimage was the one to take part in. But, when they reached the old pilgrims' hospital that was here then, they thought that it was not in good enough condition for such a laudable mission. So they had this place built.'

'Fit for royalty, Frankie. Oh, well.'

'Anyway, why did you return here if you thought it too grand?'

Sonia unstrapped her rucksack and struggled to pull out a chair. Noticing her difficulty in moving the heavy seating, a member of staff immediately came to lift it and position it for her. Seated, she put one hand up to her face and began to speak in a lower tone of voice, 'I am worried about Nuala. She seems to be having nightmares. She's been talking in her sleep.'

'Have you discussed this with her?'

'Believe me, I've tried. I've even invited her to join me in listening to my mediation tapes. She doesn't seem to want to know. Maybe, because she's Irish, she's different—'

I laughed 'We are indeed a very strange race of people, us Irish, aren't we? But you've got me curious now. What else is strange about Nuala?'

'Forgive me. I know that you're Irish. I didn't mean to—'

'No offence taken, Sonia, go on, though. What else has Nuala done that you are concerned about? Enough to lead you to follow her inside this classy hotel?'

'Well, when we first started the Camino at the end of the day, she'd strip off in the bedroom and wander naked to the shower. I suppose that is alright, but, well, I don't. But then she didn't seem to wear much in bed either.'

'Did you talk to her about that?'

'Well, yes, of course. What would Our Lady do? Purity—'

'I see. We're all so different. I hope that—'

'Look, Karam and Bahis are here too.' Sonia signalled to them to join us. Karam pulled a chair out and invited her to go to them instead.

When Sonia left us, Catherine and I discussed how difficult it must have been for Nuala and Sonia to share their bedroom.

'Typical convert behaviour,' I said. 'Extra devout. But there is an innocent appeal about her.'

'I heard a ping. Is that your mobile or mine, Frankie?'

When I looked at my mobile, I saw that the message was from Joe.

He asked me to meet him alone. I decided to tell Catherine that it was from my husband asking me to buy him a tie-pin. Catherine said that Emma wanted her to help her find the same Torta de Santiago that she purchased yesterday. That made it easy for me to go off on my own to find Joe.

Joe was in the garden of a cafe that was remote from the Plaza. His jacket was zipped up, in spite of the fact that the midday sun had settled. He didn't notice me approaching. He was moving invisible crumbs up and down the table. When he lifted his face, it seemed that he was rolling his lips over each other, possibly preventing tears from emerging.

'I saw you in the Parador. I…' I hesitated then added: 'With Nuala.'

Joe let out a long sigh.

'Something happened? You look a little shaken, Joe.'

'Nuala is a lovely person. We've… well, I thought that we had grown close. We had. We spent a grand amount of time together. Maybe, I shouldn't say… What she said is confidential.'

'You don't need to say anything that you don't want to, Joe. Richard and I know where you are coming from. We both love and look out for you.'

'I know. That's why I asked to meet you, Fran. I feel crushed. Sick inside. I don't know what I feel or what's happened.'

I watched Joe stare into space and let tears trickle down his face. When a waiter came near, I ordered two glasses of wine and some nibbles.

For a long time neither of us said anything. Then Joe began, 'Promise me that you won't tell anyone. I need to unburden, but…'

'I promise that I won't even tell Richard if you prefer that I didn't. You can trust me, Joe. I promise.'

'Well, you know that Nuala already guessed that I had been training to become a priest.'

'Yes, Joe. Those of us who have left don't realise that we sprinkle clues in our conversations.'

'Unconsciously. It's about the reason why she left me in the Wellness Clinic. You remember?'

'Yes, Joe. We came up with a few feasible explanations, didn't we?'

'You and Richard put my mind at ease. I was content and I felt that I would have to wait a while before I could approach Nuala to discuss what happened. As yet, neither of us have revealed much about our past lives. I suppose I didn't really want to know what kind of fellows that Nuala might have dated before we met.'

'I think I'd have done the same, Joe. You haven't really known each other for that long.'

Joe fiddled around with the nibbles and sipped the wine.

'Imagine then today, when we met for coffee, how

bewildered... frightened. I don't know. Confused. It's a cocktail of feelings, making me feel drunk with anxiety and bewilderment.'

'Jesus Christ. What on earth happened? You look shocked. The blood has drained from your face, Joe. What could possibly be so awful?'

'Nuala is a sexaholic. There.'

'Explain? Did she elaborate? I've not heard of this, Joe.'

'She's classified as a sexaholic.'

'What on earth does that mean, Joe? Sex is one thing... is she?'

'Addicted to sex, just as an alcoholic is to drink.'

'But Joe, surely a sex drive... well, you and I wouldn't be here. Everyone knows that. Where did she get that label? Has it come from the Church dumping guilt on her?'

'Of course I know all about that, Frankie. Procreation and pleasure. In the seminary, our friendships were curtailed...'

I grabbed some nibbles and swigged the wine. I smiled.

'Joe, do you remember the ruling that was brought in by the church about no physical contact? I can understand why those in charge of a group of young people in training, and living in closed communities, might need to be monitored and supported. However, a grown woman is surely free to befriend whoever she feels attracted to?'

'You are right, Frankie. I put essentially the same arguments to Nuala when she revealed that she was unable to have a relationship with any other person because she is a sexaholic. She went on to explain that she was powerless over lust, and that one of the many consequences of that is that when she meets anyone, she immediately views them as being naked.'

'And? Were you... you look as though you were about to add something else, Joe?'

'Yes. She reminded me of the consequences of this tendency being known by the authorities and parents in the Catholic school where she teaches.'

'Of course, Joe. But is this a condition or inclination that has to be declared?'

Joe is looking down and avoiding eye contact. He's leaving gaps between his answers. Is there something that he is not telling me? Perhaps he is not at liberty to tell me?

'Frankie, I feel that you suspect that there is a further explanation, and there is. I came to the same conclusion. Nuala broke down and sobbed when she was explaining. After a while she asked me not to probe any further. But it is the word that she used next that brought the fear of God into my heart.'

'Oh, Joe. Something happened to her. You must respect confidentiality. I don't expect you to confirm or deny if the word she used is 'abuse'.'

'Thank you, Frankie. Will we leave it at that.'

'We will. Each of us is vulnerable. What is the phrase? Yea. 'To err is human; to forgive, divine.' Nuala was honest with you, Joe.'

'There's that, but why do I feel like a devout ejeet? I genuinely feel sorry for her, but why did she encourage our friendship? Frankie, when she touched me I was... aroused I suppose. She's ruined this whole pilgrimage. Along with that, my leg is caput.'

I refrained from replying.

'I was so happy. I had imagined myself perhaps married to a lovely Irish colleen. Oh, what has happened? My sponsors will be furious if they ever find out that I haven't even merited a certificate because I didn't walk all the way either.'

'I would be very angry if I were you, Joe.'

After another long silence, I said, 'You've read John Brierley's Pilgrim's Guide. Remember, he said something about life being a risk, and that only the person who risks is truly free.'

'He's probably right. I'm sorry for unburdening, Frankie. But I feel much better for it. I know that I can trust you.'

I was satisfied that Joe looked less shaken. We finished the wine, hugged, and went off in different directions.

Old habits linger. I feel the urge to pray about what Joe has just revealed. Okay, it's off to the Cathedral.

In the middle of the afternoon, when I approached the huge Cathedral, it seemed to tower above me. To my right, I saw queues of pilgrims waiting to the visit the relics of Saint James. I went over to read the relevant information:

A green light indicates the door leading to the small chamber of the Apostle St. James. For centuries, after many hard days of travelling, thousands of pilgrims have been filled with emotion as they embraced this statue of the saint. If you are a traveller on your way through, but would still like to show your respect for the saint and the ancient tradition, feel free to go on up and perform this simple but significant gesture.

Next to the exit from the chamber, there is another green light that indicates the way down to the crypt where the remains of the saint are buried.

Above the altar of this small chapel, beyond the grille and the prie-dieu where worshippers kneel to pray, lies a richly embossed silver chest. Inside this fine piece of 19th-century silver-work there is a cedar box, divided into compartments containing the remains of the apostle and his two disciples.

When I looked at the pilgrims, I noticed that some seemed to be devoutly fingering their rosary beads.

Relics? Every Saturday night my mam made sure that I pinned my miraculous medal onto my clean vest. I wore a scapular for many years. In the convent again, I pinned a bag of medals onto my chemise. One of the arguments that was prevalent in the Church during the Reformation was that Catholics were selling relics, and granting plenary indulgences, that assured total forgiveness of sins. Nowadays, the Catholic Church is less likely to endorse the authenticity of early relics. I wonder if the remains of St James are here? Does that matter?

Pondering on this, I entered the enormous, seemingly empty and darkened Cathedral with shafts of light peeping through stained glass windows. I seated myself facing the elaborately styled high altar. After my conversation with Joe, it took me a while to settle. Gradually, my vision accustoming to the sparsity of light, I began to observe the mixture of architectural styles, huge columns, vaulting arches, countless statues of saints and angels, intricate carvings, coats of arms, splashes of bright colours, gold, silver leading the eye towards the massively ornate high altar.

While my opinion aligned with those who criticise the Catholic church for using vast riches and large sums to build such huge, adorned churches and regard such opulence as a hindrance to faith and neglect of fundamental Christian duty to care for the poor, I also consider that the very splendour of these places of worship arouses and stimulates our appreciation of man's talent and artistic skill and ability. I recognise that many of those who criticise have come to wish that more churches were as spectacular as those sprawling Cathedrals of old.

Mesmerised by my surroundings, I gradually became aware of the remote sound of footsteps and doors opening and shutting. When I peered further into the darkness, I detected movements over the high altar, and realised that some of the pilgrims that I had seen queuing outside the Cathedral were now walking behind the altar in order to venerate the relics and kiss the casket containing the bones of St James.

So much for peace and quiet conducive to prayer and reflection, even in what appeared to be an empty Cathedral. I'm distracted now.

But maybe I don't need to be? What was it that Marion said about an inner journey? I have benefitted from the periods of quiet reflection that I sought during the Camino. I want to enjoy opportunities to pause and reflect when I return back to the bustle of my busy life at home. Yes. I want to bring the Camino home with me. Can I be still in the midst of activity? If I can't do so in a comparatively empty holy place, mid afternoon, what hope is there that I will succeed back in ordinary circumstances?

After some time I found that I had centred myself, and was able to reflect on what Joe had told me about Nuala.

So on meeting people, Nuala sees them as being naked. What's wrong with that? In fact, it is a well known technique recommended by some of those who advise speakers who are daunted when facing large audiences.'You may not find your audience so intimidating if you imagine them as being young children or embarrassingly stark naked,' is their advice to would-be-speakers.

So that can't be what is troubling Nuala. Joe didn't contradict me when I used the term abuse. Has Nuala been sexually abusive? Perhaps she had falsely been accused? Has pornographic information been found on her computer? Whatever had happened, Nuala is suffering the consequences, and Joe has fallen in love with this lovely Irish colleen.

The Gospel account of the woman taken in adultery comes to mind. Jesus's recommendation that we should hate the sin and love the sinner: "Neither do I condemn you; go, and from now on sin no more."

Either way, no matter whether Nuala is guilty, has a tendency towards pornography or, in the worse scenario, has abused someone, she needs support. Moreover, by helping Nuala we will be helping Joe. I need to discuss this with Richard. Maybe this is our challenge? Surely, making an effort to walk in other people's shoes leads us to a deeper understanding of life? In fact, if we do that we will hopefully take what we have learnt on the Camino into our day-to-day living.

31

DISCREET

*S*atisfied that I was becoming more aware that both the journey to Santiago de Compostela and my arrival there was purposeful, when I emerged from the Cathedral I discreetly tried to merge with the shoppers.

'Frankie! We were just talking about you and Joe,' Catherine called over to me. 'Was he helping you to choose the tie-pin? My husband is a golfer, so he usually chooses his own at golf events.'

Oh my God. What'll I say?

'I see that you have a big bag, Catherine. Yours is bulging too, Emma. No doubt, you've found the best Torta de Santiago in town.'

'Yes. We enjoyed a few samples, of course,' Catherine said. 'But that was a while ago.'

No more probing about Joe, thank goodness.

'Time for tea, then?'

Catherine, Emma, and I began looking around before deciding where to indulge in tea and cake, when Emma noticed some of the rest of our group.

'I spy Bahis and Mark. And there is Karam, and he is signalling to us. Shall we join them?'

Glad that we would be together, we found a cosy restaurant. I was happy to see that Joe appeared to manage to conceal his fragility. Nuala seated herself next to him, but I observed that they did not hug each other. Once again, everyone seemed happy for David to order and collate the payment. Then we dispersed to complete a final pack and check-out of our hotel.

'Joe was subdued, Frankie. I suppose he's a private kind of guy. Did he say anything to you?'

Oh, Lord, I'll have to come up with something?

'Yes, Catherine. He wanted to ask if Richard would run him home when we land. Of course, I told him that he can stay the night with us. He said something about Nuala's friend driving her home.'

'Oh well. I expect their lives will return to normal. I have learnt over the years that holiday friendships rarely continue when we get back into the swing of our various routines.'

'*Parting is such sweet sorrow!* Shakespeare says it all.'

'He does. I want to tell you, Frankie, that I am delighted that I was partnered with you. I confess that I don't like sharing. In fact, when I travel with another friend, I insist that we have our own rooms. But—'

'You've had to put up with me and my snoring—'

'Quite the contrary. You remembered to lay on your side, most nights. Besides, when I looked around at the others, I consider that I was very fortunate in being partnered with you. Perhaps, we can keep up contact when we are back in England.'

Whew! Hopefully I have avoided any further questions from Catherine about Joe. Although I am longing to share the confidence that Joe has entrusted me with, that will be with Richard.

When I was on my way out of the hotel lift, Joe was waiting for me.

'Frankie, I realise that I have burdened you with my problems. I wanted you to know that I intend phoning Richard. I hope that is okay. We three have a lot in common. You both have supported and really helped me.'

'We understand each other, Joe. Would you like to come back with us when Richard arrives at the airport? You'd be more than welcome.'

'Oh, you don't know how much I would appreciate that, Frankie. Nuala was supposed to drive me home. I was dreading that. Honestly, I am exceedingly grateful. Go raibh maith agat, is aingeal thu.'

'Come on now, Joe. Me, an angel! Sure you'd do the same for me. And I'll hold you to that.'

When I contacted Richard that night, as I had expected, he was astounded on learning what Nuala had revealed to Joe about herself. After we had discussed the term Sexaholism and the possibility of abuse, Richard went on to say that Joe had told him why Nuala left him in the Wellness Spa.

'He didn't tell me that, Richard.'

'He's so distraught. He said that when Nuala saw Joe standing over her in the spa, she felt that he represented the Catholic Church accusing and damning her for her failures and sins.'

'I suppose by that time she had put two and two together and concluded that Joe had either trained to be a priest, or may indeed have left the priesthood.'

'How awful, Frankie. After having fallen in love with each other, she still felt condemned, burdened with guilt, and prevented from indulging in genuine, natural feelings.'

'When will those in the Catholic Church, who keep accusing folk of sinfulness, come to accept that every single human is frail? We are all far from being perfect.

Who would want to be, anyway?'

'I love you as you are, darling!'

'Go on with ya... Beauty is in the eye of the beholder!'

'Seriously though, Frankie. Sexaholism? I'll try and find out more about it. I've never blamed alcoholics for the affliction that they suffer, so perhaps what they have experienced is something that we can learn from and, hopefully, support both of them.'

'The other... perhaps abuse?'

'I agree with you, whatever it turns out to be, Nuala will need our support.'

32

NEL MEZZO DEL CAMMIN

On the flight home, I started to reflect on this famous quotation from Dante, 'Nel mezzo del cammin di rostra vita.' In the middle of life's journey.

Possibly, I am midway through my life. Before I started out on the Camino, I wanted a challenge. Something or someone to release me from the mundane, the humdrum, the business of life. I was aware that some of my friends had begun to make changes in their lives. They talked of downsizing, mid-career breaks, moving house. One even mentioned seeking a divorce. On the pilgrim path, I discovered that I enjoyed being able to see the beauty of the world around me. I value space to reflect, meditate, and absorb my environment and indeed, the diversity and uniqueness of those who walk beside me. This pilgrimage has made me realise that life itself is a pilgrimage… That's it. When life begins to spin around me, I will allow myself time to get off, opt out, and refuel.

During the Camino, I came across more people who have committed themselves to differing rules, regulations, and religions. I remember reading somewhere the advice that the great Spinoza gave when he was questioned about God. Something to the effect that God would tell us to go out into the world and enjoy life: *Have fun, sing, and appreciate everything that I have made for you. My house is in the mountains and woods, rivers, lakes and beaches.* He said something about love, too. I will have to find the quotes. Of course, I value the opportunity I have had to mingle with so many people during these past days. We gain so much from each other. Pilgrims on the Camino are on their own inner journeys, too. Now, I am about to embrace my own special people, Richard and Dante.

Once off the plane and all the way to the Reclaim luggage carousel there were hugs, kisses, thank yous and promises to keep in touch were exchanged. 'Back to Reality' was the phrase echoed in different forms.

A different reality. I have changed so my life will, too.

'Help! Someone. Help.'

What's that? That's Sonia. No mistaking her shrill tones.

There she is, standing where the luggage arrives from the plane to the carousel. Such a commotion. What's happening? She's pointing to her huge bright pink case and shouting for someone to help her haul hers off the carousel.

Oh no. She's running by the side of the carousel, following her case as it's moving along. No. She's pushing everyone out of her way in the process. Her blonde pony tail's swinging from side to side. Her face is red. Her unzipped green anorak is flapping about.

Thank God, a big muscular chap's hauled the case off the belt.

She's shouting, 'Thank you, thank you, sir.' She's clapping and addressing the other travellers, 'This strong man has helped cancer patients. Yes. Our fundraising group is returning from walking the Camino just for that. In helping me, he has helped us all. So if any one of you wants to donate to Oasis Cancer Centre, we will be delighted.'

What a commotion. How embarrassing. If only I hadn't handed my luggage in so early at A Coruña Airport, I would have already gone through the Nothing to Declare customs channel. I should have remembered that if you hand your luggage in early, yours will arrive last off the carousel.

When the strong man saw that nobody else was responding to Sonia's plea, he emptied his pockets of coins before pushing his trolley on towards the departure channels.

Sonia. She's well meaning. There she is, standing by her huge case, holding out her hand for donations.

Sonia waited until I had reclaimed my luggage, then she came over to give me a huge hug. When we reached the exit barrier, we found that the group had waited for us. Sonia handed the coins that she had collected to Karam. She was about to inform the group of how she acquired them. However, Karam was conscious of our waiting relatives, so he quickly thanked her, and went on to remind everyone that they would receive an invitation to an evaluation and feedback event. He added that there would be a celebration when the amount that they had raised for the cancer centre was totalled. He thanked everyone.

I tugged Catherine's sleeve to tell her what had happened with Sonia. She was grateful that she had escaped in time to avoid witnessing that scene.

When I thanked Catherine, she whispered, 'I am delighted to see Joe and Nuala embrace each other. We needn't have been concerned about them.'

'Yes, Catherine. They seem to be happy. She's a lovely teacher, from her school, who was part of their sponsored music event.'

No one need know what they are coping with at present. Richard and I will see them through this period of their journey.

Enfolded in the arms of Richard and Dante, I was in no doubt of our love.

Once back in our home, Dante succeeded in diverting any tension. He was delighted with the puzzle of Spain, depicting the various Camino routes, that Joe had brought back for him.

In bed that night, Richard and I discussed our concerns about Joe.

'He looks tearful, Frankie. He'll need some time before he will be able to relax. His eyes are flicking and blinking. He keeps rubbing his hands together.'

'He seems to be forcing himself to laugh, or even smile, sometimes. This revelation from Nuala looks as though it has really shaken him to his core.'

'We return to school on Monday. The weekend might not be enough time for him to recover. He said something about his first teaching session being on Wednesday. If he agrees to stay here in our house until Tuesday, that might give him time to unwind. What do you think, Frankie?'

However, on Sunday evening when Richard, Dante and I returned from church, we were surprised to find Joe was waiting for us with his case packed.

'Shall we eat first, Joe? Everything is ready.'

Joe agreed. Once we had eaten, and Dante had been coaxed to bed, I watched Joe's legs shaking and him rubbing the back of his hand across his lips.

Richard starting projecting pictures from the pilgrimage off a USB stick onto the wall.

'Gosh. When did you do that Richard? I didn't even miss my camera.'

'I thought I'd surprise you, love.'

I watched Joe stiffen up at the edge of his seat.

'If you don't mind, I'd rather not be reminded. I've messed up and...'

Richard switched the projector off. I handed Joe tissues

to stop tears flowing down his cheeks.

'I don't know. I didn't even manage to walk. It's...
I've failed. I... Nuala isn't to blame. It's beyond me... I...'

Richard placed a glass of wine in front of Joe. He and
I moved nearer to him.

'Joe, I want to congratulate you for succeeding to
persevere on the most difficult walk in life.'

'Oh, Richard...'

'I witnessed you on this pilgrimage. Physically and
emotionally, you achieved more than any of the rest of us.
I saw the pain on your face when the strain on your leg
forced you to stop.'

'My leg. Okay, I realised before I agreed to take part
that my knee might not take the strain, but what happened
with Nuala. Why?'

'Neither of you are to blame, Joe. I've been researching
this sexual condition. Sexaholism. You were physically
affected by the deteriorating condition of your knee. Nuala
came to your rescue. She is a caring person. But she is also
vulnerable.'

'But, Richard, why didn't she tell me that? I really
thought that she loved me. I wouldn't have responded in
the way I did had I known.'

'Maybe she should have said something?' I added.
'But, if you were her, would you have admitted that you
had that particular condition?'

'It's embarrassing, but I was so easily aroused, Frankie.
I am... my body... It's just... I can't explain. I don't have
the words.'

'You do realise that all three of us are in the same boat
as regards not having vocabulary enabling us to express
ourselves in these matters?'

'Precisely, Frankie,' said Richard. 'Monasteries and
convents didn't discuss sex. Their preoccupation was with
celibacy, chastity and purity. How many lectures did you

and I have in our time, Joe?'

'No wonder I feel guilty about being excited and loving. Oh, how am to deal with this? I want to go to Confession, but I also enjoy falling in love.'

'Guilt is going to get us nowhere,' I said. 'You have learnt a great deal on this pilgrimage, Joe. That, after all, is the purpose of a pilgrimage.'

'Look at my hands, Frankie. My legs too. I'm an ejeet. A complete amadán. My teacher was right. I'm pure stupid.'

'Just the opposite, Joe,' Richard said. 'In spite of very little involvement with a person of the opposite sex, you have bravely reached out, and risked expressing your love for Nuala. Why can't you fulfil your dreams? God Almighty, haven't you every right to feel free? That's how we grow and discover, isn't it? That's what we encourage our little son to do.'

'Richard is right, Joe. Maybe that's what Nuala did? What did she tell you about sexaholics?'

'I was in a state of shock. I have told you. I can't…'

'Joe, I said that I had done some research on this condition.'

'Richard, you both have school tomorrow. Would it be okay if I slept here for one more night? You've made me think. Enough for tonight? Thank you. You need to rest.'

'Of course you can stay, Joe. Besides, it's an inset day tomorrow,' I insisted.

'Fine, Joe. We've begun a discussion tonight. Before we go to bed, would it be okay if I just read out the 12 Steps set out for Sexaholics?'

'Okay. I don't know what I can take in though, Richard.'

'Here we are: The Twelve Steps and Traditions of SA

The Twelve Steps
1. We admitted that we were powerless over lust—that our lives had become unmanageable.

2. Came to believe that a power greater than ourselves could restore us to sanity.

3. Made a decision to turn our will and our lives over to the care of God as we understood Him.

4. Made a searching and fearless moral inventory of ourselves.

5. Admitted to God, to ourselves, and to another human being the exact nature of our wrongs.

6. Were entirely ready to have God remove all these defects of character.

7. Humbly asked Him to remove our shortcomings.

8. Made a list of all persons we had harmed, and became willing to make amends to them all.

9. Made direct amends to such people wherever possible, except when to do so would injure them or others.

10. Continued to take personal inventory and when we were wrong, promptly admitted it.

11. Sought through prayer and meditation to improve our conscious contact with God as we understood Him, praying only for knowledge of His will for us, and the power to carry that out.

12. Having had a spiritual awakening as the result of these Steps, we tried to carry this message to sexaholics, and to practice these principles in all our affairs.'

'Thank you both. There's a lot of mentioning of God in there. What kind of God, though? We haven't said anything about abuse either.'

'Correct Joe,' I said. 'Did God create our bodies the way they are and expect us to live miserable lives? Not my kind of God. Try to sleep. Feel free to wander around if you can't. Make yourself a cup of something. Empty the wine bottle.'

'Thanks, Frankie.'

When Joe had gone to bed, Richard read the following to me.

Stop blaming me for your miserable life; I never told you there was anything wrong with you or that you were a sinner, or that your sexuality was a bad thing. Sex is a gift I have given you and with which you can express your love, your ecstasy, your joy. So don't blame me for everything they made you believe.

When Einstein gave lectures at U.S. universities, the recurring question that students asked him most was:

- Do you believe in God?

And he always answered:

-   I believe in the God of Spinoza.

33

CONSEQUENCES

'We're up. Come on in, Joe. We've just begun breakfast. Did you manage to sleep at all?'

'I did... eventually.'

'I see that you're all ready for action. Fully dressed already. An bhfuil ocras ort?'

'Strangely enough, I am hungry, Frankie.'

'It's Flahavans's Porridge oats, then for you boyoo. Sit yourself down here, will you?'

Joe is still wide eyed and taking tentative steps. His leg must be paining him, too. Richard will gently coax him, while I prepare a bowl of good Irish porridge for him.

When Dante was wakened, the usual school morning got into swing. He was breakfasted, dressed, and all three of us set off, leaving Joe at home in our house. As it was an Inset day at school, Dante was dropped off at a friend's home and we continued to join the staff training designed to provide time for teachers to continue to improve their practice, keep up to date with changes in education, and ensure that they are ready to deal with the challenges of their job. Before we left home, Richard and I had encouraged Joe to try to take things easy, maybe go for a walk and relax until we returned.

That evening after we had eaten and Dante had gone to bed, Richard and I tentatively encouraged Joe to continue discussing our dilemma regarding his relationship with Nuala.

'Well, Joe, did you phone Nuala today?'

'Now that's the hardest thing about this. She made it quite clear that she can no longer be in contact with me.'

'What?'

'Yes, Frankie. Joe's correct. That's what I read about this condition. If she were to be with Joe, all those feelings of arousal would be kicked into play.'

'God Almighty, how does she live? It must be—'

'Horribly painful, Frankie. She will have been advised not to watch television, or even look at photos in a book.'

'So what can she do, Richard?'

'Look, whatever about me, it's very hard for her.'

'I can't figure it out at all, Joe,' I commiserated.

'What a life? When she's teaching her music, wherever she goes, she's restricted.'

'But Richard, she must have known all this before she opted to go on the Camino?'

'No doubt, Joe. Don't forget that the Camino was a pilgrimage for her, too. I was looking at the rules of Sexaholics Anonymous today. Step 6 says: 'Were entirely ready to have God remove all these defects of character.' I guess that when she set out that she wanted to try to do that.'

'Now that I think of it, she insisted in being a back marker. Then, of course, as well as wanting to be with her when my knee caved in, I was always lagging behind. If only I had known. I wouldn't have let myself fall in love with her.'

'Could you?' I asked. 'Love is crazy. It's potent. After all, it's what makes the world go round, Joe.'

'Frankie's right, Joe. Bishops, priests, nuns. So many are not suited to abstinence. Look at the two of us. It didn't work for us. Some priests, who could not cope, became abusers. They are sexually frustrated. Of course there are many for whom a life of chastity is fine.'

'I never used to understand homosexuality, and the other sexual orientations, Joe. But who am I to pronounce judgment when scientists do not know the exact cause of sexual orientation? There are many theories about the causes of the complex interplay of genetic, hormonal, and environmental influences. At one time, some folk tried to use psychological and other methods to try to change these sexual orientations.'

'I'm of the same opinion as Frankie.'

'I'm ashamed of myself. You two must be... I don't know...'

'Come on, Joe. I had to check myself many a time from feeling jealous, and even doubting Richard's love for me. I feel so embarrassed even now in admitting it.'

'When, darling?'

'Remember when you were with that nurse who was looking after your aunt in Florence?'

'That was my fault, leaving you on your own to care for Dante and everything else. That was thoughtless of me.'

'Jealousy, infatuation, are all part of life, Frankie. Remember, Brother Paulo, Joe? I loved the way he swaggered about, his husky voice, his good looks...'

'Italian, suave, dapper chap with any amount of gorgeous black curls, Richard.'

'I began to wonder if I was homosexual back then, Joe.'

'L'amor che move il sole e l'altre stelle.' The love that moves the sun and the other stars. That's from Dante

Alighieri.'

'What's the other quote from Dante about the journey of life, Richard? I was trying to remember it all on the plane on our return flight.'

'*Nel mezzo del Cammin di nostra vita mi ritrovai per una selva oscura…* halfway through life's journey. I found myself in a dark forest, for I had lost the path that does not stray. The first lines of Dante's Inferno. Then, after a long and very difficult journey, Dante ends up pleading that he be taken to St Peter's door…'

'So I'm on a journey?'

'We all are, Joe. Frankie and I too. The Camino led to the field of stars. But, where will our lives lead us?'

'D'you know what, Joe? When you get that leg of yours sorted, how about we walk to the end of the earth? Finisterre?'

'Wow! That'll spur me on, Richard. I heard so many pilgrims saying that after visiting the Cathedral and the tomb of St James, they planned to continue to the place where he is supposed to have landed out in Cape Finisterre. The end of the world.'

34

REUNION PARTY

'Come on, Frankie, I am looking forward to meeting all your pilgrimage friends. I want to compare the before and after. See if they have changed. I think that you have.'

'In what way, Richard?'

'Hard to say. Let me think. God Bless him. Dante's patiently waiting for us in the car, getting his dinosaur to growl out of the window. In you go, madam. Let me tuck your flowing skirt in before I close the door for you.'

'Good boy, Dante. I see that you have belted yourself in. Off we go now, we only have half an hour to get to Bahis's house for the reunion.'

'Watch out Daddy, Diplo is breathing down the back of your neck! Grahh! See his glowing green eyes, Mummy!'

'Ohooo! He looks fearsome.'

'Tell Mummy how many species of dinosaur there are, Dante.'

'Some say seven hundred, but not everyone agrees.'

'As many as that? Do you happen to know the main types?'

'Of course, Mummy. The species listed are Brachio-saurus, Dilophosaurus, Proceratosaurus, Gallimimus, Tyrannosaurus, Velociraptor, Compsognathus, Stegosaurus, Metriacanthosaurus, Triceratops, Baryonyx, Parasaurolophus, Herrerasaurus, Segisaurus, and Corythosaurus.'

'Wow! You have been doing research. Bravo, Dante.'

'See, Frankie. Maybe, we have a little genius in the back of our car?'

'He definitely must be taking after me, darling!'

'Of course. A renowned pilgrim genius.'

'Richard, I'm really glad that you asked Sr Sheila to join us today. I heard her telling the school staff.'

'Well, it was in response to Bahis' request for someone from Spain to join us. As we don't know anyone from as far north as Galicia, I thought of Maria Sánchez. Then, when I suggested her to Sr Sheila, she offered to bring her. Her parents asked if she could wear her First Communion dress, and we all agreed that this would add another dimension to our multicultural event.'

'Grand. Besides, Sr Sheila was such a good headmistress. She always encouraged and supported us. She was so pleased when you replaced her as Head. It's a pity though that she won't be wearing their old nun's habit. Religious habits are no longer worn by so many religious nuns and priests.'

'Here we are Richard. The house with all the flags flying, Dante.'

'Do you realise that your Italian green, white, and red flag looks similar to my Irish green, white and gold one?'

'Not when you get up close, Frankie. Anyway, when all the flags are flying, they will merge into a rainbow.'

'It's our turn to park. Bahis is waving to us, Richard. Oh, it's going to be great catching up with everyone.'

'Didn't Bahis say that there will be a Rabbi there, too? I know that he wanted Judaism to be represented.'

'Look what they've done, Richard. He's put scallop shells and yellow arrows up to guide us into his car parking area.

'Oh, Richard, Bahis has placed a blackboard over there with fridge magnets on it about the Camino. He must have bought them in Galicia.'

'Let's get out of the car and have a look, Frankie.'

'That's horrible, Mummy. That foot with a plaster. Yuck!'

'You've seen Mummy's feet, Dante. Remember she told about her blisters. That foot-shaped magnet is just to remind everyone how hard all that walking was for all those taking part in the pilgrimage.'

'Wow! Doesn't Bahis look smart in his long green tunic and trousers?'

'That must be his wife, Richard. Isn't she beautiful? She looks so stylish in that grey and pink kaftan style tunic. Her face is so pretty, framed in that silky headgear. Oh, Sister Sheila, you're here already.'

'Yes, Frankie, one of the Sisters drove me and collected our little Spanish Maria en route.'

'Is that her over there making friends with the other children?'

Having greeted Sister Sheila, Richard took leave of us to follow a very excited Dante, eager to play with the other children.

'Yes, indeed, Frankie,' confirmed Sister. 'So many costumes. Lovely.'

'And headgear. That lady, Sister, must be Bahis's wife. He was one of our leaders on the Camino. The lady wearing the pink head covering that I'm pointing to.'

'Beautiful. I was thinking, Frankie, that it is not dissimilar to the bonnet and veil that we wore in our convent. Some people say that they can't tell that we are nuns, now. The only sign that we have is a little silver crucifix brooch.'

'That's as it maybe, Sr Sheila, but somehow the peace that you radiate still distinguishes you. There's a holy air about you.'

'Here comes Maria. Doesn't she look lovely, Sister?'

'Mind that white dress, Maria.'

'This is not my real one. My mum said that it doesn't matter if I get this one dirty, Sister.'

Sister Sheila clasped Maria's hand and walked around with her to introduce her to the others.

In no time Emma's eleven-year-old twins, Emily and Eve, encouraged by their father, John, had put themselves in charge of the trampoline. Queues were formed for the slide, and Dante mingled eagerly with Karam and Daljeet's son, Geet. Basil's son, and Maria, joined in, too.

Richard returned to me.

'They're fine now, love. Dante's safe enough on that trampoline. Did you see Karam, darling?'

'I did. Don't they both look amazing in their Sikh outfits? That purple colour really is lovely on Daljeet. Such a lovely couple. He was a good leader. He carried a great deal of responsibility.'

'My eyes are on Joe, now, Richard. I bet he's wondering if Nuala will turn up.'

'I hope that she does.'

'Oh no. I thought I heard Sonia. She's always so well turned out, but my, that voice of hers.'

'She's heading towards Joe.'

'Leave it to me, Richard.'

I sneaked up on Joe sitting alone on a bench. Before he realised that I was near, I crept up behind him, tapped him on his shoulder, and said, 'Aon scéal?'

I was delighted to witness his crumpled face breaking into a smile.

''Tis many a story that I have to tell. Pick one, will you?'

Undeterred, Sonia proceeded towards us and seated herself on the other side of Joe.

'Hola! Everyone seems to be here except Nuala. I expect you've spent the last few days reminiscing over your time together. She's really fallen for you, Joe. You make a lovely couple.'

'When did you say that she'll be returning from Ireland, Joe? I suppose it depends if her mother's condition improves, Joe.'

'Yes, indeed, Frankie.'

'I didn't realise that her mother was not well, Joe. So sorry.' Sonia looked puzzled.

'Shall we mingle, Sonia? It's good to meet everyone again.'

Joe and I watched Sonia walk to the right. I pulled Joe to the left.

'God, you were quick off the mark, Frankie. When did you concoct that sceal?'

'Maybe I am getting good at telling lies? I knew that there would be no end to her quizzing. Stay near Richard and me, and you'll be fine. There's Richard waiting for us.'

Richard pointed to David's sporting his Scottish kilt. Blue tartan. 'Would you look at those pleats?'

Richard and Joe went over to greet David. I saw Catherine.

'Congratulations Granny, or is it Nanny, Catherine?'

'Nain. As I'm from north Wales. It's Taid for grandad, but it's Mamgu and Tadcu in south Wales. We're all delighted that a bonny baby boy weighing eight pounds, eight ounces, was delivered. No name yet.'

'Any names mooted?'

'Well, they were talking about Owain, Elis, James. I'm hoping that they'll end up choosing my late husband's name, Dafydd shortened to Dai. But who knows what the little fellow will be christened?'

'I expect that you'll only be sure when he is baptised, Catherine.'

Catherine was delighted to inform me that she had decided to become a volunteer at the Oasis Centre.

'It's payback time for all the support that they gave me. I'm grateful that I'm alive to welcome my grandchild. Joy, too, has offered her counselling skills, Frankie.'

Most of the people were mingling around the long tables covered with a vast number of dishes. There was of a variety of food and plenty of all kinds of drinks.

I noticed that Joe and Richard had moved at a distance from the buffet. I wandered over to join them. Joe turned to welcome me.

'Well, Nuala didn't turn up. And I'm glad that she didn't. She spared me lots of embarrassment.'

'Perhaps it was just as well, Joe.'

'Thank you, Frankie, for being so quick off the mark with an adequate and believable explanation.'

'I'm becoming a competent liar. But it was a really good day. Perfect. Bahis and his wife went to great lengths to provide everything possible for us. Delicious food and drink. Even assuring that the array of our national flags were hung up the correct way on the various poles. Credit and praise is due to them.'

Bahis silenced the guests so that he could thank Karam for leading the pilgrims. Eventually, the clapping died down, and Richard invited Joe to accept a lift back to our home. Fortunately, Dante succeeded in distracting him by chatting on our car journey back to our house. Moreover, once we entered the house, exhausted Dante willingly asked his dad if he would put him to bed with one of his favourite bedtime stories. I switched on the news on our television, and Joe and I sat in front of it until Richard joined us. With a glass of wine, Richard gradually, gently, encouraged Joe to unwind.

'Karam was duly praised. From all accounts he seems to have been a very competent and compassionate leader. The money raised appears to be mounting up. Everyone has succeeded in raising over six thousand.'

I agreed. Joe nodded.

'Now, Joe, I suspect that you may still be feeling distraught. Possibly angry?'

'That, I am, Richard. I have a lot to learn.'

'So have we all. You're not alone. Wasn't it deaf and blind Helen Keller who said something like, together we can do great things?'

'Such a courageous woman. Inspirational. I owe you two a huge debt of gratitude. Really, I do.'

'What did the consultant at the hospital say about the condition of your knee?'

'It's deteriorated enough to merit a knee-replacement operation, but as I am apparently too young to have this operation on the NHS, I am way down the list.'

'That's what Frankie told me. So we have decided that we will pay for you to go privately. Would you accept that, Joe?'

'Oh Jee, haven't you done enough for me?'

'Actually, I'm being selfish. You see, I want to walk the Camino. I even want to go as far as Finisterre. Who better to guide me than you, Joe.'

'Me? Well, the shells and arrows point the way. So, yes. That would be beyond wonderful.'

'If you have recuperated from your operation sufficiently by our spring half-term break, next April, we were wondering if Dante and I could come, too. Of course, we would only walk for short parts of the pilgrimage.'

'You and Dante, Frankie. I'm overwhelmed. I really am. You're prepared to go to Finisterre. Aptly named, the end of the earth, for me. I really don't deserve this. But I'd love nothing more.'

Laughingly, I reminded them that John, one of the Oxford Dons met us after we came out of the Cathedral he suggested that I go to Confession after pretending to be Roberta in order to get a certificate for her. I added that the other thing John said is that his group of friends would be willing to contribute to our fundraising for cancer patients' therapies in the Oasis Cancer Centre on the condition that at least two of our group met them in Canterbury Cathedral. On the feast day of St Thomas a Becket on 29th December.

'That would be a wonderful way of preparing for our pilgrimage, Joe. What do you think?'

'You and I, Joe, could celebrate the efforts that we made on the pilgrimage that we have just finished too.'

'Ah well now, Frankie. Maybe you could celebrate, but sure, mine was a botched job, a poor effort. I'd need to be doing penance…'

'Now come on, Joe, you along with Roberta, did your very best.'

I reminded them that I told them that the Oxford Don that I met on the pilgrimage spoke about the Canterbury Tales. The Canterbury Tales is a realistic microcosm of Chaucer's society. So although each pilgrim is an individual, each one also represents the struggles that every human experiences.

'Very good. So are you saying that the Canterbury Tales actually relate to problems and issues that we find in today's society?'

'Indeed, Joe. And d'you know, Joe, I'm determined to write about our pilgrimage and what's more I am going to entitle it, *The Camino Tales*.'

'Sure, that's a great title, but I'd imagine you'll have to leave the bit about me out of your account.'

35

CAMINO AND CANTERBURY TALES

As music teachers, it was almost inevitable that Joe and Nuala would bump into each other, especially during the many musical events leading to Christmas. Joe even enjoyed a pleasant yet tantalising experience when his music skills were required in the school in which she taught. Tantalising, because Nuala embraced, kissed and looked genuinely delighted to welcome him into her school environment. When he reported how confused he felt about Nuala's behaviour to Richard, I suggested that it might be good to invite her to join us when we visited Canterbury Cathedral. He wondered if she would accept.

A week before Christmas, Joe underwent his knee-replacement operation. He enjoyed celebrating Christmas with Richard and me while he was recuperating. Being prevented from travelling to County Limerick until he had recovered sufficiently, Richard cooperated with Joe's parents in setting up communications through Skype.

The weather forecast on the 26th December predicted that snow was threatening, so having booked into a small hotel in Reculver near Herne, we packed and set off on the 27th. As both Dante and Joe were not able to walk with us, Richard arranged that they stay in a hotel near the Cathedral. Dante brought his new toys and Joe his crutches.

Each year some of the Oxford Dons, including Elizabeth and John, whom we had befriended on the Camino, walked the ten miles, taking three and a half hours from St Mary's Church, Reculver, to Canterbury Cathedral.

They had chosen this location as a starting point because this church was on the site of a 7th century monastery given by King Ecgberht, after which it had been under the jurisdiction of various archbishops of Canterbury.

Accounts of St Augustine accompanied by forty monks being sent by Pope Gregory as early as 597 to Canterbury to set up a Benedictine monastery has, for many centuries, inspired people to hold Canterbury in high esteem as the birthplace of Christianity in the South of England. Augustine was, after all, their first Archbishop. The Pope is often reported referring to the resident Anglo Saxons inhabitants as being 'Not Angles, but angels.'

Fortunately, it did not snow. After an evening recalling memories of the Camino interspersed with singing carols around an open fire, Richard and I thoroughly enjoyed the company of the retired Oxford Dons. Booted, togged and with adequate supplies the next morning, six of us set off following a route that the Dons had mapped to Canterbury Cathedral. The carol that we chose to sing repeatedly en route was 'Good King Wenceslas'. It was of course deemed appropriate because it was the feast of St Stephen traditionally venerated as the first Christian martyr from the fifth century.

The final verse seemed particularly apt:

The journey took us longer than we had expected. I suspected the reason being that we paced ourselves a little slower to accommodate Richard, who was breaking-in a newish pair of boots.

When we arrived near the precinct of the Cathedral, Dante and Joe were looking out for us. Immediately, Dante saw us. He left Joe to jump into my arms and delighted in Richard swinging him around. It was bitterly cold, so we were grateful that the Dons had booked a place for us to enjoy a hearty meal in a nearby restaurant. Richard, Dante, Joe and I left the Dons after agreeing to meet them the following day in the Cathedral.

We had purposefully arrived at the Cathedral on the eve of the feast of St Thomas so that we could wander around freely before the crowds arrived. When we approached the entrance, an official informed us that various choirs would be rehearsing and, at present, a Spanish a cappella group were singing a beautiful Latin chant specially chosen to commemorate the murder of St Thomas:

R. The grain of wheat lies smothered by the chaff,
the just man slain by the sword of sinners.
Changing his house of clay for heaven.

*V. The vine-keeper dies in his vineyard,
the general in his camp, the husbandman on the place
of his toil.
Changing his house of clay for heaven.*

Although they had visited the Cathedral during their training for the priesthood, Richard smiled when he heard Joe asking another guide to direct him to the window depicting Adam Delving.

'Come on, Richard, for old times' sake, let's show Frankie and Dante this beautiful stained glass window, called Adam Delving.'

Right on cue, Dante asked, 'What's Adam delving, Daddy?'

They burst out laughing and then had to explain to Dante the faux pas that Joe made in asking the same question. Moreover that was when he was much older and in a group of trainee priests being guided around the Cathedral.

'Dante, that man is digging a hole in the ground. He might be beginning to lay the foundations of a building, or just planting vegetables. Look at me now, delving into my pocket to search for my hankie. Delving is a grand word with so many meanings.'

'Okay, Joe. But he's got hardly any clothes on, and he has a whopping big spade. Did he help build this big church?'

'Now Dante. Remember his name is Adam...'

'Oh, he's looking after Eve. I'd forgotten, Mummy.'

'That's one reason why I like this window, Dante. You see, my dad is a builder and builders work hard.'

'A builder. Is he, Joe?'

'That's also what's important about this window, Dante. It's often called Digging with dignity, because it reminds people that every kind of work is important. Whether you are a teacher, a judge, an artist or working hard digging, you are important.'

'I like it, Daddy. I like the blue colour… oh look, the sun's shining and it's brighter blue now.'

Joe began singing and using one of his crutches as a shovel pretending to conduct, he started Christy Moore's song where he instructs the labourers not to forget their shovels if they want to get to start 'Diggin!'

We laughed so much that one of the guides came over to remind us to quieten down. Once we complied, he told us that this stunning glass window was created around the year 1176. He said that in Medieval Britain there were three orders of people: the Church, the knights and labourers like Adam.

'Eve was naughty. She ate the apple.'

'Quite right, son. The story in the Bible tells us that, because both Adam and Eve ate the apple that God instructed them not to eat, they were punished and made to do hard work like digging.'

I was anxious to locate the precise place where Thomas a Becket was murdered. I was about to ask the guide when I overheard another guide telling a small group that he was going to show them that exact spot. When I asked if we could join them, he welcomed us to do so.

We gathered round the guide in front of a sculpture and altar. Aware that young Dante had joined the group, the guide endeavoured to simplify his account and involve him, 'Who was Thomas a Becket? What year was he murdered? Do you think that there would have been an altar here then?'

Prompted by Richard, Dante was able to reply, 'Archbishop of Canterbury, 1170, and no the altar wasn't there then.'

'Excellent, young man.'

'Why was he murdered?'

'Ah well, young lad, that was because he said things that King Henry did not like. Lots of people think that the king did not want to kill his old friend, but the four men that he sent to warn Thomas came with swords, and when Thomas refused to say that he would obey the king, they chopped off his head.'

'Uck! That's horrible.'

The guide then pointed to the four swords positioned in a cross shape above the altar to remind everyone that no sword was ever to enter the Cathedral again. Then the guide made everyone wonder what he meant when he asked Dante if he wore underpants. When Dante proceeded to tell the guide that his were a different colour each weekday, the guide informed the group that under his Monk's dress, Thomas wore a sackcloth shirt that reached to his knees, and swarmed with all forms of wildlife.

'Daddy, is that true?'

'Shish. Listen.'

'What do you think that you would you do with the filthy dress that Thomas had worn after he had died, Dante?'

'Smelly. Dirty. Burn it or…'

'Now you are going to find this very strange, little man. But, because the other Monks thought that one day Thomas might become recognised as a saint, they cut up his clothes and even tried to save some of his blood. Do you collect footballers medals, fill a sticker album, or keep football programmes? You probably know that a famous player's shirts or the boots that they wore when they scored the winning goal could be worth two or more hundred pounds.'

'Yes. Daddy and I save our Chelsea programmes. Don't we, Daddy?'

'Okay then, in the time that Thomas and the other Monks lived what they cared for most of all was getting into heaven when they died. If they had a piece of what a saint wore, they hoped that keeping that near to them might remind them to live good lives. They called these cloths 'files of blood', and even parts of the dead saints' body, precious relics.

'Now to the adults among you. Would you mind me asking what religious denomination that you belong to? Are there Catholics and members of the Anglian Church here?'

The guide then proceeded to invite a Catholic (me), and a chap named Charles from the Anglican Church, to kneel side by side on the prie-dieu, or kneeler, that was positioned in front of a table or small altar just below the four swords, forming a backdrop to the area assigned to remembrance of St Thomas. Then he reminded us that Pope John Paul II and Dr Robert Runcie, Primate of the World-Wide Anglican Communion, had knelt side-by-side on that very same kneeler.

'What about Saint Alphege, Sir? Wasn't he the first to be martyred in this cathedral?' enquired a man in the group.

'You're correct, sir. In fact, it is said that three days before his death, on Christmas Day, Thomas preached a sermon on the martyrdom of St Alphege. Some believe that Thomas may have been foretelling his own death. Thomas might even have been holding the Psalter of St Alphege when he was murdered.'

When the man asked about the Psalter, Richard looked as though he was tempted to explain that this book contained 150 Psalms, and that the Monks would be praying some of them during Vespers in preparation for the feast of St Thomas later that evening. Joe winked at Richard in acknowledgement that he too had restrained himself from giving an explanation. Neither of them found it easy to reveal that they had spent their earlier lives in religious institutions.

'Mummy, you are called after St Francis. Did Thomas become a saint?'

'Thank you for reminding me… your name is Dante, am I right? Yes, Dante. Soon after his death, Thomas was recognised as a Saint or canonised, by Pope Alexander III.'

36

MULLING OVER

*B*ack in the Canterbury Hotel that evening, after dinner and once Dante had snuggled down, Richard and Joe and I relaxed at the far end of an adjacent common room.

'Come on will you. Cop yourself on, Paddy flaithiuil, throwing your money around to impress us, is what you're doing. 'Tis mighty expensive in this hotel. The cost of that Guinness must have emptied your pockets.'

'Sure, what else would I be spending my money on, Frankie? Amen't I being found and fed in your lovely home. No 'tis my small way of repaying you both for putting up with a lonesome fellow.'

'Do you think Nuala will turn up in the Cathedral tomorrow, Joe?'

'No, Richard. She's most likely back home in Listowel. She's hinted at the fact that her family run a dairy farm. But, d'you know, I really don't know that much about her. I've never even been invited to where she lives in Balham. And, of course, with me living in a room in the Salesian Priests

House, I've never felt free to invite her back to mine.'

'Do the Salesians know your background, Joe?'

'Yes, Frankie. The Carmelite Priory, or as we were known as 'The Friars' was listed as my previous abode. I usually join the Salesians at Lauds and Mass before I leave for school each morning. Old habits die hard, or in my case, get cast aside!'

'Richard, do you think it's about time that we told Dante about our backgrounds?'

'Not yet. I'm not ready… not sure. Wait a while, shall we, Frankie?'

Joe, observing the sensitivity that Richard and I felt about this topic, began to describe what it must have been like to be a stonemason back in the day that the stone would have been hauled from miles away. We discussed how long it probably took building just one of the many walls. The work must have been monotonous. They would have been exposed to all the elements. The stones are heavy. Lifting them day after day, backbreaking. They would not have known how much of the building would be completed in their lifetime. It is recorded that some men died as a result of the strenuous work entailed. However, it gave them employment. It paid the bills. Hopefully, some of the builders might have been happy to know that they were building a cathedral, and see themselves as important as the guy making the stained glass windows, or even the architect.

Richard, who had researched the history of the Cathedral, related that the venerable Bede, living between 673 and 735, recorded that Augustine reused a former Roman church. Joe had discovered that the oldest remains of the Cathedral were found during excavations beneath the present nave in 1993 were, however, parts of the foundations of an Anglo-Saxon building that had been constructed across a Roman road.

The following morning, a ceremony had been arranged by the Oxford Dons to reward various charities with funds that they had raised throughout the year on sponsored walks. One of the smaller chapels was set aside annually for the representatives of these charities to assemble. The title for the group adopted by the Dons is Gaudete, translated as Rejoice. So appropriately as the representatives were entering the chapel a choir was singing the medieval hymn, Gaudete, gaudete Christus est natus, a cappella. Each verse sung first in Latin and then in English:

'Rejoice, rejoice! Christ is born of the Virgin Mary. Rejoice.'

Once everyone was seated, the names of the charities were announced. Then, while a representative from each charity approached the altar to receive a donation, the choir sang hymns and carols:

O Come. O come Emmanuel, For us a Child is Born, Oh Holy Night, Adeste Fideles (O Come all ye Faithful). Richard was surprised when an Italian carol, *Tu Scendi dalle Stelle*, was the last carol sung.

After the ceremony, we were all invited to a buffet lunch provided in a room leading off from the chapel. It was there that we discovered that each of the charities had received a thousand pounds. Richard, Joe and I were delighted that the forty thousand raised from the Camino for the Oasis Centre was now augmented.

Richard was even more elated when he asked their Camino friends, John and Elizabeth, why the hymn selected to end the ceremony was *Tu Scendi dalle Stelle*. They explained that the previous year when they had visited Assisi, and were in Greccio, they were reminded that Saint Francis of Assisi is credited with creating the first live nativity scene in 1223. Francis has been inspired to do so by his visit to the Holy Land, and was shown Jesus's traditional birthplace.

'Frankie, they say that God works in miraculous ways. This is extraordinary.'

'I know, Richard. That hymn. *Tu Scendi dalle Stelle…* 'You come down from the stars, Oh King of Heavens, And you come in a cave…' We sang that hymn in the Duomo in Florence when you first invited me over to Florence to spend Christmas with your family.'

'We've come full circle. We're back to aunt Margherita, and her cancer, and our inspiration to fundraise for Oasis.'

Richard began to hum, 'Tu Scendi…'

'That sounds lovely, Richard. It sounds like a lullaby.'

'You're right, Joe. Children sing it in most schools. It's that and St Francis and his love of animals that makes it so attractive.'

Richard and I decided that the celebration of the feast of St Thomas might be too long and take place too late in the evening for Dante to be present. Fortunately, our friend Elizabeth's daughter arrived to join us, and agreed to look after him along with her daughter for the duration of the evening service in the Cathedral.

When Richard, Joe and I arrived at the Cathedral for Evensong, we discovered that it was standing-room only. However, Elizabeth, John and group had reserved seats for us near the choir. The Archbishop presided, and it seemed that representatives from many parts of the world were present to commemorate the life and the martyrdom of St. Thomas of Canterbury.

The service was lit by candles, with each member of the congregation igniting their own candle at the appropriate point in the service. Many of the hymns were sung in Latin plainchant. There were readings from T.S. Eliot's *Murder in the Cathedral.* At the appropriate moment, the congregation processed from the choir to the very place where Becket was murdered. The congregation heard the words taken from the section of Eliot's play where

St Thomas is purported to have called out that the doors should be thrown open. He reminded all that he did not wish to witness the church of Christ turned into a sanctuary. He vouched that even if the building were to destroyed the church of God would endure.

When, after the service, Richard, Joe and I returned to our hotel, each of us said that we were delighted that we had witnessed the re-enactment of St. Thomas's death and elevation to sainthood. The service with its beautiful polyphonic choral piece and congregational hymns reminded us of our lives in religious institutions.

'Once a Catholic always a…'

'Ah, Richard, once you have been a member of a Religious Community, bells, and especially the sonorous sounds of that music, will never leave you!'

'Soul searching, beautiful music. Music is so powerful, isn't it, Joe?'

'Correct, Frankie. Wasn't it way back that Plato said: "Music gives a soul to the universe, wings to the mind, flight to the imagination, and life to everything."'

'WOW. With those positive thoughts I'll sleep well, tonight, Joe.'

37

CONFRONTING THE PROBLEM

During January, when Joe returned to work as a peripatetic music teacher, his local education authority sent him to various schools and music centres. Much as he tried to forget Nuala, he longed to discuss her addiction with her. Whenever he met Richard to prepare to walk the Camino, they often puzzled over how crippling Nuala might find the restrictions imposed on her.

I was glad that Richard gave me such a clear account of what was happening between Joe and Nuala that I felt that I was actually witnessing how their relationship progressed:

Eventually, determined to meet Nuala, Joe waylaid her at the end of a school day when he knew that she would be leaving to drive home. When she appeared, dangling her car keys, she saw Joe standing near her car. He was pleased that she smiled back at him. He invited her to share a meal at a nearby restaurant. She seemed delighted and acted as though it was normal for them to spend time together.

While they enjoyed their meal, they chatted about their school work and compared their experiences. Nuala enquired about how Joe was adjusting to his knee operation. They seemed so relaxed and at ease with each other that Joe began to wonder if he had been mistaken about what Nuala had said about her inability to continue their relationship. He was even more taken aback when she raised the topic of the Camino.

'You must have wondered, Joe, why I didn't make it to the reunion of the Camino pilgrims. I did not respond to the invitation to meet at Canterbury Cathedral, either.'

'I would have been great if you had been there, but you told me the reasons why… well.'

'Joe, I love you. That's why I don't want to spoil your life with my problems.'

Tears flooded Joe's eyes. She handed him tissues. He mopped his face. Nothing was said. When she saw the waiter approaching their table, she shooed him away.

'Love. I love you, Nuala. I couldn't stop myself. I am sorry.'

'It's I who should be sorry, Joe. You are not to blame.'

'A cure? Is there a cure, Nuala?'

'Believe me, Joe, if there was, I would be first in the queue. I hate to see you like this.'

'I can't imagine what it's like for you, Nuala. It must be pure torture. Have you been like this all your life?'

'I don't talk about it… but, I feel that I owe you something that might shed some light…'

'Nuala. I really don't want to hurt you. I love you too much for that.'

'I know, Joe. You're a kind and gentle fellow. Okay. I didn't realise that I was any different until a member of staff in my previous school reported that there was pornographic material on my computer. This chap was the school's technician. Until then, I had no idea that what I was doing was wrong. The head believed my explanation. He advised me to go for counselling. He actually recommended a counsellor. However, I was eventually asked to leave the school.'

'God, that must have been hard, Nuala.'

'My father keeps asking me if I have met that someone special yet. Mammy talks about hiring an ancient castle for my wedding. Can you imagine what they would say if I ever told them, Joe?'

'Was it the counsellor who diagnosed... that's the wrong word.'

'Yes. But when the cost of counselling mounted up it was my counsellor, Fiona, who suggested that I would most likely find the Sexaholic meetings helpful.'

'What's Fiona like, Nuala? She isn't by chance a member of a religious community?'

'I was afraid of that. I didn't want to be indoctrinated, or reprimanded for my morality. No, what drew me to her was that she is Irish, and a deserter of the Catholic faith. More than just a lapsed Catholic.'

After this response, Joe decided that it might be better not to probe any further. They finished their meal and promised to keep in touch from time to time. Nuala advised Joe to widen his circle of female friends. She reiterated her concern for his future without the hassle of supporting a struggling, addicted friend.

Joe wasted no time in contacting Richard and arranging to meet him the following day to practise walking in preparation for the Camino. As Joe was still recovering from his knee-replacement operation, he hoped that they would have plenty of time to chat. They arranged to meet at a cafe in Battersea Park.

When Joe saw Richard walking across the grass, he ordered coffees for both of them.

'Good to see you smiling, Joe. Have you come off painkillers?'

'This new leg's improving all the time, Richard. I'm

sure you don't want to see the scar but any amount of pain is a worth putting up with in order to be better able to walk. Besides, I've got good news for you. Important news.'

'Let me guess. You have spoken to Nuala?'

'Not only that, but we've dined together.'

Joe gave Richard an account of what Nuala told him about how she had accepted that the diagnosis that she was a sexaholic.

'Are you coming to the same conclusion as me, Richard?'

'Yes, if you are also wondering that on the basis of what her counsellor says, we could all be suffering from the same affliction, Joe?'

'Indeed. Are we all sexaholics?'

'Well, there's a few matters that I question, Joe. When a person has reached an age when they might be overeager to meet a partner, they might also be wondering why they have not succeeded so far. That may lead them to researching relevant information. They could innocently come across sexually arousing photos or images.'

'And, if they are steeped in religion, they would feel guilty. Now, Richard, that leads me onto the fact that her counsellor is an Irish, lapsed Catholic. There's no such thing as a lapsed Catholic. I doubt if that counsellor will be able to escape from drummed-in guilt and scrupulosity.'

'Taking pleasure in sexual arousal was, and possibly still is, considered to be sinful by the Catholic church. Married couples were constantly reminded that the prime purpose of sexual intercourse is procreation.'

'That's what I deduced, Richard. Nuala could well be beating herself up for some God-given built in sexual attraction and arousal.'

'That's a fair conclusion. We might be correct, but we will have to tread carefully. We're not privy to what goes on inside Nuala's mind. Her reality is her own, as are her perceptions. Nurture and or Nature, and all of that.'

'True, Richard. Come to think of it, when we were in Canterbury Cathedral I wondered if Thomas Becket was convinced that he should become a martyr. Did he set himself up to be killed in order to merit a heavenly reward? Nowadays, there are those suicide bombers. No matter how hard we try, we will probably never succeed in probing the minds of these people. Each of us, after all, is alone in our own mindsets. We essentially have to work things out for ourselves.'

'I agree, Joe. Even if you are married, or have children, we are lone beings. When I used to ask my aunt Margherita why she always seemed so content while she was on her cancer journey, she repeatedly reminded me that she had chosen to think positively.'

'That's probably why she coped with that awful disease, Richard.'

'What do you think about asking Nuala to walk the Camino with us, Joe?'

'The very thing. Exactly what I was thinking. Even if she didn't want to walk the whole way, she might be encouraged to join us from Santiago out to Finisterre.'

'That's a wonderful idea, Joe.'

'Yes. I'll go very gently. Maybe use WhatsApp occasionally to keep in contact. Eventually, slowly, and carefully mentioning and hinting.'

After that discussion, Joe and Richard walked slowly around the park. Later, when Richard returned home and related all that they discussed with me, I came to the same conclusions about Nuala.

'So there we are Frankie. Of course Joe wanted me to keep you up-to-date with how they are coping with their relationship. He is so grateful that we are both behind him.'

A fortnight later, Karam emailed each of the group who had taken part in the Camino inviting us to join the annual 'Away Day' organised by the Oasis Cancer Centre. The topic for the day was to be on an Indian ancient holistic health system.

Joe hoped that this approach to health might attract Nuala to attend the day. Richard recalled that Aunt Margherita was convinced of the merits of complementary treatments. She regarded body massage, reflexology, acupuncture as being complimentary for patients on their cancer journey.

That weekend, I invited Joe to our home to join us in celebrating Marion's seventieth birthday party. Marvelling at Marion's robust health eventually led us on to discussing the ancient Indian holistic health programme.

'It isn't by any chance called Raymoundra?'

'You're a mind reader, Marion. How do you know about it?'

'Our local U3A Group…'

'U3A, Marion?'

'Oh, Richard. U3A. You're all too young to subscribe. You have to be retired to be eligible to belong. U3A stands for University of the Third Age. I heard that they dropped the word 'university because it seems to deter folk who think that it only relates to academic pursuits. It's a nationwide organisation run by retired people. We have lots of courses. Artistic, social and well, all kinds of subjects and activities. Recently, our group invited a representative from Raymoundra to address us. Most of us concluded that it appears to be a wholesome approach to life.'

'That's coincidence, Marion. On their website it states that it is a complete way of life. It claims to provide both physical and mental support by creating harmony between a person's body and nature.'

'Quite right, Frankie. They advocate things like yoga,

massage, detoxification, herbal remedies, meditation. Raymoundra claims that this holistic life style improves not
only a person's health, but also their well-being, behaviour
and state of mind.'

'Well guys, are you thinking what I'm thinking?'

'Nuala. It might well be the answer, Joe.'

'Thank you, Marion.'

'From what you've told me about Nuala, this might be
the answer to our prayers. Our bodies are sacred vessels...
There's that hymn, Earthen Vessels. 'We hold a treasure,
not made of gold, in earthen vessels…''

'I remember that lovely hymn, Marion.'

'Beautifully sung, too, Frankie.'

'Maybe you could begin to drop a few hints to Nuala,
Joe?'

'I was thinking that, Richard. But I wonder if it might
turn out to be counter productive? She might think that we
are coaxing her into another belief system. Maybe similar
to yet another religion?'

The destination chosen by Oasis for their Away Day
was a huge barn, often hired for events situated in the
Surrey Hills. On the day set aside, I drove Richard and Joe
through winding one-way lanes to our destination, high on
hills, overlooking much of Surrey.

Just as Karam was being invited to face those
assembled in order to thank him for leading the Camino
pilgrimage on behalf of Oasis, Joe heard whispered in his
ear, 'Conas tá tú?'

'Tá mé… well, if it isn't yourself. Nuala, push in here
beside us.'

Richard and I were delighted that Nuala had joined us.
We were pleased too that during the question-and-answer
time at the end of the talk, she posed her own questions to
the speaker.

After lunch, when the others chose to walk over the

luscious, green, meandering Surrey hills, Richard and I joined Joe and Nuala sitting on a bench near a lake. It was during that conversation that Nuala related how she had discovered that various meditations and reflections on a way of life recommended from many sources had helped her experience the beginnings of mental harmony. She felt that she was already beginning to taste liberation and positive support and encouragement. She admitted that she was still questioning the reason why she felt that she craved bursts of sexual arousal to quell her longing and loneliness. Joe put his arm round Nuala and asked her:

'Did you find the talk helpful, Nuala? Do you sense that this approach to life will help you move away from what is disturbing you?'

'There is no one approach, Joe. But I feel that I am taking baby steps on a journey of discovery. Because I am a unique human being, I want to work out what is right for me. It's like the Camino, Joe. It's miles long over so many different kinds of territory in a different country. I'm just at the stage of getting my kit together... I've not even tied up my boot laces yet.'

'Nuala, would you walk the Camino again? Richard and I have planned to.'

'D'you know, I think that I would, Joe. Yes, Richard. Yes Frankie. I will walk the Camino again.'

With tears of contentment and happiness, Joe embraced Nuala, and Richard and I encircled them both in a huge circle of love.

'My darling, Joe. My love. I will walk with you to the end of the earth.'

'Together we'll pass the Compostela, flickering stars of the field of gold, out to Finesterre, the end of the earth.'

BIBLIOGRAPHY

1. A Pilgrim's Guide to the Camino de Santiago, John Brierley (6th Edition)

2. The Way DVD, written and directed by Emilio Estevez, starring Martin Sheen

3. Buen Camino, Natasha & Peter Murtagh

4. The Last Relic of Thomas Becket, Christopher de Hamel

5. The De La Salle Brothers Music. A religious congregation of men within the Catholic Church. The hymn: Laudato Sii6. Quotes taken from Dante Alighieri, Italian poet, prose writer, literary theorist, moral philosopher, and political thinker. Best known for The Divine Comedy.

7 Ayurveda medicine. Alternative medicine

8 Having recovered from breast cancer I became a fundraiser and volunteer for the Fountain Centre in St Luke's Cancer Centre in the Royal Surrey County Hospital NHS Guildford Surrey.

I have walked the final hundred miles thrice, the last time finishing in Finisterre. Following the French Route twice and the Portuguese route.

Acknowledge permission from Kevin Mayhew Ltd

ABOUT THE AUTHOR MARION DANTE B.ED.

Marion Dante hails from Limerick and has lived in England since 1955. When her family arrived in Shepherds Bush, London, there were signs on some door saying 'No Blacks. No Dogs. No Irish.'

Aged fourteen she began training to be a nun in the Salesian convent in Chertsey, Surrey. After her aspirantade and noviciate, Marion made her vows of poverty, chastity and obedience in Friar Park Henley-on Thames in 1965. (This premises was later purchased by George Harrison.) She finished her three year teacher training course at Digby Stuart College in 1970. Having taught in Chertsey, Henley on Thames, Battersea, Rotherhithe, Glasgow and Farnborough she gained her degree in education (Bachelor of Education) London University in 1979 and continued to teach when she left the Salesian Order.

Many changes brought about in the Catholic Church as a result of the second Vatican Council resulted in Marion pondering on her future role in the convent and the realisation that she did not have to be a nun in order to live a fulfilling life. Mother Provincial of the Salesian Sisters strove to help her to prepare for life outside the convent. Initially, Marion was sent to Ireland to study theology and related religious studies. She graduated from Maynooth University, Kildare 1987. The following year she completed a Secretarial and Business, Pitmans word-processing and typing Course at Language, Secretarial and Business Centre, Balfe Street, off Grafton Street, Dublin 1988.

On returning to England at some financial cost to the Salesian Sisters, Marion benefitted from further support, counselling and various therapies in a Heronbrook House in the Midlands. While there she became convinced that she could no longer remain in the convent and eventually wrote to the Pope to be dispensed from her vows in 1991.

Anxious to equip herself for her future life, while still teaching, Marion gained further qualification from several courses: Two years at Tavistock Clinic to meriting Counselling Aspects in Education certificates. City and Guilds Further Adult Education run by University of Surrey in Family, Language and Literacy. TESOL qualification enabling her to teach English to speakers of other languages. Information Technology at Brooklands College Surrey.

While teaching in St Patrick's School, Farnborough, Hampshire, Marion was diagnosed with breast cancer in 1995. She eventually retired but continued to teach privately. Soon after becoming a member of Camberley Writers she began to pen her autobiography. Encouraged and supported by Charlotte McDowell, who had been her radiographer and became co-founder of The Fountain Centre in St Luke's Cancer Centre in the Royal Surrey County Hospital, Guildford, she enlisted and continues to be a volunteer helping to raise funds for this therapeutic centre. To this end she was sponsored when she climbed Machu Picchu and on three occasions endeavoured to trek the last hundred kilometres of the Camino Compostela in northern Spain.

Marion Dante's autobiography 'Dropping The Habit' was well received in Ireland, England, USA and was translated into Polish. She is invited to give talks to many different groups:

Women's Institute, The Townswomen's Guild, Probus, Rotary, Inner Wheel, Tangent and various retirement groups.

Marion was on RTE television and radio as part of the publicity at the launch of her autobiography.

She has featured in BBC Programmes such as Heart and Soul BBC World Service, Radio Four Saturday Live and this February 2017 to speak on BBC Radio Surrey taking part in the BBC Listening Project. (Stored in the British Library).

She is a member of The Three Counties Cancer Support Group, The Kindred Spirits Choir, Camberley and Farnborough U3A in which she takes part in Italian, yoga, walking and ukulele groups. Marion also attends aqua aerobics and is a Member of National Women's Register, discussion, dining and reading group. She has been engaged as a public speaker for many years and has recently managed to continue to do so through the medium of Zoom.

As a public speaker Marion has been recognised and approved by the Surrey Federation of Women's Institute 6 Paris, Parklands, Railton Road. Guildford Surrey GU2 91X

Marion Dante is also the author of:

Dropping the Habit
Her autobiography

Novels

Searching for Love
A Love as Strong